THE LETTER MAN

OTHER BOOKS BY
JEFF VANOUDENHOVE

THE DARK SERIES:

** *Book 1 - DARK PLACE*

** *Book 2 - DARK LANE*

** *Book 3 - DARK QUEEN*

** *Book 4 - DARK CHILD*

** *Book 5 - THE FINAL DARK*

SCREAMS IN THE DARK AND OTHER TWISTED TALES

THE ALPHABET KILLER

JUST LISTEN

For signed copies of the author's books, please visit:
javo-publication.square.site

THE LETTER MAN

JEFF VANOUDENHOVE

Javo
PUBLICATION

Westfield, MA

JAVO Publication
Westfield, Massachusetts 01085

This is a work of fiction. The characters, places, and events portrayed in this book are either the product of the author's imagination or are used fictitiously. Any similarity to real persons, living or dead, business establishments, or events is coincidental and not intended by the author.

ISBN
979-8-9865975-8-4

Library of Congress Control Number:
2024912957

Cover design by JAVO Publication

*For Patti Green,
whose larger-than-life personality
is surpassed only by her love for her family*

<u>****SPOILER ALERT****</u>

This is a direct sequel to The Alphabet Killer.
Events in this book give away major plot spoilers of the
original storyline.

If you haven't read The Alphabet Killer,

STOP NOW!

You'll want to read that one before devouring this one.

Prologue

K

I knew what I was walking into the moment I received the address. The call came in as a wellness check when the victim hadn't shown up to work for a few days. Since her boyfriend had left her six months earlier, she'd been alone with her grief, and I'd been worried about her. I would occasionally stop in to check on her. It had become a routine of mine, perhaps borne out of guilt. I felt it was my responsibility to make sure she was doing okay; especially after everything that had happened. My only regret was that I didn't stop in frequently enough, and now because of it, this had happened. I should have pieced it together sooner; all the clues were there. I'll never forgive myself for dropping the ball on this one. As I said, I knew what I was walking into the moment I received the address. I just wasn't fully prepared for what I found.

"Shit." I was left shaking my head in disbelief.

"Tell me about it; it's a freaking mess in here."

"I was thinking more about how I was going to break the news to the kid."

"*You're* gonna do that?" Officer Sanchez questioned.

"It's gotta be me," I returned. "I owe him that much. I shouldn't have let this happen."

"This isn't on you, Mick; you couldn't have known."

"*Shouldn't* I have?" I exclaimed a little louder than expected, causing forensics to stop what they were doing to glance over. "The Southbridge PD received a letter soon after we took The Alphabet Killer down. It was some fucking psycho claiming he was going to continue the killings. I was practically hand-fed the evidence. We knew it was only a matter of time before this shit started up again. Of course, it was her. It was always going to be her. And like everyone else before her, she was just the next letter on the list. The son of a bitch did exactly as he said he'd do - he started where the kid left off. K for Karen. And he even said he'd use a knife. The sick bastard."

I'd seen victims with knife wounds before - stabbings and slashings and the like, but nothing as gruesome as what I encountered when I stepped through the front door into the dried puddle of blood that migrated from her mutilated body. She was lying on her side in front of the television, her legs extended, her arms stretched straight over her head, and her cold, pale skin covered in lacerations. Forensics confirmed she'd been stabbed seventeen times in the neck and chest, her midsection eviscerated, and her internal organs on display for those who could stomach it. Her hands and feet were cut from her limbs and placed on the living room coffee table. In front of them, fifteen digits - ten fingers and five toes - were removed from their respective appendages and lined neatly in a row as if to make a statement. It was unnecessary. For me, the statement had been received the moment I saw Karen's face. It was untouched, save for the lone marking cut into her forehead, the killer's calling card, the letter K.

After seeing that and recovering my heart from my stomach, it wasn't hard to surmise the fifteen fingers and toes represented the balance of what had now been restarted. Karen was the first. And with her death, letters L through Z remained - the last fifteen letters of the alphabet. It had begun again, only this time, I found myself caught in the thick of it.

"I don't know anything about all that," Sanchez stated. "And maybe you shouldn't be telling me right now. But I can tell you this, Mick - you're not looking too good. Maybe I shouldn't have called you in on this one."

It was true; I usually couldn't handle a scene such as this without losing the contents of my stomach. But this was Karen. Jimmy told me shit like this would get easier in time, and in honor of his memory, I had to suck it up. I just never thought it would be a case involving his ex-wife.

"No, I'm glad you did," I responded. "Jimmy and I were tight. You know that."

"I know, buddy. You were the first person I thought of when dispatch radioed me. But you shouldn't have seen her like this. I should have waited until I knew the situation. I had no idea it was . . , well, I had no idea."

How *could* he have known? It had been over two years since the alphabet killings. People have tried to forget about what had happened. Not to mention, this wasn't the killer's usual stomping grounds, and the Southbridge PD hadn't heard a peep since receiving the last ominous letter from someone claiming they were going to continue the slayings. After months of tense anticipation where nothing happened, we all believed it to be a hoax. But now . . , this.

It could have been some sick, twisted individual trying to duplicate the murders. And had it only been the letter carved into Karen's forehead, that's what I would have believed. But that wasn't the only message the killer left. There was another, handwritten in blood on the wall.

IF YOU'RE READING THIS, CONGRATULATIONS! YOU'VE WITNESSED THE FIRST OF MY HANDIWORK. IT WON'T BE MY LAST. I WARNED THEM I WAS COMING. I GAVE THEM TIME TO PREPARE. BUT NO AMOUNT OF PREPARATION WILL HELP FOR WHAT I HAVE IN STORE. THIS WAS JUST THE BEGINNING. THE BEST IS YET TO COME.

α

Nobody outside of the Southbridge PD knew about the previous letter. This wasn't a random copycat. This was him. And he wanted us to know it.

Just then, the Chief Forensic Officer perked up excitedly. "I think I've got something."

We both immediately turned our attention in his direction.

"What is it, Shane?" Sanchez asked.

"We found a distinguishably different print. One that doesn't match the victim."

"Holy shit," I let out. "That was fast. We've got the fucker."

"Easy, Mick," Sanchez said. "We don't know anything yet."

"It's him," I replied. "I can feel it."

"Maybe," Sanchez responded. "But we won't know who it belongs to until we run it through AFIS. And that's if it's even in our database."

"Then, let's run it and go pick that son of a bitch up."

"Whoa! Hold on there, Mick. Even if we get a hit, I can't have you coming along on this one. You're too close to the victim, and my chief will never go for it. I'm sorry, but this isn't Southbridge."

"What the fuck, Sanchez?"

"It's out of my hands; you know that."

Sanchez was right. I was out of my jurisdiction, only present for a wellness check that turned out to be a crime scene; this wasn't my city.

"Fine," I said, my voice elevated. "You go and get this guy and bring him in. I'll go and deliver the bad news to her son."

"You mean that fucking freak, The Alphabet Killer?"

"Yeah," I replied, showing my distaste for his callous words.

"And his name is Ben."

Chapter 1

Visiting the Past

It had been a while since I last visited. Out of respect for his old man, I had made an effort to stop in regularly during the first year of the kid's incarceration, but admittedly, I had let my schedule slide over the past six months when it seemed Karen needed more of my attention. Still, I had visited him more than his mom ever had. I understood her reasoning; she'd told me his actions disgusted her. She had tried a few times in the beginning, but I think the sight of him and the thought of what he had done sickened her more than most people would be able to comprehend. She never spoke of it with me in detail, but I think she felt responsible in some way and that seeing him was a not-so-subtle reminder of that fact. Ben hated her for it - probably more than he should have. He made that quite clear the last few times I'd seen him. I couldn't say as I blamed him, but she didn't deserve to die for it.

With his father dead, and now his . . , I couldn't even bring myself to think it . . , I was all Ben had left - good ol'

"Uncle Mick." Except, even that was a farce. The title was given to me by his dad, who had hand-fed it to the kid when he was young. We weren't blood relatives; I was just one of his dad's childhood friends. Still, the title stuck. I guess, in some way, that made us "family." That was why it had to be me who delivered the awful news. It wasn't going to be easy.

I had called the warden in advance to explain what had happened. I couldn't go into details, only to let him know that the kid's mom was found dead. He offered his condolences, knowing she was a friend, and he allowed my request to go in and sit with Ben for a bit. Sadly, now that I was here, all I could think about was getting up from my seat and running for the nearest exit. Unfortunately, I was too stupid to listen to my rational thoughts.

The rattling chains were what first caught my attention. He rounded the corner into the visitor's hall, escorted by one of the Corrections Officers, his wrists and ankles shackled together, causing him to step awkwardly to keep from falling over. They say prison changes you; you're never the same person as before you went in, but Ben looked like he'd aged five years since I last saw him. And it wasn't just his unshaven face. He was different, hardened. I wasn't met with the same optimistic smile as during my previous visits. His cold stare stabbed into me like icicles. This was no longer the Ben I knew.

He was delivered to the table where I sat, strong-armed by the officer at his side, and forcibly plunked into the chair across from me. Glancing up at the officer with a disdainful glare, he tugged his arm from the CO's grip in hateful defiance and dropped his clenched fists to his lap, maintaining his stare until the officer backed away to give us privacy.

"Mick," Ben began with an emotionless tone, turning his attention to me and nodding. "Long time no see."

I noticed right away he dropped the "uncle" from his greeting.

"Hey, kid. Yeah, it's been a minute, hasn't it? The job's been keeping me busy."

"That's right," Ben responded, "the job. It's always the job with you guys."

I didn't take the comment or his tone personally. It was a remark directed more toward his father than to me. I was merely the available target for his pent-up anger.

"Yeah, it's been pretty hectic since I made detective."

"Detective? Well, I guess congratulations are in order. Hoo-ray." He raised a hand above the table's surface and sarcastically twirled his index finger in a circle before returning it to his lap.

Remaining silent for a moment, I returned a half-hearted smile.

"So, what's this you've got going on?" I questioned while rubbing my fingers across the non-existent facial hair of my cheek, trying to lighten the mood.

"I figured it was time to change things up," he replied. "Call it the new me."

"It's grown in nicely," I said, nodding. "Looks good."

Another bout of silence took the next moment hostage while we stared uncomfortably at each other, uncertain of what to say. Ben came around quicker than I did.

"Why are you here, Mick? I doubt it's to discuss my beard."

I immediately felt my stomach drop. I imagine my expression fell with it. Before I could reply, Ben spoke again.

"Nevermind. Your poker face needs a little work. She's dead, isn't she?"

Caught off guard, I shifted my eyes to the table and silently nodded, stumbling for the words.

"When did it happen?" he asked.

"The coroner thinks she'd been dead about four days. Maybe five. I'm so sorry, Ben."

He tightened his lips and shook his head. "It was only a matter of time, right? Was it him?"

"Who?" I asked.

"C'mon, Mick. Do you honestly think I'd forgotten about the letter? I'm surprised you guys didn't have a police presence keeping tabs on her."

"How could we have..?" I stopped when the realization hit me. "Wait; did you know your mom was in danger this whole time?"

"You *didn't*?" Ben questioned, smirking. "It was practically spelled out for you. 'That bitch of a woman,' 'The dirtiest K of them all.' How could you *not* have seen it? I think your detective skills need some refining, Mick. Especially if you're expecting to catch this one. I'll forgive you since you're still a little green at the new job. But tell me, what's Richie's excuse?"

I felt my blood begin to boil - not because Ben knew Richie's health had deteriorated, forcing him into early retirement, but because he'd known what was coming all along and said nothing.

"What's happened to you?" I questioned through clenched teeth. "All of this could have been prevented. *You* could have prevented this from happening. And now she's dead. Don't you get it, Ben? Your mother is dead, and you might as well have been the person holding the knife."

A devious smile crept onto Ben's face.

"So, the killer did what he said he'd do. You know something, Mick? I wish it *had* been me holding the knife. The bitch got what she deserved."

I couldn't take it anymore. I'd heard enough. I stood from my chair, staring at Ben's smug face as he smirked back. I now knew why Karen couldn't stand the sight of him. She'd already known what I was just now learning. Her son was dead, and in his place was this.., evil thing.

"You know something, Ben?" I said heatedly. "When we were all on that rooftop, your dad was right about something; you *are* sick. But there was also something he was wrong about; there's no getting help for you."

I nodded for the Corrections Officer to take him back to his cell. As I turned to walk away, I couldn't help but feel Ben's demented smile ripping into my back. The tormented kid I once knew, who struggled with what he had done, was gone, and in his place was an uncaring monster devoid of feeling. Even worse, there was another just like him out there somewhere, stalking his prey. I hoped the fingerprint panned out - because this sure as hell wasn't what I signed up for.

Chapter 2

L

was excited to receive a message from Sanchez that they had gotten a match on the fingerprint. It belonged to one Lyden Foster. The psychopath was already in the system, having been arrested on multiple counts of assault and battery with a dangerous weapon, including the last two times with a knife. You didn't have to put two and two together to realize he was our guy. It also didn't come as a complete surprise to learn that the man was one of Southbridge's very own.

He lived up on the north end with all the other high-society schmoozers who thought their shit didn't stink. People in that neighborhood thought they were above the law. It was easy to understand why. The north end was Victor Ramos' territory. He was one-third of the city's triumvirate of scumbag crime lords. He was everything Papa Rio was not. Born into a Columbian drug cartel, Victor was raised into money. He didn't have to work for what he had; he was the heir to his family's dynasty. How he ended up in Southbridge is anybody's guess. Some say he was run out of his country by the expansion of the Mexican cartels. Either way, the man was untouchable. He had the corrupt politicians in City Hall on his payroll, and the residents on the north end paid him handsomely to make sure their hands remained clean. It's how people like Lyden Foster remained on the streets without doing any serious jail time. But Lyden slipped up; he crossed city limits into Larson to kill his victim. Victor couldn't help him this time.

When I heard the Lieutenant was sending a unit over to aid Larson PD in picking him up for questioning, I volunteered to be their babysitter. Though he was only a person of interest at this time, I was hoping Lyden would put up a stink about coming in and perhaps get a bit physical; it would give me a chance to rough him up for what he did to Karen. Thinking about what I'd like to do to that scumbag made me feel better.

I pulled up along the nicely-edged sidewalk and parked behind our boys' squad car. Two Larson PD cruisers were in front of us, encroaching on the neighbor's property. Sanchez parked his cruiser in the driveway behind a white Jaguar, and he was standing with the other officers at the base of the perfectly groomed lawn, waiting to converge on the front door. I stepped out of my vehicle and gave Sanchez a nod.

"I had a sinking suspicion you'd be tagging along." He said.

"Yeah, well, I had to make sure you Larson boys did this by the book," I returned.

"I *bet* that's why you're here," Sanchez responded sarcastically. He nodded toward the front door, "Let's get this over with, shall we? And can you try to keep it civil?"

"I'm all about civil," I replied.

Sanchez and I, along with another uniformed officer, started up the lawn while the other three officers congregated in the driveway keeping their eyes focused on the side door. We'd seen no activity thus far; there was a chance Lyden wasn't even home.

We made our way to the front steps when Sanchez suddenly stopped.

"What the fuck?" he stated alarmingly. "Is that blood?"

He pointed to three streaks of faded red just below the doorknob that looked as though they'd been smeared onto the wood by bloody fingers. The streaks disappeared where the door met the casing, suggesting that they wrapped around to the inside. Sanchez immediately drew his sidearm and signaled to the officers in the driveway to cover the side door. With his service weapon by his side, he and the uniformed officer cautiously ascended the steps while I stayed behind.

"Mr. Foster," Sanchez yelled, knocking on the door, "this is the police! Can you come to the door, sir?"

He listened for any movement within. When he heard none, he turned to me and shook his head. He then knocked a second time.

"Lyden Foster, is everything all right in there? This is the police."

Again, he waited for a response, and again, none came.

"I don't like this, Mick," Sanchez noted. "I don't want to step on your toes; this is your jurisdiction. It's your call."

"Shit," I let out, deciding what our next move should be. "You sure that's blood?"

"I'm no expert, but it sure looks it to me."

"All right, no mishaps on this. Let's do this right. Have one of your men check with the neighbor over there," I pointed toward the house adjacent to the driveway. "I'll send Marcus over to that one," I nodded in the opposite direction while patting the rookie officer on the shoulder. "Let's find out if anybody has any information on our guy. Maybe somebody's seen something unusual. I'll call my Lieutenant; we may have to go in."

"I've got a bad feeling about this, Mick," Sanchez said, shaking his head.

"It's nothing yet," I tried to reassure, though I was thinking the same. "Wait until we hear something. Now go."

Officer Marcus started toward the neighbor on the left; Sanchez stepped away to relay the order to one of his officers. I pulled my cell phone from my pocket and dialed Frank.

"Yeah, Lieu – it's Mick. We've got a possible situation here. We're at Lyden Foster's residence. There's a vehicle in the driveway, but nobody's answering. We've got officers checking with the neighbors now, but I'm not confident they'll have anything for us. And Lieu, there's blood on the outside of the door. There may be something more going on here."

After a few seconds of the Lieutent's expletive-filled rantings, I continued.

"What do you want us to do if the neighbors don't pan out?"

Sanchez made his way back to my side. My cringing face told him an undesirable story.

"Okay, Lieu; I'll keep you posted."

I hung up and let out a deep breath, turning my stare to the smeared blood on the door.

"Well, what did he say?" Sanchez questioned.

"He said to wait until we hear what the neighbors had to say."

"They're not going to know anything," Sanchez said.

"I think you're right, but we've got our orders. We'll wait."

We waited for the officers to return and report what we already knew; the neighbors hadn't heard or seen anything from our Mr. Foster here. Things had been quiet.

"So, now what?" Sanchez asked.

"Now, we call it probable cause. Check the knob."

Sanchez grabbed the doorknob, and I watched it twist freely in his grip.

"It's unlocked," he said.

I sighed, then nodded.

Slowly, with his gun poised, Sanchez cracked the door a few inches and shouted, "This is the police; we're coming in. Keep your hands where we can see them."

When he opened the door, I could tell from his horrified expression that my wish for roughing up the suspect was no longer an option; someone had beaten me to it. Sanchez stumbled backward from the doorway, bumping into the officer behind him.

"Fuck! Shit! Fuck!"

"What is it?" I asked, springing up the steps to see for myself, even though I already knew. I squeezed past Sanchez, who was leaning over the step's iron railing to catch his breath. Officer Marcus was staring into the doorway, covering his mouth. I knew it couldn't be good. And it wasn't. For the second time in as many days, I stepped into something for which I was completely unprepared.

"Oh, my God!" I mumbled. "Call it in."

Chapter 3

The Little Pieces

I woke in a cold sweat, the visions of what I'd seen wreaking havoc in my brain. I now knew what people meant when they'd say they wanted to gouge their eyes out. I'd do it right now if I thought it would do any good. Unfortunately, with or without eyes, I'd never be able to *un*-see what I saw at Lyden Foster's residence.

"Honey, what is it?" Gina asked, having woken from my sitting up abruptly.

"It's nothing," I replied, swinging my legs off the bed. "Go back to sleep."

"Is it Karen?"

"No, I'm fine, babe. Really. I just need something to drink."

I hoped she couldn't hear the dishonesty in my voice. I hated lying to her, but I couldn't tell her the truth. I didn't need her getting worked up, and I didn't need her worrying about me. Being stressed couldn't be healthy for the baby. She was going to learn the truth soon enough, just like everyone else in this city. She might as well get a couple more nights of decent sleep before the shit hits the fan.

I made my way to the kitchen, where the feel of the cold linoleum under my bare feet had a soothing effect. It wouldn't be enough, but it was something. I poured myself a glass of ginger ale to calm my churning stomach, and then I sat at the table and stared at the rising carbonation bubbles while my thoughts wandered back to the scene.

"Call it in."

"What the fuck is going on here, Mick?" Sanchez yelled, recovering from his initial shock. "I ain't never seen anything like what's in there." He pointed toward the door.

"That makes two of us," I responded, stepping back onto the top step and closing the door. "Nobody goes inside until the medical examiner and forensics get here to give the okay. Now call it in," I said louder, practically screaming.

"You're goddamn right; I ain't going inside," Sanchez expressed vehemently. "What kind of sick fuck . . ?"

"That's exactly what we're dealing with," I cut him off, "a sick mother fucker. And worse, he's just getting started. And for Christ's sake, Marcus," I screamed at the uniformed officer, "will you call it in already? Fuck!"

In hindsight, I was probably a little hard on the rook. We'd all just stumbled upon a gruesome scene. There was no way for him to know how to react. Nothing at the academy ever trained you for what we'd encountered.

I took a sip of my drink and pressed the cold glass to my forehead to help ease the oncoming headache. Still, I couldn't wipe the memory from my thoughts.

"Well, I don't think you needed me here to declare this man was dead," Barry said.

Barry Hinkman was the newly appointed Chief Medical Examiner. He'd been the Assistant ME for years until the whole debacle with Lenny, the former Chief ME, thrust him into the forefront. The Alphabet Killer case took its toll on many of us; Lenny wasn't immune. He was relieved of his position after some disturbing behavior involving evidence tampering. It was just as well - Barry was a little less strange.

"We know he's dead, Barry," I stated. "What can you tell us about his death?"

"Oh, you know, the usual decapitation story - with a demented twist."

Barry's attempts at levity weren't doing the trick. It'd been two days, but even now, just the thought of the graphic image was enough to make my stomach flip. We'd all seen some nasty shit before, but I don't think any of us had seen anything like what we saw in that house.

"I don't think whoever did this liked the vic very much," Barry added.

"Oh, you don't say," Lieutenant Garrett stated sarcastically, stepping through the door into the crime scene. "Smartass."

"Oh good, the gang's all here," Barry jested.

I was trying desperately to keep it together. The smell alone was enough to cause me to gag. The sight was even worse. Sanchez was the smart one who decided to remain outside with Officer Marcus. And I'm pretty sure Marcus threw up on the lawn.

"As I was about to tell Mick," Barry began, "whoever did this was meticulous. This wouldn't have been easy; it took some time."

"No shit," I responded, covering my nose with my sleeve.

"Yeah, the smell," Barry said, noticing my reaction. "That's the beginning stage of decomposition. Given the color of his skin and the blackened, decayed flesh around the cuts, I'd say our friend here has been dead for about two days. The heat in here, and the body's . . , condition, certainly aren't helping matters. Consider yourself lucky this isn't day four. That's when putrefaction sets in, and the smell intensifies."

I took another sip and then placed my glass on the table. While I sat in partial darkness, my only light being the dim glow from the overhead sink fixture, the sound of the ticking secondhand from the wall clock clamored in my ears like a jackhammer. I couldn't piece together what had happened. Our person of interest - the man I believed to be responsible for Karen's death, had instead become the killer's second victim. And in the most horrific of ways. I should have known it wasn't going to be that easy, but damn, I didn't know if I was ready for all of this.

"I'd say our killer has a flair for the dramatic," Barry continued. *"Or an incredibly twisted sense of humor."*

"You think this shit is funny?" Frank growled.

"Oh, not me, Lieutenant Garrett," Barry answered, *"but it's quite obvious the killer did this for his own distorted amusement. And he had no problem leaving his tool behind for us to find. No guesswork needed on this one; the bloody hacksaw is in the other room on the kitchen table."*

"The sick fucker," the Lieutenant mumbled. *"Who does this sorta shit?"*

This "sorta shit" was an understatement. Lyden Foster had not only been killed but dismembered. His arms and legs had been severed from his body, and his head, which had an L carved into his forehead, was cut from his shoulders, leaving only the torso. But that wasn't all. The killer took the time to pose Lyden's body parts, propping them up into a seated position on the couch. His left leg was placed normally, bent at the knee and over the cushions so the foot was planted firmly on the floor. His other leg was in a leisurely folded position over the left. His left arm resided by his side, while his right was outstretched onto his leg, his hand manipulated so that he was flipping his middle finger. You would've thought the killer was trying to say "fuck you" to us if it wasn't for Lyden's head placed conveniently on the coffee table directly in front of the obscene gesture. As if that weren't enough, fourteen teeth were removed from Lyden's mouth and located neatly on the table in front of his head. Yeah, we get it, you sick fuck – fourteen letters left.

I propped my elbows onto the table beside my glass and rested my head between my palms. My hands were cold, but it wasn't from my drink. Was this what Jimmy had to deal with? It now made sense why he was always angry and brooding. But we all had the scoop on the alphabet killings; nothing in Jimmy's case was ever this bad.

"Hold on," I said. "I can't wrap my head around this. We thought this guy was our killer. We found his finger-prints at Karen's house."

"Ah, that would explain this," Barry said, lifting Lyden's left forearm from the couch to display a hand with blood-stained bandages wrapped where an index finger once existed. "I was wondering where it might be. Did you happen to find a severed finger at the last victim's house?"

"Ten of them, actually," I replied. "But they all belonged to the victim."

"Oh, damn, sorry."

"So what the fuck does this mean?" Frank questioned. "Our killer cut off this piece-of-shit's finger and went back to Karen's house to plant evidence for us to find?"

"I don't think so," Barry began to explain. "Ligature marks on the wrists and ankles suggest Mr. Foster here had been bound. Who knows for how long? But the fact that the finger - or where the finger used to be - had been treated and bandaged tells me the killer didn't want him bleeding out. At least, not until he was ready to kill him."

I jumped in immediately. "So, you think the killer tied Lyden up, cut off his finger, then went and killed the first victim and used the severed finger to plant evidence?"

"That's my guess, Mick," Barry answered.

Before I could get the words out, Lieutenant Garrett jumped in. "Then, the son of a bitch came back here days later and finished what he'd started."

"It's just a theory, at this point," Barry stated.

"How the hell did that fucker know we wouldn't find Karen's body sooner," I asked, "before he killed this guy?"

"Karen was called in as a wellness check, right?" Frank questioned. "Find out who called it in."

"I'll get Sanchez," I said, quickly turning for the door. I couldn't get out of there fast enough. Sanchez wasn't going to like what I had to tell him. He looked like he was in rough shape.

"Sanchez, my Lieutenant needs you inside." I saw his shoulders drop like he thought he'd done something wrong and his punishment was having to endure standing near the dead victim. I didn't have the heart to tell him dealing with Frank could be a worse punishment.

"Fuck me," he responded, shaking his head as he followed me back inside.

As we entered, I noticed Sanchez doing all he could to avert his eyes from the gruesome scene. Lieutenant Garrett didn't care; he wanted answers, and he was going to get them whether Sanchez could stomach it or not.

"Officer Sanchez," the Lieutenant barked, "who called in the wellness check on the first victim?"

Sanchez didn't respond at first, staring across the room, looking confused.

"I asked you a question, officer," Frank bellowed. "Who called for a wellness check on Karen?"

"Wh-what?" Sanchez asked, still staring straight ahead. "I... I'm sorry," he muttered, pointing where he'd been staring. "That picture..,"

He was pointing to a five-by-eight unframed photograph, standing vertically, leaning against the television screen.

"What about it?" Frank asked.

"I know that kid," he replied. "I used to look after him when I was in the Big Brothers program. But, I don't understand; why would it be here?"

Barry stood from his squatted position and stepped toward the television to retrieve it.

"It does seem a bit out of place, doesn't it?" he questioned, snatching it from the entertainment center. "Let's see what we've got here. Well," he nodded, "he's a good-looking kid." Then, he flipped the picture over, and his expression quickly soured.

"What is it, Barry?" I questioned.

"You're not gonna like it," he answered, pulling a pair of blue latex gloves from his jacket pocket and handing them to me. I quickly put them on and held out my hand, to which he responded by slowly passing me the picture while his eyes remained fixed upon it. I wasted little time turning it over as Sanchez peered over my shoulder. I wasn't surprised by what I saw; I was expecting it. Lyden's dismembered body wasn't the only message the killer left for us.

WELCOME, OFFICERS! I'M SURE THIS WAS QUITE UNSETTLING FOR YOU. I DO APOLOGIZE, BUT AS YOU CAN SEE, I'M NOT PLAYING GAMES. I

HAVE NO USE FOR HUMAN FILTH. IF YOU WON'T TAKE OUT THE GAR-
BAGE, I WILL. I'VE GOTTEN THE TASTE FOR IT, AND I WON'T BE
STOPPING ANYTIME SOON. ONE BY ONE, THEY'LL ALL FALL BY MY
HAND — OR SAW - AS THIS ABUSER OF WOMEN RIGHTFULLY LEARNED.
YOU CAN SEE BY MY WORK, I'VE CHANGED THE RULES A BIT. I WON'T
BE LABELED A COPYCAT. I KILL HOW I PLEASE. JUST THINK, THERE ARE
SO MANY OTHERS AWAITING THEIR TURN. AND AS YOU'VE PROBABLY
GUESSED BY NOW, YOU'RE HOLDING ONE OF THEM. I HOPE YOU DON'T
MIND, BUT I'VE HAD A HEAD START. GOOD LUCK WITH YOUR HUNT.

α

"No, no," Sanchez shouted. "We need to get to him before that maniac does. His name is Matthew. Matthew Lynch."

"Where does he live?" Lieutenant Garrett questioned boisterously.

"I haven't seen him in years," Sanchez answered. "He'd be twenty-five or twenty-six now. There's a chance he might still live with his mother in Larson."

"Get on the radio with your boss; have him send a unit over there right now."

Sanchez nodded and ran out the door. I looked at the Lieutenant's face and saw something I hadn't seen from him before - fear.

"Lieu, I . . ,"

"Don't!" Lieutenant Garrett yelled, putting his hand up in front of me. "I don't need this goddamn shit again."

"You want me to go to the kid's house?"

"No," Frank answered. "I want you and Sanchez to find out who called in the wellness check. We don't have *time for subtleties. I don't care if you have to haul their ass in; I want some answers."*

"You got it, Lieutenant."

I handed Barry the picture and turned toward the door. And as I was about to walk out, I heard Lieutenant Garrett speak in a hushed tone.

"This son of a bitch is even worse than the kid was. God help us all."

I forced down the last of my drink and placed the glass on the counter before making my way back to the bedroom where thankfully, Gina had fallen back to sleep. I stood at the foot of the bed, watching her chest gently rise and fall. She looked so peaceful. She didn't yet know what was out there, and I envied her for it. She'll be pissed when she finds out, though, knowing I didn't tell her. I hoped she'd forgive me.

I let out a quiet sigh and returned to my side of the bed. I went through the motions of lying down, pretending I'd get some sleep, but it was no use. As I stared at the long shadows on the ceiling, my mind continued to race. I thought I'd seen the worst with Karen and Lyden's deaths. I wasn't so fortunate; my nightmare wasn't over. How could I have known what was coming next? How could any of us have known?

Stop thinking about it and get some sleep, my thoughts pleaded. Easier said than done. When Sanchez and I left Lydon's house, we had yet to see how sick that fucker could be. But he was about to show us.

Chapter 4

M

The night hadn't been kind. I'd barely gotten any sleep before my alarm so rudely blared out. As strange as it sounded, though, I welcomed it. The longer I was away from the job, the longer that homicidal maniac was loose on the street. I needed to get back to it, especially after the mess this guy was leaving in his wake.

Gina hadn't woken up before I left for work this morning. I let her sleep. After today, she'd be too worried to sleep through the night. Unfortunately, as demonstrated in my restless evening, I was already at that point.

I sat at my desk, my eyes glossing over while I stared at the report in my hands. Members of the State Police were coming in this morning, and Frank and Captain Redfern expected my full report, including the previous night's horrifying discovery – the main reason for my lack of sleep. I thought I'd seen it all with Lyden's death, but now I knew how wrong I was. We now knew what kind of demented fucker we were dealing with. And soon, the whole city would know.

I scanned the report to make sure I'd captured everything. How could I not have? The images had been forever burned into my brain. I couldn't forget what I saw if I tried. Instead, the events that took place at Lyden's house, and those that took place after we left, continued to replay in my thoughts on a constant loop. And so vividly, as if seeing it for the first time over and over again. Lucky me.

"Is this it?" I asked Sanchez as he pulled up along the front lawn.
"This is the address," he replied. "Lisa Steadman, 23 Chestnut."
"Well, let's get this over with - see what she has to say."
We stepped from the squad car and made our way across the lawn. I watched a wide-eyed boy stare nervously out the front window through a gap in the curtains as we approached the front steps. As he pulled himself away and threw the curtains closed, I heard his voice clamor.
"Mom, the cops are here."
We didn't get a chance to knock as the front door flew open.
"Is he dead?" The woman at the door asked.
"Excuse me, ma'am?" I questioned.
"My husband. Is he dead? The son of a bitch didn't come home last night. It would serve him right. He was probably out with that tart from his office again."
"I'm sorry, ma'am," I interrupted. "I don't know about your husband. We're here for a different matter."
"Oh," she replied. "What then?"
"Are you Lisa Steadman," Sanchez asked.

"I am."

"You called in a wellness check for one of your associates?"

"Oh, yes. Karen Haddick. I hadn't heard anything since. Is she all right?"

Sanchez and I glanced at each other, making our reaction rather conspicuous.

"Oh my God, is SHE dead?"

"I'm afraid we can't discuss any details," I answered. "We do have a few questions we'd like to ask you. If you wouldn't mind."

"Of course," she nodded, her face showing concern.

"What made you call it in?"

"As long as I've known her, Karen has never missed a shift at the hospital without calling in. I tried calling and texting her a few times, but she didn't answer."

"How long had it been since you last heard from Karen?"

"Um..," she brought her right hand to her mouth and began tapping her bottom lip with her first two fingers. "I'd say it's been about four or five days now. It's just not like her to not tell someone or have someone cover for her if she was going to miss work. I shouldn't have waited so long; I should have called right away. Oh, God, did something bad happen?"

The woman was becoming fidgety and hysterical.

"It's all right, ma'am; I understand your concern," I said, nodding. "And what about...?" My words were cut short as Sanchez's radio blared.

"We found the kid's car abandoned on Ledgehill Road. No sign of the owner, but you'll want to get over here and see this."

Sanchez spoke into his mic, "We're on our way." Then he nodded his head toward his car. I took the hint and turned back to Mrs. Steadman.

"Thank you for your time, ma'am. We'll be in touch. If you think of anything else, please contact the Larson PD."

"I will," she said as we walked away. "And if you come across my husband, tell him his ass is in a sling when he gets home."

The woman seemed to be more worried for her colleague than she was for her husband. I threw my hand over my shoulder to acknowledge her comment but didn't bother to turn or reply. My thoughts were elsewhere.

Ledgehill Road was a long dirt road on the outskirts of Larson that cut through the middle of the woods. It used to be the access route to the old mines before they were shut down and closed off in the ninety's. There wasn't much more out that way except for a few grown-in trails that even the Appalachian Mountain Club had since removed from their list. I was now worried it could also be a place to hide a body.

When we arrived, there was a cruiser parked behind the abandoned, dark blue Corolla, and two officers were standing by the vehicle's open driver's side door. I recognized one of them - Officer Peters; we'd gone to the academy together. As Sanchez and I exited to talk with the two officers on the scene, another cruiser pulled in behind us, along with a K-9 unit behind it.

"So, what have we got?" Sanchez inquired.

"The car's registered to Matthew Lynch," one officer spoke. "It was like this when we found it. The engine's cold. From the look of it, I'd say it's been here awhile."

"What led you out this way?" I questioned, directed toward Peters, since I knew him.

"The kid's mom. She told us he liked to hike out here regularly."

"No sign of the kid, though, huh?"

"No, but you might want to check inside. On the dash. We didn't touch anything after we saw."

"What the hell is it?" Sanchez questioned, leaning inside to see for himself. A few seconds later, he shuffled back from the doorway with a shocked look on his face. "What the fuck?"

I didn't ask what it was, instead squeezing between him and the door to get a look myself. It was probably a mistake.

On the dashboard were thirteen Polaroids lined side-by-side, similar to the items at the previous two crime scenes. The pictures were of little boys, maybe between the ages of six and eleven, in various stages of undress – some of them completely naked and in provocative positions. I lost my breath for a moment, thinking what it could mean. I pushed myself from the open door to gather some air.

"What the hell is going on here, Mick?" Sanchez questioned loudly. "What is that about?"

"How the fuck should I know? We need to find Matthew. Now!"

"That's what Hunter is here for," the K-9 officer said, stepping forward, holding a leash to a large German Shepard. "If the owner of that vehicle is out here, this boy will find him."

The officer, who wore dark sunglasses (even though the sunlight was quickly fading), and whose badge read "M. Shea," was yanked passed me, pulled along by the anxious dog. Hunter lifted himself onto the bottom of the open door frame with his front two paws and sniffed around the front seat. After a few seconds, he dropped down and immediately ran to me and Sanchez, circled us twice, and then let out a loud bark. Officer Shea tilted his head downward and lowered his sunglasses just enough to peek over the frames to glare at us.

I put my hands up and shrugged my shoulders. "We were just in there."

The other two officers chuckled. Sanchez gave them a dirty look before peering back at the canine officer.

"Come on, Mike; He's gotta do better than that. We need to find this kid."

"Hunter!" the officer shouted, tugging on the leash. "One more time, boy."

Hunter repeated his car sniffing routine, sniffed the ground below the door, then sprinted to the driver's side of the road, pulling Officer Shea with him.

"All right, boy, let's go."

The leash was given some slack as Hunter darted into the forest with his handler in tow. The rest of us followed in a fast-paced walk. I wasn't sure any of us noted the time when we started, but it must have been a good fifteen minutes later that Hunter ended his tireless pursuit at the base of a large oak tree. The vehicle's owner had been found.

Matthew Lynch stood naked against the tree, his arms wrapped around the trunk in a hug. His wrists were bound together with rope, used to pull him tightly against the bark's rough surface. It appeared the rope was meant only to temporarily restrain him until the killer could enact a worse punishment, as, from his hands to his shoulders, Matthew was pinned to the tree *with long framing nails, no doubt from a nail gun. The boy's legs were similarly secured with a track of nails from his ankles to just below his buttocks. A large tree branch, about an inch in diameter, had been forced into the boy's anus. As if that wasn't bad enough, his eyes had been gouged out, and his open mouth revealed that his tongue had been sliced from it. Across the pale skin of his bare back, written in blood, the letter "M." Beneath it, the word "pedophile." And finally, the finishing touch to the gruesome scene was an axe embedded into the back of Matthew's skull. Above the boy's head, nailed to the tree, a blood-spattered note.*

"Oh my God," Sanchez let out in a muted voice. "Matthew."

"Take it easy, Sanchez," I said. "Peters, call this in," I shouted over Hunter's barks. Then, to whoever would listen, "Get the medical examiner out here," I bellowed.

"Take it easy?" Sanchez snapped. "Jesus fucking Christ, Mick. Look at this shit. The kid's dead. Fuck!"

It was bad enough that I couldn't think straight with the dog's non-stop barking. I couldn't deal with Sanchez losing it as well.

"Mike," I shouted, "can you shut your fucking dog up?"

The K-9 officer was tugging at Hunter's leash, trying to calm him down.

"He's not usually like this," the officer spoke. "He's riled up today."

"Then get him the fuck out of here. And take Sanchez back with you, for Christ's sake."

He nodded and wrangled Hunter up tight to his side. "C'mon boy; good job." Then he slapped Sanchez on the shoulder, "You too, Rubio."

"Detective Dooley!"

The Lieutenant's shout startled me, shaking me from my recall.

"Let's go. We're going to need you in here."

Having been lost in my thoughts, I hadn't seen the state police unit arrive.

"I'll be right there, Lieu," I answered, shoving pages back into the file folder. As I got to the last paper - a photocopy of the original - I paused, staring at the words on it mingled with drops of blood around them.

I'VE LEFT YOU A TREAT. THIS ONE LIKED TO LOOK AT AND FONDLE LITTLE BOYS. HOW MANY LIVES HAD HE DESTROYED BEFORE I PUT AN END TO HIS SICK WAYS? I'D SAY HE'S LEARNED HIS LESSON, WOULDN'T YOU? HOW MANY OTHER LESSONS WILL I HAVE TO TEACH? THE CITY IS RIPE WITH THE WRETCHED, WAITING FOR ME TO PURGE THEM FROM EXISTENCE. SO MANY LETTERS TO GO. WHO WILL BE NEXT ON MY LIST? YOU'LL HAVE TO WAIT AND SEE. EVEN THOUGH I'M SURE N WILL NEVER SEE IT COMING.

THE ALPHABET KILLER WAS A CHILD PLAYING A MAN'S GAME, AND FOR HIS EFFORTS, HE ROTS IN A CELL. I HAVE NO PLANS OF JOINING HIM. THE STREETS WILL RUN RED WITH BLOOD. THE SINNERS WILL LEARN OF MY WRATH. THEY WILL ALL FEAR MY NAME. AND UNTIL MY VENGEANCE IS THROUGH, SO SHALL YOU. CALL ME - THE LETTER MAN.

a

I shook my head in disgust and slid the killer's note into the folder. Whoever the bastard was, he thought he was doing good. He wrote about teaching lessons. If anyone needed to learn a lesson, it was him. I wanted to be the one to teach it to him. Bad people or not, we couldn't have vigilantes out there deciding people's fate. It was fucked up what he did to that young man, even if we learned Matthew was guilty of what the killer claimed. As nice as having one less pedophile on the street sounded..,

With that burning thought, I tucked the folder under my arm and started for the briefing room.

Chapter 5

United We Stand

It was happening all over again, the meet and greet with the officers from the state police barracks. The FBI would be next. Captain Redfern hadn't pulled the trigger yet, but I was sure it was happening after today's briefing. In the six years before the Alphabet Killer murders, I'd never worked a case involving the Feds. Suddenly, I'd found myself dragged into a situation where I'd be working with them for the second time in two years. It didn't seem possible, yet unfortunately, it was all too real.

Southbridge had the lucky distinction of being located between Larson to the west and Devers, where the state police barracks was headquartered, to the east. Because of that, Chief Copelli invited both the Larson PD and the state police to meet at the Southbridge police department for a briefing. Neither outfit put up a stink about it; that was a good start.

I stepped into the room, and all eyes of the seven officers present shifted in my direction. They must have thought I had something to say. They were going to be sorely disappointed; after what I'd seen over the past couple of days, I wasn't sure if I was even able to form a coherent sentence. Not to mention, with who was currently in the room, I had just become a small fish in a very large pond – one with a hook embedded in my cheek, and I felt I was about to be reeled in and cooked for dinner. Looking at their faces, everyone looked over-eager for answers. Perhaps being cooked wouldn't be the worst fate. These large fish looked as though they wanted to eat me alive.

In attendance were Lieutenant Garrett, Captain Redfern, and Chief Copelli from the Southbridge PD, Captain Norris and Chief Sutton from the Larson PD, and Lieutenant Frangione and Captain Bessell of the state police. Then there was me – a nobody. What the hell was I doing here?

"Gentlemen," Captain Redfern started, "this is Detective Mick Dooley. He was one of the officers responsible for bringing in The Alphabet Killer."

It sounded like gloating to me. That was Captain Redfern's way. He used it to establish superiority for the Southbridge PD. His story was a bit of a stretch, though. The only hand I had in taking down the killer was slapping handcuffs on him after he'd succumbed to grief for shooting his father.

"Detective Dooley," Captain Bessell stated, extending his hand to greet me, "good to see you again. I'm sorry it couldn't be under better circumstances. I heard about Detective Haddick's wife. I wanted to offer my condolences."

That was unexpected. The last time we worked with the state police, Captain Bessell had a hair across his ass. Maybe it was just Jimmy's sparkling personality that brought the worst out in people.

"Thank you, sir," I replied, shaking his hand. "I'm still a little numb from it all."

"Understandably. I know you were close."

I dropped my chin to my chest and nodded. "I just want to catch the son of a bitch who did it."

"We all do, son," Chief Sutton jumped in, grabbing my upper arm and gently squeezing. "That's why we're here. We know what you folks went through with the Haddick boy. Now we've got this similar lunatic threatening *both* of our cities. We've got to put an end to this quickly."

"And that's why I've already contacted the Bureau's field office," Chief Copelli announced. "We let things get out of hand last time. We won't make that mistake again. We need everyone in on this from the ground floor."

"The FBI has already been notified?" I questioned.

"That's right. I'm not taking any chances with this case. They should be here anytime now."

That was it, then. If I felt like a small fish before, I was soon to be a bottom feeder. I was happy they didn't remove me from the case, though. I shifted my glance to all the officers before focusing on Lieutenant Garrett.

"Where's Sanchez?" I questioned. "Shouldn't he be here?"

It was a question directed toward the Larson officers, but admittedly, I felt more comfortable staring at Lieu.

"I gave him the day," Captain Norris chimed in. "He took the Lynch boy's murder pretty hard. He's with the boy's mother now. I've shared Officer Sanchez's report with your superiors," he continued, stepping forward and nodding his head toward the three Southbridge officers, "as I see you've brought yours, as well."

I pulled the newly created manila folder from under my armpit and tapped the spine against my palm a few times. "I think it's everything we know. Which is to say, everything we know about the crime scenes and the victims. We've got squat on the killer."

"We've got a team combing every square inch of that kid's vehicle," Lieutenant Frangione added. "They'll find something."

"No, they won't," I stated confidently. "Larson's forensics crew has already been over it. There was nothing - not a print, not a hair, not a goddamn thing. What we *did* find were two sets of tire tracks. Two vehicles stopped at that location on Ledgehill, but only one left - backed out from the look of it. The killer was never in the kid's car except to place those Polaroids on the dash. Hell, they didn't find anything at Kare..," I froze for a moment, getting choked up on my words, "at the first victim's house, except for what the killer wanted us to find, and he was at her place for a while. It was the same with the second victim; our forensics team came up empty-handed. And we probably wouldn't have learned about victim number three for days if the killer hadn't practically held our hands and led us to him. No, they won't find anything with the kid's vehicle. This guy, this.., *Letter Man*, is too smart for that. He's already got it all mapped out; he's been planning this for too long to make a mistake."

"What makes you think that?" Captain Bessel questioned. "This lunatic could have dreamt this whole thing up two weeks ago for all we know."

The room became silent as those of us on the Southbridge force shifted our stare to one another. It was a telling moment.

"What's going on?" Captain Bessel asked. "What are you *not* telling us?"

Captain Redfern put his hand up toward me and Lieutenant Garrett as a way of silencing us. It wasn't necessary for me; I'd already said too much.

"Some time ago," Captain Redfern began, "we received an anonymous letter from someone claiming they were going to continue the alphabet killings."

"Jesus Christ!" Bessell shouted. "And you're just sharing this now?"

"It was a year-and-a-half ago, for Christ's sake. We didn't know what we were dealing with. It could have been some goddamn prank. And after six months of nothing, that's what we thought it was. You would have thought the same."

"The hell I would have," Bessell snapped. "It's this sort of irresponsibility I expect from..."

The state police captain's words were interrupted by the briefing room door bursting open.

"Gentlemen!" the suited man walking in exclaimed. "We got here as quickly as we could. Can we please start from the beginning? Also, perhaps you'd consider keeping your voices down to a reasonable decibel. We heard you screaming from halfway across the department floor."

And just like that, the FBI had arrived.

Chapter 6
Divided We Fall

He exuded authority from the moment he entered, the broad-shouldered man who lacked any form of human expression. If ever there was a stereotypical federal agent with the non-descript black suit and heavily tinted shades, he was staring me in the face. Even if he *hadn't* looked the part or immediately offered his identification upon his entrance, the agent following him through the door would have blown his cover.

Special Agent Marion Hayes was all too familiar with the unsmiling features her colleague presented. *Her* cold demeanor prominently displayed itself during the Alphabet Killer case. I understood why, especially after our conversations at the hospital. She'd worked harder than most of her peers to garner a fraction of the respect. I admired her for that. I think Jimmy did, too. He didn't show it; it just wasn't his style. Though, I think he would have come around had he known she waited with the rest of us the entire time while he was in surgery. She earned a lot of officers' respect that day. Yeah, Jimmy would have appreciated that.

The intimidating figure slowly removed his dark glasses to reveal his equally dark eyes and chiseled features. With an intense stare, he carefully scanned those of us in the room as he folded his spectacles and slid them into his breast pocket.

"Judging by the looks on your faces," he began, "I'd say you're not too happy to see us. That's fine; you don't have to be happy. We're not here to make friends. I'm Special Agent Gunner Lowe, and as of right now, we'll all be working together on this case."

The man knew how to make an entrance. If he intended to stir the pot, he was well on his way to doing so.

"I believe some of you may have already met my colleague, Special Agent Marion Hayes."

"Hello, gentlemen," she said, nodding toward the state police and Larson officers. "Chief Copelli," she added, glancing in his direction, "you did the right thing by contacting us sooner this time."

"Time will tell on that one, won't it?" Chief Copelli replied. "We've got a live one on our hands. Three murders so far in two jurisdictions. Both the Southbridge and Larson Police are sorting through what little evidence we have, searching for traces of anything the killer might have left behind at the scenes."

"And what have you found?" the stoic agent asked, stepping forward as if to assert his command.

"Besides three dead bodies," Lieutenant Garrett jumped in, "we've got dick. Pardon my language, Agent Hayes."

"It's quite all right, Lieutenant; I've heard worse."

"Yeah, I imagine you have," he replied.

"Can we dispense with the pleasantries and unproductive chit-chat?" Special Agent Lowe remarked.

I didn't care for the stiff agent's attitude, as I imagine most of the brass didn't, but I was curious as to why Hayes hadn't shut that overbearing machismo down immediately. It wasn't like her to let someone else step on her toes. From what I remember, she was all about collaboration, not hostile takeovers.

"We're going to need both departments to catch us up to speed with everything you have on this case," he continued. "And I do mean *everything* - the names of the victims, any suspects you might have, locations, times; it all comes out on the table, gentlemen. If you know what the victims had for their last meals, we'll take that information too."

"Now, hold on a minute," Chief Sutton argued, stepping forward and pointing his finger at the demanding agent. "I don't care how expensive your fancy suits are; you can't march in here flashing your FBI badges and expect us to just hand everything over to you. If that's what you're assuming, my people are perfectly capable of handling this case without your involvement. You're supposed to be working *with* us, not *against* us."

"Right, and who are you?" the unabashed agent asked, his eyes narrowing.

"I'm Chief Sutton of the Larson PD. It was my men that found the first body."

Chief Sutton was blowing smoke, probably hoping Agent Blowhard would choke on the fumes. His statement wasn't exactly accurate. Although the first murder did take place in Larson - that much was true - it was both Sanchez and me who stumbled across Karen's body. Either way, I had to give the man credit. He wasn't afraid to get in the tall agent's face. For a short, unassuming-looking, rapidly balding, gray-haired man who was far past his prime, Chief Sutton had been around the block a few times. Everyone in the room knew him as a hard-nosed yet compassionate figure of authority who commanded the respect of his officers. Unfortunately, I don't think that mattered much to the FBI.

"Well, Chief Sutton," the agent responded, peering down at the shorter, aged man, "let me make this clear to you." He then raised his chin to address the room. "Let me make this clear to *all* of you. Agent Hayes and I *are* here to work with you, but whether you like it or not, this case has now fallen under federal jurisdiction. The Bureau expects full cooperation from both local authorities and the state police, and any attempt to hinder our investigation can and will result in a full criminal inquiry into your departments. I'm not here to be a hardass; I'm only telling you like it is. Believe me when I tell you this, gentlemen; you do *not* want to be in the hot seat when the hammer comes crashing down."

"All right, all right," Captain Bessell chimed in. "We don't need the speech, Special Agent Lowe. None of us are looking to hinder any investigation. We all want the same thing. But you need to understand that many of us have been through this shit before, and it didn't end well for one of our colleagues."

I noticed Agent Hayes dip her head at the Captain's comment.

"Furthermore," he continued, "it would serve you better if you dismounted from that high horse you seem to have ridden in on. Many of us have experience dealing with the likes of a sadistic serial killer – or spree killer – whatever the fuck you want to label these freaks, so whether *you* like it or not, you're going to need *our* help as much as you seem to think we'll need yours."

I saw Hayes flash the slightest hint of a smile, though she tried hard to disguise it. I think I had the same reaction. I had to give it up for Captain Bessell. He came across as such an asshole when last I worked with him, almost as much as the agent he was confronting. Now, he seemed more like one of us than I'd given him credit for. The Alphabet Killer case sure changed a lot of us.

"I understand your concern, as unwarranted as it is, Captain," Agent Lowe retorted, "and I appreciate the fact that many of you have had to deal with a similar situation." The stiff agent swerved his stare back to the older chief. "But that isn't the case with you, Chief Sutton, now is it? The Alphabet Killer's stomping grounds were limited to Southbridge. Larson remained wholly untouched."

"The fuck it did!" Chief Sutton barked. "You didn't have to see the horrified looks on the faces of those in my community every day. The residents of Larson were not only devastated by what was going on in their neighboring city, but they were also fearful it could spill onto their streets and into their homes. And what did the FBI do to make everyone feel safe? Nothing. It wasn't even the FBI that caught the son of a bitch; it was one of Southbridge's own. So you'll need to forgive me if I don't seem overwhelmingly enthused about your sudden arrival. Now, if you'll excuse me, I've got a department full of officers to get back to with real police work to do."

Without another word, but instead, a simple nod to his second in command, Chief Sutton stormed past the taller agent, making sure to nudge him with his shoulder on the way by. Captain Norris followed in his commanding officer's footsteps, only without the shoulder nudge. With a sideways glance, Special Agent Lowe watched as the two men left the briefing room. When the door closed behind them, he turned back to those of us remaining.

"Well, now that we know where Chief Sutton stands," he began, "are there any others among you that would like to speak their piece before we get on with it?"

Chief Copelli motioned with his hand as if he were about to raise it, then quickly lowered it to his side before announcing his thoughts.

"I'd like to say something," he started in his usual, mild-mannered tone. "Before you pass judgment on who you think we are, know that these men are all good officers. As Captain Bessell stated, we all want the same thing: to catch the bastard who's killing our good citizens. That includes Chief Sutton there." He pointed his finger toward the closed doors. "I'd had the distinct pleasure of working with Chief Sutton many years ago when we were both lieutenants in Fullerton. He's as fine an officer now as he was then. Also, not many here know this, but Sutton was an officer on the Milwaukee force in '91 when Jeffrey Dahmer was taken into custody. So, yeah, he's seen his fair share of sick shit."

"That's all well and good," Agent Lowe replied, brushing aside the Chief's words, "but we're a long way from Wisconsin and an even longer way from '91. Try to remember, it was *you* who contacted the FBI - not the other way around. And, now that we're here, we have a job to do. We *all* have a job to do." His eyes shifted to the other officers. "Like it or not, your departments *will* give us your full cooperation. And yes," he threw his thumb over his shoulder, "that includes Chief Sutton and his officers.

Now, if there's nothing more, I'd like to get down to what we're all here for. We don't want a repeat of last time."

The no-nonsense agent turned his stare to me. "Is that the full report, officer?" he asked, pointing to the folder under my arm.

"It's Detective Dooley, sir," I answered, jumping forward, shocked he had suddenly singled me out. "I'm sure it's not everything, but it's *my* full report, anyway."

"Let's have a look."

He put his hand out, signaling me to surrender the documents. With everyone's temperatures flaring, I wasn't sure where things had left off. I looked to Captain Redfern, who was in my direct line of sight, for guidance. His affirmative nod was all I needed. I passed the folder to the demanding federal agent and stepped back several feet while the other offices huddled closer. Once outside the "circle of important people," I stepped back a few more feet, a move that didn't go unnoticed by Special Agent Hayes.

Stepping away from her fellow agent to let the "boys," as I'm sure she'd refer to them, have their discussions, she approached me with a sympathetic smile.

"Officer Dooley.., Mick. So, detective now, huh?"

"Yeah, it's been about five months. I'm still getting used to the gig, you know?"

"You deserve it," Hayes remarked. "But if I'm being honest, you look like shit. Have you been sleeping?"

"That's the question, isn't it?" I replied. "I'm guessing, by my looks, you already know the answer."

"Has it been that rough?"

"This fucking guy.., I swear, I don't know what it is, but he's worse than Ben was. I don't know. I could be making shit up. The Alphabet Killer was more your and

Jimmy's case. It's just.., the messages he leaves.., The Letter Man – that's what he calls himself - there's such anger and hatred in them. And then *this* uptight douchebag," I waved my finger at her male counterpart, "why haven't you taken control of the situation?"

Hayes glanced over at her partner before returning her attention to me.

"Well, quite frankly, it's not my situation to gain control of. Special Agent Lowe is the man in charge."

"What are you talking about? I thought you were like, you know, the head agent or something."

She let out a chuckle and looked down at the floor. I could tell she was frustrated.

"Yeah, well, things have changed a bit, Mick." She lifted her eyes back up to meet mine. "After The Alphabet Killer, things didn't exactly play out nicely. I thought I handled the case the best I could have. The Bureau thought otherwise. They told me they should have sent a 'more capable agent.' Can you believe that? Not to mention, I may have done a few things since that case that hadn't exactly been to the Bureau's liking. Since then, they've had me pulling back-up duty. Oh sure, they let me keep my title, which they think I'm supposed to be thankful for, but instead, I've been a sidekick to just about every other 'more capable agent' they've paired me with. I'm afraid I'm number two on this one." She glared at Agent Lowe. "In more ways than one."

"Shit!" was all I managed to let out before realizing how that must have sounded after what she just said. I wanted to say more. I should have, but my brain and tongue weren't working together.

"Exactly," she replied.

"No, I didn't mean..,"

"It's okay, Mick," she smiled, "I knew what you meant."

I didn't say anything more. I just put my head down and nodded. What were we to do; we'd both been dealt shitty hands. How we played them, though, that was up to us. And, as Hayes pulled at my sleeve, bringing me back to our present situation, I decided right then that I wasn't going to fold. The FBI wasn't going to steamroll us; fuck that. There was a psychotic fucker out there killing people. He killed that kid. He killed Karen. With or without the FBI's help, I was going to nail his ass to the wall.

Agent Hayes nodded her head toward the others. I understood; it was time to get back into Agent Lowe's little game of "I'm in charge." And as we joined the group, I couldn't help but think a single thought. The Letter Man had better be ready for me because *I* was ready for *him*. Shitty hand or not, I was all in.

Chapter 7

The Funeral

Gina squeezed my hand as I placed the rose on Karen's casket. We said our final goodbyes, then stepped back with the rest of the mourners who were there to pay their respects. It was a good turnout from the department. Even though Karen and Jimmy divorced some time ago, it didn't matter; she was a cop's wife, and the death of an officer's spouse always brought us together. Even Agent Hayes showed up. Sanchez, too, though I could tell he was uncomfortable after what he'd gone through with his wife and son. Poor bastard. I couldn't imagine what I'd be like if I lost Gina, never mind my kid. Still, I appreciated him for taking the time to be here.

I still couldn't believe this was real. We buried Jimmy's ashes only two years ago, and now we were putting Karen in the ground. Something about that seemed fucked up. I wanted to lose my shit, but I had to keep it together for Gina's sake. She'd already had her meltdown when she found out I'd kept the news from her - that there was another sadistic killer on the loose who picked up right where the kid left off. I should have known better, but I'd never been the brightest guy when it came to women. I couldn't say anything anyway, no matter how smart I was. She understood, even though she didn't like it. I sure got lucky with Gina, though. I thank God for her every day. I felt myself following her lead and returned a gentle squeeze to her hand. Out of the corner of my eye, I caught her looking up at me, but I couldn't look back for fear the floodgates would open. I knew she saw it in my face when she hugged my arm with her other hand. As I said, I sure did get lucky.

The minister said his final prayers and offered his heartfelt condolences to those friends and family in attendance. Then, just like that, it was over. Most people were quick to disperse, offering a quick goodbye handshake to those they hadn't seen in a while, making empty promises to get together other than at the next person's funeral. Frank said a few words to Karen's older brother, who'd flown in from Denver the day before, then made his way over to me and Gina. He looked distraught.

"This was a tough one," he said, letting out a heavy sigh while shaking my hand and staring at the casket with flowers draped over it. I didn't realize Frank was that close to Karen. I wonder if it was a feeling of guilt for all the years he'd given Jimmy shit. Either way, I was glad he took the time to make it.

"It sure was," I replied. "First Jimmy, now Karen. I can't believe they're both gone."

"Yeah," Frank said, nodding, still focusing on Karen's casket. "I'm going to head back to the station. Special Agent Lowe is still rustling through paperwork and being a pain in my ass. You coming back today?"

I looked at Gina first. She nodded.

"Yeah, I'll be back there in a little bit. I just.., I need a little more time here, if you don't mind, Lieu."

"Take what you need, Mick."

He patted my arm, then turned to Gina and gave her a sorrowful look before taking her hand, leaning in, and giving her a peck on the cheek.

"I'll walk with you, Frank," Gina said, nodding toward me, letting me know she knew what I needed. My lips formed a slight smile.

As they walked back toward the vehicles, following a line of officers who'd already started heading out, they stopped to chat with Hayes. She'd been, for the most part, left alone at the rear of the departing crowd, probably feeling out of place. Frank did what he could to show his appreciation. He bent his arm, gesturing for her to grab hold to join him and Gina. She smiled and graciously accepted, sliding her arm through the opening. It was good to have her on board.

I turned back to Karen's casket looming over the hole that would become her final resting place and watched her brother place his hand on the lid while bowing his head. I'd only met him once before - at Karen and Jimmy's wedding. From what I understand, they weren't that close. But, hey, at least he made it.

Finishing his thoughts, he turned in my direction, gave me a quick nod, and then strolled past me, leaving me alone. Or, at least, I thought I was.

"Hey, buddy," the voice quietly spoke, "how are you holding up?"

It was Sanchez, approaching from behind. He'd stayed even as the rest of the attendees were driving off.

"It's a shame," I answered, maintaining my stare on the casket's flowers as Sanchez made his way beside me. "This shouldn't have happened."

"Come on, man," Sanchez responded, "you can't keep doing this to yourself. If it was going to happen, it was going to happen. There's nothing you could have done to change that."

"I know you're right," I replied. "It doesn't make it hurt any less. It's funny, but I keep looking at her casket, thinking she's still here - that this is all a practical joke or a bad dream or something. How did you get through it with your wife and.., with Miguel."

His response began with a heavy sigh as he dropped his chin to his chest.

"It took me a long time to get over Maria's death. I couldn't stand to watch the cancer eating away at her. I wanted her pain to stop – her suffering to end, but then, when it did, I realized she was gone for good, and I had a son to raise. Only then, I was on my own. I loved that woman more than I probably showed, but I hated her for leaving us. Fucking cancer, man. So, there I was a widowed father with no freaking idea what I was going to do without my wife. Suddenly, I'm the only person my eight-year-old kid has got; you know what I'm saying? I didn't know how to raise a kid by myself. Fuck! Maybe if I did, I would have seen the signs."

"I'm sorry, Rubio," I offered. "I didn't mean to..."

"No, it's good, Mick. It's been two years. It's good to get this shit out of me. If I didn't, I'd probably explode."

"Miguel was a good kid," I responded. "You should be proud of the job you did."

"Oh, he was a *great* kid," Sanchez added. "He just never got over his mother's death. I knew he was depressed; we both were. I thought it was something he needed to work through, you know? I thought he'd come out stronger once he did. I'll tell you, though, I'll never forget that night I got home from work. The goddamn kid couldn't tie a knot to save his life but somehow figured it out well enough to hang himself. Christ! Sixteen years old. He had his whole life ahead of him. I'll never get over his death."

It suddenly became silent while Sanchez wiped a stray tear from his eye. I could tell his thoughts remained tormented no matter how much time had passed.

"Did you know he left me a note?" he continued. "He said he couldn't deal with it anymore - that he missed his mom and wanted to meet up with her again. If only I'd seen how much he was hurting inside. But I didn't see it. Or I didn't *want* to see it. What's that say about me?"

I turned to my friend and placed my hand on his shoulder, his eyes bloodshot and snot leaking from his left nostril, mingling with the top of his mustache.

"Hey, now who's being too hard on himse..."

I stopped mid-sentence, my thoughts suddenly lost. Something over Sanchez's shoulder grabbed my attention. He noticed immediately and turned his head slightly to see what distracted me.

"What?" he questioned, wiping his nose with his thumb and forefinger. "What is it?"

"Who is that?" I nodded.

"Who?" Sanchez answered, now turning fully to see what diverted my attention.

"Who the fuck *is* that?" I repeated, dropping my hand from Sanchez's shoulder and stepping by him.

In the distance, a lone, lime-green vehicle sat conspicuously parked along the cemetery roadway, its occupant, a hooded figure, leaning against the rear passenger door, staring at us through binoculars. It seemed too strange for me to ignore. I continued walking in the person's direction even as Sanchez voiced his opinion.

"It's probably nobody, Mick," Sanchez stated, slowly following me.

"Then what's with the binoculars?" I questioned.

"All right, sure, it's a little weird; I'll give you that. But, come on, man - he's probably not even looking at us. Maybe he's one of those bird watchers or some shit."

"Bullshit!" I said, hastening my pace. "He's looking right at us."

Sanchez reluctantly followed my lead, griping under his breath at my stubborn insistence while I weaved around headstones. As we started up a small grassy hill, a gradual incline leading to the roadway, the curious figure pulled the binoculars down to glare at us over the top of them. Though I couldn't get a good look at the man's features from this distance, his undeniably suspicious actions made me believe something was amiss. He hurriedly ran around the trunk to the driver's side, got into his still-running vehicle, and sped off. I frantically sprinted the rest of the way up to the roadside, hoping to get a license number. It was no use; he was already too far away, exiting the property. All I got was the make of the vehicle: a Hyundai.

Sanchez finally joined me on the pavement, looking a little ragged as he bent over and rested his palms on his knees, trying to catch his breath.

"Shit, Mick," he began, gasping for oxygen. "I'm not in that kinda shape anymore. Do you want to tell me what's going on? What was that all about?"

"I don't know," I replied, shaking my head. "I just didn't get a good feeling about that guy."

"Because he had binoculars at a cemetery? Fuck, Mick, it's not illegal. You probably scared the guy half to death, running at him as you did."

"I know, I know."

"Listen, buddy," Sanchez said, pushing himself upright, "I know Karen's death has your head all messed up right now, but you gotta get control of that shit."

"I just... I don't know." I hunched over and took a moment to rub the sweat from my forehead. "Sorry, Rubio. Everything's just got me on edge right now. I can't even think straight. It's like everything is something, you know?"

"Hey, it's okay, man. I get it. But not everything is about this case. Sometimes it's just regular shit."

He shook his head and smirked.

"Now come on," he patted my upper back, "let's get you to your vehicle."

"Yeah, okay," I said, standing up and glaring toward the cemetery gates. Rubio was right; I had to let things go. I realized I was getting too attached to the case. I had to keep a clear head and remove myself from the victims. There was no difference between this and any other homicide case. Yeah right. Someday, I might even find myself believing that.

With Sanchez at my side, I turned around, and we began walking down the roadway toward our vehicles. We remained silent for a fair distance until Sanchez spoke up, no doubt, to lighten the dour mood.

"Do you have lightning in your pants or something?" he said, grinning. "You were like The Flash back there."

"Shut up, Sanchez," I remarked, shaking my head and rolling my eyes.

"I'm serious, man. I've never seen you move so fast. You were like Speedy Gonzalez. You probably put that Bolt guy to shame. You know, that Olympic runner."

"Am I going to have to put up with this from now on?" I questioned, giving Sanchez a friendly shove.

"I don't know," he replied, snickering. "Are you going to be running again anytime soon, Roadrunner?"

I gave him a sideways glance. "You done?"

"Depends if we come across any coyotes," he answered, shrugging his shoulders. He responded stone-faced, which only added to the humor.

Sanchez was just being stupid, but I appreciated that he was trying to take my mind off the situation. The least I could do was join him.

"At least I wasn't a snail, like someone I know."

"Ouch! That hurt, man."

"Hey, at least I didn't say a winded, out-of-shape snail."

"Fuck you, Mick," he said, smirking. "I work hard at keeping this pear shape. I even lift weights."

"Oh, I know; 12 ounces at a time."

"You beat me to it," Sanchez laughed, reciprocating the shove as we reached my car.

I shook his hand and thanked him again for coming, then got into my car. We both had to get back to work, something neither of us was looking forward to. In a way, Sanchez was lucky he wasn't in the detective bureau. He could get back to his daily routine. He didn't have to keep his hands in the muck. The FBI and the detectives in Southbridge and Larson would handle most of the heavy lifting. Unfortunately, that meant *I* couldn't escape it. But with everything weighing heavily on me, I was more determined than ever to see it through. I wasn't going to let Jimmy and Karen down again, and I wasn't about to let myself down.

As I drove off, I watched Sanchez getting into his car and couldn't help but think of everything he had lost - his wife, his kid. It made me realize my focus was misaligned. It wasn't that I was so determined because of Jimmy and Karen's deaths. It had nothing to do with them. It was Gina. She was my rock. I couldn't stand the thought of her worrying about things. That about summed it up; it was all for her. I wasn't going to let *Gina* down. And I sure as hell wasn't going to rest until I put a stop to that psychopath out there killing people.

Chapter 8

The Silent Hours

I could hear the guys at Detective Frazier's desk placing wagers on whether the killer would strike again. It had been three weeks since the last murder, and we hadn't heard a peep out of the guy. Normally, that would be a good thing, but the case had run cold, and we needed something to get us back on track. None of the crime scenes offered anything except what the killer wanted us to find. We had no leads, no suspects, and no direction in which to go. Even the FBI was becoming restless. Special Agent Lowe had already exhausted his resources at the field office, and Washington was threatening to reassign him and Agent Hayes if there was no further activity. If we didn't need the federal resources, that wouldn't have been such a bad thing. Vera and her crew took their best crack at Lyden Foster's place, determined to find something that might have been overlooked. Sadly, they were unsuccessful.

I think Vera was taking it the hardest. We all knew she thrived on that stuff, and the fact a serial killer was involved made it more exciting for her. She got off on that shit. She said it made her "tingly." There was no doubt the woman was messed up (she'd be the first to admit that), but she was passionate about her job. She wanted to catch the guy as much as the rest of us, though she'd have to take her place in line behind me.

The respite had, at least, offered *something* positive (besides the fact nobody had died in the past three weeks). Chief Copelli was able to smooth things over between the two departments and the FBI. Even Chief Sutton managed to cool down and get on board once Special Agent Lowe backed off his narcissistic stance and apologized. I think Special Agent Hayes had something to do with that. She might not be the one in charge anymore, but I bet she could still knock a man down a peg or two if she wanted. And believe me, she wanted.

Everyone on the force was on pins and needles, waiting for the hammer to drop. We all had other cases to work on; uniformed officers were still on the street doing their jobs, but you could feel the tension in the air. We were all waiting, anticipating the killer's next move. We all felt it was going to happen, but we didn't know when. It was *that* helpless feeling that was more excruciating than the crime scenes.

Captain Redfern had been on daily conference calls with the Larson PD and state police, checking to see if they'd had any movement in the case and updating them on our unchanged progress. Special Agents Lowe and Hayes had appropriated the briefing room as their makeshift command center, updating Washington every day with the slightest details, making it look like they were still needed here. The truth was, unless (or is it, *until?*)

this "Letter Man" struck again, we were all left holding our dicks.

"Jesus Christ, Mick," Lieutenant Garrett shouted from his doorway, "you got a problem with your hearing?"

"What do you mean, Lieu?" I asked, sitting upright in my chair.

I could hear the snickering behind my back.

"I've been standing here calling to you, and you've been staring out into space like a fucking moron."

"Sorry, Lieu. I was distracted. I guess I had some things on my mind."

"Well, get them off your mind," he barked.

"It won't happen again," I assured him. "What do you need?"

"I need you to get your ass downstairs to find out what Vera is chirping about. She's been blowing up my goddamn phone."

"You got it, Lieu," I replied, jumping from my chair as he disappeared back into his office.

"You gonna be able to find your way, space cadet, or does someone need to hold your hand?" Detective Frazier joked while the officers around him chuckled louder.

I turned my head slightly to acknowledge his comment while continuing forward, "Shut the fuck up, Frazier, or I'll tell everyone what I caught you doing in the men's room the other day."

I caught a glimpse of the others turning their curious stare toward him, wondering what that was about. I felt myself smirk as I turned my attention forward. Truth was, I didn't catch Frazier doing anything, but the others now thought I did, and they wouldn't believe him no matter how much he denied it. *Say something else about me, fucker*, I thought, as I rounded the corner to the staircase, a pleased smile on my face.

It wasn't often I made my way to the Dragon's lair. The cases I'd worked on prior didn't need the crime lab's assistance. I'm sure Vera was thankful for that; she had enough going on without me feeding her anything more. Speaking of which…

"Holy fuck," the shrill voice clamored from the open lab door, disrupting my thoughts. "Do my eyes deceive me? Is that Matt Damon coming to visit me?"

"No, Vera; it's me, Mick."

I noticed her roll her eyes while she leaned against the door, keeping it propped open. "No shit, Sherlock."

"As always, it's nice to see you, too."

"What the fuck do you expect, Mick; you caught me just as I was heading out."

"But Lieutenant Garrett said you wanted someone down here."

"Well, you sure took your sweet-ass time," she replied. "That was half an hour ago. Shit-for-brains up there has been ignoring my calls all morning. He must still be sore at me for beating him at poker the other night."

"Well, I don't know anything about that," I said, "but I'm here now. Is it something quick?"

Vera glanced up the stairs, sighed, then nodded her head sideways into the lab. "Come on. I don't want the bosses hearing this."

I felt my eyes widen at the thought of what it could be as I stepped by her into the lab and she closed the door behind us.

"What? What is it, Vera?"

"This stays between you and me," she began. "Oh, and Danny over there," she peered over my shoulder, "but he doesn't count."

I turned and saw her lab tech standing at a table, looking up from a microscope after having heard his name. He gave me a quick wave, then went back to staring into the lenses.

"Listen, I'm going batshit crazy here," she continued.

"What do you mean?" I asked.

"I mean, I need something on this Letter Man case. I'm sooo bored. This other shit we're doing doesn't compare. Give me something, Mick; anything."

"Sorry, Vera," I responded. "We've got nothing."

"Shit, fuck! That's it, then; you're going to make me say it, aren't you?"

"Say what?"

"You're not gonna like this, and I almost hate even thinking it."

"Well, what is it already?"

"It's like this - I'm gonna need you to go out there and kill somebody."

I shook my head and leered. "That's not even funny," I replied.

Her shoulders dropped in disappointment. "Aw, come on, Mick. It can be an ugly fucker. Anybody."

"You're too much, Vera."

I knew she was joking, and had it been anyone else, I probably would have punched them. It still lacked taste. Speaking of which...

"Fine," she replied, interrupting my thoughts again before I could get my words out. She grabbed the door and swung it open, "I'll stick with this boring shit." She gave me a little shove and walked out with me. "I don't mean to rush you, but I've got a dentist appointment I need to get to. I chipped my tooth on a bone last night." She then gave me a dirty look. "I can tell what you're thinking, smart ass, but no; it was an *actual* bone."

I wasn't thinking anything, but speaking of which... I paused for a moment, thinking I might get interrupted yet again. It didn't happen.

"Hey, Vera - I've been meaning to ask you – would you like to come over for dinner?"

She stopped in her tracks and raised her left eyebrow, a mischievous smile on her face.

"Did you just ask me out on a date?"

I felt my face become flush. "What? No, I..," I suddenly became nervous and tongue-tied. "I was asking you over for dinner."

"Sure sounds like a date to me."

"It's not," I quickly responded. "You know I'm married."

"And that means what exactly?" she naughtily replied.

"Quit it, Vera," I said, shaking my head nervously. "Gina's been asking me to have you over since you helped her with her forensics paper."

"Fuck; your wife's gonna be there?"

"Of course."

"Listen, Mick - I didn't mind it when I thought I'd be riding your pony solo, but I'm not into that 'three-way with a married couple' shit." She paused for a second or two before rolling her eyes and showing me a huge grin. "All right, you caught me; I totally am."

"Are you done fooling around, now?" I questioned.

"All right, fine. You cooking?"

"No, Gina's cooking pork chops."

"Aw, hell no. You lost me at 'Gina's cooking.'"

I shook my head and exhaled heavily, "Why does everyone say that?"

"Don't get me wrong, kid, I love your wife, but that woman's got no business in the kitchen. Do yourself a favor and get some take-out on the way home. I gotta get going."

She smacked me on the arm and strolled past me, making her way up the stairs. I dropped my chin to my chest, feeling sorry for myself.

"Fuck!" I whispered. "Her cooking really *is* that bad." I turned my head to the glass walls of the lab and saw Danny awkwardly staring at me. Again, he gave me a quick wave before turning his attention to a centrifuge. I rolled my eyes and started my trek back upstairs. All I could think of was how bad my wife's cooking was.

Like Vera, I was bored with the mundane cases. I needed to get my head back in the game. I felt like I was losing it. Maybe the woman was onto something. Suddenly, killing someone didn't sound like such a bad idea. I joke, of course, but it sure beats sitting around twiddling my thumbs, waiting for our guy to do the dirty work. I thought about checking the obits and recent arrests – maybe I'd get lucky and find our killer there. I knew he hadn't moved to a different area; what he was doing was too personal for that. No, he was still out there.

I knew I shouldn't think that way. We should all be thankful it's been quiet these past few weeks. That was the problem; it's been a little *too* quiet. If there's one thing I've learned, that's never been a good thing. It usually meant something bad was coming.

I only hoped I was wrong.

Chapter 9

N

The days felt longer when there wasn't much to do except compare notes with the other officers who had even less information about the case than I did. The only thing that kept me sane was thinking about getting home to my wife. She'd be disappointed Vera couldn't make it for dinner, but it was probably for the best. I'm not sure how well that woman would have been able to keep quiet after tasting Gina's food. She'd never been one to hold back. Whenever Gina cooked pork, it was almost like eating a mystery meat. Then again, maybe Vera would've felt right at home. It might have taken a forensics expert of her caliber to determine what it was.

I walked in the front door and immediately felt the weight of the day lifted from my shoulders. The sight of Gina had a way of doing that to me. The smell of the food on the stove, however, did not. I did my best to block that from my mind as I draped my jacket over the kitchen chair. She turned from stirring what I assumed was gravy (though I couldn't tell from the color of it) to greet me.

"You look ragged, hon," she said with a sympathetic voice, showing me eyes that matched.

I shook my head and smiled, "Not anymore; just glad to be home. How's my little girl today?" I bent down and kissed Gina's stomach before standing and kissing her cheek. Gina sighed while circling her hand around her belly.

"She's been active today," she answered. "I think she wants out as much as I want her out. Either that, or she wants to be a soccer player in the worst way."

"If she takes after you, maybe," I responded.

Gina was an athlete in high school, excelling at track and field. The only thing I excelled at was passing my homework in late. And that was if I passed it in at all.

I placed my hand on the front of Gina's stomach. "You've got a couple more weeks to go, little lady. Stay in there until you've finished cooking. We don't want you half-baked like your old man."

"Stop it," Gina said, smiling, pulling the dish towel from her shoulder and gently whipping my hip. "But seriously," she continued, rubbing her palm across my cheek, "you look so tired."

"I'm all right," I assured her as I leaned in and gave her another kiss. "I promise." I flashed her a teasing smirk, "At least until after I eat your food."

I backed away a step in case she took a swing at me. Playfully, her mouth dropped, and with it, her eyebrows.

"You *like* my cooking," she said, her voice elevated.

I smiled, "Of course I do. I'm going to wash up."

I turned to make my way to the bathroom. I didn't want her to see my guilty face. Liking her cooking was the only thing I'd ever perpetually lied to her about. And if I knew what was good for me, I'd keep up that lie.

Looking at myself in the mirror made me realize Gina was right. I *did* look ragged. It's been the constant worrying. The killer was still out there, and he wasn't through. The last note he left confirmed that much. "*The streets will run red with blood,*" he wrote. He even went so far as to throw it in our faces, "*N will never see it coming.*" Yeah, the fucker was out there, probably laughing at us.

I splashed my face with cold water to give myself a little jolt. I took a deep breath and slowly let it out, then swiped a hand towel down my face to wipe away the excess liquid, hoping it would also wipe away the stress. It was an unsuccessful effort. I hated for Gina to see me worry. She never liked me being a cop in the first place but learned to live with it and supported my decision to stay on the force. She's one hell of a lady.

As I stepped from the bathroom, my cell phone rang. I saw it was Lieutenant Garrett. Foolishly (or maybe desperately), I answered.

"Hello? No, it's okay. What's going on?"

Gina peeked around the corner from the kitchen and leaned against the wall, her arms crossed about her chest.

I tilted my head to the side and shrugged my shoulders apologetically while I listened to what Lieu had to say.

"I understand," I said. "Yeah, I'll be down there."

I hung up and gave Gina a sorrowful stare, unsure of how I should break the news to her. She made it easy for me. She could see it on my face.

"He's back, isn't he?"

I nodded. "Someone called it in; another body turned up."

I watched Gina's shoulders drop. She knew I had to go.

"Be careful, Mick. You know I won't be able to relax until you get home."

I stepped beside her, placing my hand on her free shoulder, trying to maintain a positive attitude. I saw in her eyes that she could tell I struggled with it.

"I'm always careful," I answered.

As I walked by her and grabbed my jacket from the chair, she didn't budge, continuing to stare forward. I knew she was worried, but there wasn't anything I could say to change that. I had a job to do, a killer to bring down. She knew that. It wasn't about me; it was about keeping our little girl safe – safe from being brought up in a world where scumbags preyed on the innocent. I wasn't going to let that happen. I opened the door and glanced back, saw she was still facing away from me, and thought I should say something, but the words never came out. I silently walked out the door.

* * *

I pulled up to the Yorkshire Building on the corner of Franklin and Murcer and parked behind the FBI's non-discreet, black Escalade. Two cruisers were parked just beyond the building's front entrance, a third across the street. The medical examiner's van was out of the way along the sidewalk on Murcer. It looked as though I was the last to join the party.

I stepped into the lobby, where a uniformed officer was stationed to keep the public from wandering into the crime scene. The receptionist at the front desk was flush and on the phone – a personal call from the bit of conversation I heard, telling the person on the other end that she was going to be late - no doubt asked to stay for proper questioning. The staunch officer standing beside the desk held up three fingers and silently lipped the words "third floor" so as not to disrupt the distraught woman's call. I nodded my response and veered toward the elevator.

I could only imagine what I was about to step into. The last three crime scenes were the worst I'd seen, and after weeks, they still kept me up at night. But this was a different setting altogether. The other murders took place in secluded, private locations; this was an office building. How the fuck could this happen?

I stepped off the elevator into a brightly lit office space of low-walled cubicles. To my far right, in a corner office, two uniformed officers were taking a statement from a seated Hispanic male. No handcuffs; he wasn't our guy. Two other officers were standing in an aisleway between cubicles in the center of the open room, staring at the small crowd of law-enforcement officials gathered inside an office along the left wall. That made it easy enough to determine the *where*. Now to find out about the *who* and the *how*.

I walked to my left, hugging the perimeter wall. One of the officers in the center of the room saw me and shook his head as if to say, "It's not good." No shit. Like any murder was? But I caught his drift.

As I approached the open doorway, Lieutenant Garrett stepped out, wiping his forehead and looking pallid. He didn't notice me at first as he dropped his chin to his chest and leaned against the short cubicle wall in front of him, his palms pressed firmly against its top to hold himself steady.

"Lieutenant, you all right?" I asked.

"Jesus Christ, Mick!" he exploded, turning toward me. "What the fuck took you so long?"

I could tell from his jumpy reaction I startled him. Whatever that was, it wasn't normal. Lieutenant Garrett wasn't a jittery man; something had him spooked.

"I left my house as soon as you called, Lieu."

He exhaled heavily and brought both hands up to rub his temples.

"Sorry, I'm a little on edge."

"I can see that. What's going on?"

"It's the vic," he began. "I knew her. She was a close friend. Well, a close friend of my wife's. Fuck! How am I going to break the news to her?"

I patted him on the shoulder, "Damn, Lieu; sorry. Why don't you stay out here; let me check things out?"

He nodded and went back to leaning on the cubicle wall. I stepped into the office doorway, looking at the backs of Special Agents Lowe and Hayes. They were blocking my view of the victim except for a sliver between them, where I could see Barry on one knee beside outstretched, stockinged legs. As I stepped forward, Agent Hayes felt my encroachment and turned to greet me.

"Detective Dooley," she said, nodding. "Not the best welcome gift."

"What do we have here?" I questioned.

Hayes stepped aside to give me the full view.

The nicely dressed woman was sitting in a swivel office chair in the center of the floor, her wrists duct-taped to the armrests. Her white button-down blouse and green skirt were stained red with blood. The backs of her hands were stabbed through with metal letter openers, where dried streaks of red splintered from the wounds, once forming droplets of blood that hung from her fingertips, clinging for dear life, before falling to the floor. The woman's head was tilted back over the rear of the chair, her mouth gagged with a floral-patterned neckerchief – her own, most likely. Two more letter openers stood vertical, gouged into the woman's eyes, where blood had trickled down the side of her face and mingled with her flowing brown hair.

Barry overheard my question and began his assessment to bring me up to speed.

"The victim's name is Nancy Osterlander, fifty-three years old. A bigwig in the company."

I peeked back at the open door and saw the attached plaque, "*Nancy Osterlander, Chief Financial Officer.*"

"The cause of death is as you see it," Barry continued. "The letter openers through the eye socket pierced the cranial cavity into the brain. She may have survived one, but not two."

Barry stood from his knelt position.

"She was alive when the stabbing happened. Based on the angle of the weapons, I'd say our killer stood behind the victim." He took his place behind the chair, re-enacting the gruesome event. "The location of the majority of blood spatter on her face indicates that the killer stabbed her left eye first. He would have pulled her hair back and down with his right hand, forcing her face upward so she couldn't move..,"

"Or so she was forced to look at him," I interjected.

"Right. Then our 'Letter Man' jabbed the implement into Nancy's eye with his left hand."

"So our killer is left-handed then?" I questioned.

"Ah, if only it were that simple," he replied. "Maybe it was out of convenience, or maybe he's ambidextrous. You see, the angles of the letter openers are opposite, which means he used his right hand for the other."

Barry made a fist and moved his hand in a stabbing motion to give us all a visual. Or, perhaps, to give us nightmares.

"How long ago?" I asked.

"Based on the state of the blood and the condition and temperature of the body, I'd say she's been dead for a few hours."

"So, how do we know this is our guy?" I questioned. "I don't see any obvious note or carved letter in the victim."

Barry shifted his eyes to Agent Lowe, who responded with a nod before a verbal approval.

"Show him."

Barry turned his eyes to me and signaled for me to join him.

"Walk this way, Detective. Just watch where you step."

I made a sweeping arc around Special Agent Lowe, making sure to avoid any blood on the carpet. When I joined Barry behind the victim, he flashed an uncomfortable smirk.

"You ready for this?" he asked.

I shook my head. "I'm never ready. But it's never stopped you before."

"Fair point," he acknowledged. He placed his gloved palms on both sides of the victim's head and lifted it forward, exposing the back of her neck.

"Yup," I stated, letting out a heavy sigh. "That's our guy, all right."

"He carved this sometime after she'd been dead for a while. That's why you don't see any blood around the N."

"What do you mean?" I asked. "Why would the killer wait so long to carve that after he'd already killed her?"

Agent Hayes stepped forward.

"Nothing in here has been disturbed. Everything is as it was when we arrived. If you look at Ms. Osterlander's rather neat desk, you'll notice the tool the killer used to carve the letter into the vic's neck – another letter opener - situated right in the center. And beside it, a solitary pen. After killing his victim, we believe this guy sat down, took his time to write a note, then carved the letter."

"Son of a bitch," I let out. "But if that's true, where's the note?"

"That's what my team and I are going to find out," Vera's voice boomed from the doorway. "That is, if Mr. Hinkman, here, is done with the body."

Barry slowly lowered the woman's head to its original position, then nodded.

"I've officially declared the woman's dead," he said. "The room's all yours. Let me know when you're through so I can take the body."

"All right, you heard the man," Vera barked. "Everybody out. That includes you, Mr. Swanky-pants," she said, looking directly at Agent Lowe.

As I said, Vera wasn't one to hold back.

"Vera!" the Lieutenant's voice rang out from the hall.

"Sorry, Frank," she yelled back. Then, looking at the agent, she reiterated her request in a more demure tone, "I mean, Mr. Agent Lowe, sir."

I couldn't tell if the sarcastic-looking smile was her own or a coincidental side effect from her earlier appointment with the dentist.

Those of us not among Vera's team of forensic experts scrambled out into the hallway. Once there, I noticed the clock on the wall and couldn't help but fire off my questions.

"So what am I missing?" I questioned. "It's only 6:47. You said Ms. Osterlander had been dead for a few hours. Plus, you think the killer took his time writing a note and then carved a letter into her. Where were the other employees?"

Lieutenant Garrett turned from the cubicle wall he'd been leaning on. "The office is closed the last Friday of every month," he stated. "I don't know; something about the end of the month financials or some shit. I was only half paying attention when she and my wife would talk shop."

"And who's that guy?" I questioned, throwing my thumb over my shoulder at the Hispanic man.

"He's from the cleaning service," Special Agent Lowe answered. "He's the one who called it in. He found her like that when he went to empty her trash."

"Can we confirm that?"

"What the fuck you think your officers are doing, Detective?"

I put my hands up in front of my chest, "Hey, take it easy; it was just a question. Christ."

I looked at Hayes, "Any cameras in the building?"

She shook her head, "None. But we'll check with the building across the street. They've got cameras. Maybe they'll have something useful."

"What about the receptionist in the lobby?"

"There's a lot of businesses in this building," Hayes replied. "People are in and out of here all day. We'll get to questioning her, but I doubt she'll have anything useful to provide."

Before I could get another word out, Vera's voice penetrated through the partially closed door.

"I think we hit the mother-load, crackpots."

Agent Lowe practically jumped to the door to be the first to learn of Vera's discovery. He stepped a few feet in, letting the rest of us gather in the opening.

"What is it, Vera?" Lieutenant Garrett asked.

"She's got a nice little mini-fridge in here," Vera began. "Too bad it's full of all sorts of freaky shit. Look at this." Vera reached in and pulled out a styrofoam cup. "Tongue, anyone?" She tipped the cup sideways to reveal a severed tongue. The killer left us a present. The Lynch boy was missing his tongue. I think we just found it.

"Jesus," Agent Lowe blurted.

"There's also an ear in here if the tongue isn't good enough for you."

The kid in the woods – Matthew - had both of his ears. I immediately looked toward the dead victim in the chair to see if she was missing one. She wasn't. That ear belonged to someone else. Another victim?

"And then we've got these," Vera continued, pulling a handful of bank receipts from the refrigerator. "Personally, I would have stocked it with vodka, but to each their own."

"Enough, Vera," Lieu barked.

On a hunch, I added my two cents.

"I'd be willing to bet you've got twelve receipts in your hand."

"Oh yeah?" she questioned, shuffling through the papers, counting them.

"...Nine, ten, eleven, twelve. Give the man a prize."

"Thirteen pictures with the last victim," I said, "twelve receipts with this one. The fucker is still counting down."

"Oh, and there is one final thing in here you'll want to see."

With her free hand, she reached in and pulled out the familiar item we'd been expecting - the killer's note.

Special Agent Lowe was the closest - and since he was already wearing gloves, Vera handed it over to his eager hands.

"What's it say?" I inquired.

LETTER N HAS SERVED HER PURPOSE. HOW SATISFYING THAT THE LETTER MAN SHOULD GET TO USE SUCH WEAPONS TO BRING HER TO HER END. THIS CHIEF FINANCIAL OFFICER WAS NOT ALL SHE APPEARED TO BE. IF YOU WANT TO KNOW WHAT I HAVE LEARNED, DIG DEEP INTO HER FINANCIALS; YOU'LL FIGURE IT OUT. I SHOULD BE THANKING YOU. IF YOU HAD FIGURED OUT HOW DETESTABLE SHE WAS SOONER, SHE MIGHT STILL HAVE BEEN AMONG THE LIVING. BUT WE WOULDN'T WANT THAT, WOULD WE? NOT WHEN SHE'S HURT SO MANY. ARE YOU LISTENING NOW? DO I FINALLY HAVE YOUR EAR? SPEAKING OF WHICH, THE ONE YOU'VE FOUND BELONGS TO O. HE'LL MEET HIS END SOON.

α

"Mother Fucker!" I blurted. "He's already got someone else."

"Calm down, Mick," Lieutenant Garrett snapped. "Vera, check everything. Find something!"

"We're on it, Lieu. If he's left even a drop of sweat, we'll find it."

Hayes spoke up. "We'll put a rush on the cameras across the street."

"We've got to do something," I said loudly. "You heard what he wrote. He's probably torturing somebody right now. We need to get out there on the street and find this asshole."

"And where are we supposed to search to do that?" Lieutenant Garrett yelled. "We've got nothing useful on the guy. He could be your goddamn neighbor, and you wouldn't know it. Now calm the fuck down."

"Well, fuck, Lieu . . . I can't just stand here doing nothing."

"Watch your tone, Dooley."

"Gentlemen!" Agent Hayes interrupted. "Enough." Then, she looked at me, "Can I speak with you for a moment, Detective?" She gestured back out into the main office space.

As she pulled at my forearm, leading me out the door, Lieutenant Garrett had to get the last word.

"Calm his ass down!"

I felt my hands roll up into fists. I'd never been a violent person, but right now, I wanted to punch something. Or some*one*.

Hayes led me to the end cubicle on the corner – far enough from the others that we wouldn't be heard, then she whipped around to face me.

"What the hell has gotten into you, Mick?"

"What?"

"This isn't like you. You're acting like you've never worked a case before."

"We can't just do nothing. Some poor guy could be dying right now."

"And what would you like us to do, huh? Use your head for a minute. I know you want to catch this guy; we all do. But we can't just run off blindly without knowing where we're running to. That's something Jim would have done."

"Yeah? Then maybe I should do it too."

"You don't want to do that," Hayes stated sternly.

"And why not? It worked for Jim."

"You're not Jim," she stated. "And look where it got him."

We both became silent for a moment.

"You're right; I'm not Jim. But I can't stay here knowing there's someone out there about to die. I've got my own ideas."

"I understand your feelings, Mick, but I can't have you going rogue on us. Don't make me do something I'll regret."

"Then don't. Just let me do my thing. I won't get in the way of the FBI's investigation."

I walked away, heading for the exit. I felt Hayes' eyes burning into my back.

"You'd better not," she yelled.

I kept walking.

I knew I wasn't the detective Jimmy was. Maybe I never would be. But, like him, I was now after a twisted fucker. I had to figure this guy out. I had to learn to think like him. The problem was, I *couldn't* think like him. It just wasn't me. And there it was, right in front of me. I didn't need to think like that sick son of a bitch because..,

I knew someone who did.

Chapter 10

Pulling the Strings

Somehow, I knew that the uncomfortable chair they sat me in wasn't going to be the worst part of my visit. I was still unsure if coming here was a good idea. It popped into my head, and I ran with it. I called Lieutenant Garrett on my way over and told him I had a plan. I didn't want to say anything more than that. He didn't stop me, so I think that meant he approved. I took that as a good sign. Or maybe he wanted me to find out on my own how much of a terrible idea my plan was. As I sat in the wobbly metal chair, staring at the empty seat on the other side of the reinforced glass, I couldn't help but think it was a mistake.

I still couldn't believe I was here. If I thought we had anything else to go on, this wouldn't even have been a consideration. After our previous meeting, I'd sworn it was my last. But things in the case had gotten out of hand, and we were grasping at straws. I was willing to try anything, even if it cost me a sliver of my humanity.

79

The metal door swung open, the third time since I'd been here, delivering another jumpsuit-clad inmate to their awaiting visitor. The previous two wore gray garbs and had smiles on their faces when greeted with the presence of a loved one. This one, *my* requested prisoner, was dressed in red and had no such smile.

The guard held his ward's upper arm tightly in his grasp, escorting him to the visitor booth, the prisoner's wrists handcuffed in front of his waist and connected to a chain that looped around his back, keeping his arms at bay. When they arrived at our assigned cubby, Ben shot me a long, displeased stare, one I half-expected, as the officer slid the prisoner's chair out from under the station platform. His apoplectic gaze eventually yielded in favor of a subtly annoyed glance directed at the guard instead, who proceeded to unlock the chained cuffs. After the guard backed away a few feet, Ben slid into the chair, his eyes refocused upon me. I picked up the phone located on my right side and brought it to my ear, waiting for him to do the same with his. He made no initial attempt, content in relaying his unspoken irritation visually until my eyes shifted to his phone and then back to his unwavering stare. He relented, grabbing for the phone, though I'm sure it pained him to do so.

"Ben," I greeted, giving a quick nod.

He remained silent, his eyes still shooting daggers at me.

"How have things been?" I asked, forcing a reply.

"Why aren't we meeting in the visitor's hall?" he countered, his voice monotone. "Do I detest you that much?"

"Ben, no..," I fell silent, his question catching me off guard. "Yes. I mean, no. Maybe. I don't know."

"Clear as mud, Mick," he replied. "Are you sure you can handle this new role you've taken on? Detective work is a big responsibility. I'm sure the force can't afford to have indecisive officers out there. Especially not in these dark times."

"I can handle it," I replied.

"We'll see about that, won't we," he answered. "So, what brings you back here?" he asked, shifting his attention to the left edge of the glass, where I watched his eyes follow the perimeter of the window up and around to the opposite side as if he were calculating what it would take to break it free from its casing.

"I'm here because I need your help."

Ben's eyes immediately jolted back to mine, his squinted stare telling of his sudden curiosity.

"You need *my* help?" he questioned. "In case you haven't noticed, Mick, I'm a little indisposed at the moment. Perhaps another time. Like maybe when you become a *real* detective."

That was an unnecessary jab. We both knew I was still learning to get my legs under me; he didn't need to take it there. Was he purposely trying to rile me? Would it please him to learn it worked?

"Goddamn it, Ben," I stated, showing my anger but trying to keep my voice down, "I *am* a detective - as real a detective as your father was."

Shit! Why was I playing into Ben's little game?

"Don't you dare compare yourself to my father!" Ben seethed through clenched teeth, not as concerned with his volume. "He was a great detective. He did what nobody else could do. He took down The Alphabet Killer."

The kid was warped, twisted, and, though he didn't know it, exactly the kind of person I needed to talk to.

"He *was* a great detective," I agreed. "I looked up to your father. He helped me a lot when I first joined the force. But he's not around anymore, and I'm trying my best to live up to the man he was – to honor his memory. But I can't do it on my own. That's why I need your help. He talked about you, you know."

"He did?" Ben questioned, looking surprised but also curious and hopeful.

"Of course," I replied, bolstering the kid's ego, no longer playing by *his* rules. "He was always going on about how smart you were. He always told us you'd make a better detective than he ever was. He said you had good instincts; you saw things that others didn't."

"I pay attention to details," he replied. "The ones that aren't so obvious."

"Exactly!" I exclaimed, pointing my finger at him. "Which is why I'm here. That other guy is still out there, killing people. The other detectives, the FBI - they can't figure him out. But I think *you* can, Ben."

"You think *I* can?" he questioned. "Why is that, Mick? Do you think all killers are the same - like we share the same motives? Even if that were true, why should I give a fu..," he paused, tightened his lips, then sat back in his chair. "Why should I care?" he corrected himself, a smile forced upon his face. "This guy has killed like, what, two people?"

"He's killed four so far," I jumped in with my response.

"Four?" Been replied. "Impressive. Still not a reason to help you."

"No? Well, how about this? He thinks The Alphabet Killer was a joke."

I noticed Ben's smile fade.

"That's right," I continued. "He also said you were only a child playing a man's game."

I could see Ben's jaw tighten at my words. I was getting to him.

"He's left more notes?" Ben inquired, his upper lip curled in anger.

"With each of his victims," I replied, nodding. "Seems like he's taken a page out of your notebook. He's copying you."

Ben smirked as he looked to his left, shaking his head. He let out a quick breath from his nose as if holding back a chuckle, then bit down on his lower lip as if debating how to respond, trying to disguise his pridefulness that someone was continuing his work.

"He calls himself 'The Letter Man,'" I added.

Ben's gaze immediately shifted back to the reinforced glass barrier between us, his eyes narrowed in disdain. I wasn't sure if he was looking *at* me or *through* me.

"The Letter Man?" Ben questioned, his stare lifeless and distant. "How sophomoric and unoriginal. And he called *me* a child. For the name alone, this guy needs to be taken down a notch."

In an instant, I saw focus return to Ben's glazed look as he glared at me with pure hatred in his eyes.

"All right, Mick," he began, "I'll help you. But I've got two requests."

"You know I can't do anything to get your sentence reduced," I jumped in, feeling that was every convict's wish.

Ben smiled and shook his head. "Don't worry, Mick; I know where I'll be for the rest of my life. I'll make it simple for you. Next time, we meet in the visitor's hall. This shitty arrangement…" he waved his finger back and forth at the glass barrier, "makes me feel claustrophobic."

"I can make that happen," I said, nodding. "And the other?"

"I want to see the notes. Not copies; the originals."

I paused, swallowing heavily. "I.., don't know if I can do that, Ben."

"Then the deal's off, Mick. You can find the fucker on your own."

"It's evidence in an ongoing investigation," I reminded him. "The FBI will never allow it."

"Well, Mick, if you want my help, you'll have to find a way to convince them, won't you? The choice is yours."

I looked down at the narrow shelf my elbow rested upon, imagining how it would all play out if I presented the request to my superiors. How many "Hell No"s and "Fuck that"s would be slung at me? That's *after* I got chewed out for even coming here, asking for the kid's help. But I *did* come here for a reason. I wasn't going to back down so quickly. I knew Ben could offer us some insight into the mind of that demented fuck. It wouldn't be easy getting top brass to agree to it (nothing in this case seemed to be), but I had to find a way. Only, there was a slight problem. I turned my eyes back up to Ben.

"I'll do it," I said, watching a sly smile return to Ben's lips. "But I can only get you three originals."

Ben tilted his head sideways, pondering my words.

"The fourth?" he questioned.

"Written on the wall with your mother's blood," I replied straight-faced.

He licked his lips, displaying little emotion. "Not quite as interesting as carving it into someone's back like

I did to that little Asian addict, but at least he showed some effort."

I shook my head, holding back my rage.

"Fine," he conceded. "I know there's pictures of it, then. You'll bring one of those."

I gave him a single nod, unwanting to open my mouth for fear of what would fly out of it. He grinned, understanding my struggle. Then, after a few seconds of silence, Ben offered his final remarks.

"Until next time, Mick," he nodded, keeping his stare fixed on me while he slowly delivered the phone back to its wall base. I kept mine to my ear, unable to remove it as I felt my hand squeeze tighter around the receiver. He turned his head toward the guard and nodded to be taken back to his cell, his eyes staying focused on my stiff reaction. The guard complied, sternly grabbing under Ben's arm and forcing him up from his chair. Ben smiled at his rough handler as he was quickly ushered away, a sign that he had become accustomed to such harsh treatment. Or that he was in control. I sat motionless for a moment before realizing I still held the phone to my ear. I watched the steel door close behind them before finally hanging up the receiver.

What just happened? What the hell did I promise? I must be out of my mind. We all wanted to catch the killer, but was I going too far? Or perhaps I was the only one thinking straight. Maybe I was the only one willing to do what was necessary to get it done. I only hoped I still had a soul when this was over.

Chapter 11

What We Endure

I leaned against the counter, sipping my coffee, my thoughts more distant than my stare. Gina noticed my glazed-over eyes the moment she walked into the kitchen.

"Wow, Earth to Mick," she stated, smirking and waving her hand to gain my attention. "Anyone in there?"

I glanced over at her as she rubbed her belly, only then made aware of her presence. The darkness I'd seen through my eyes suddenly faded with the sight of her bright features as I smiled to let her know I was still there.

"Sorry, hon," I offered with an apologetic grin. "I've just had a lot on my mind."

"I know," she said, pulling the coffee pot from the heated base and filling the empty tumbler beside it. "It's starting to show with the gray hair."

"What?" I questioned defensively, reaching up and rubbing my fingers through the hair above my ear. "That's my natural blonde."

"Yeah, okay," she said sarcastically, nodding while screwing the cover onto the travel mug. She placed it on the counter beside me, then reached for the same hair on the side of my head and began gently twiddling a clump between her thumb and index finger.

"This case is weighing on you," she said softly, standing to my right.

I sighed heavily, something she picked up on right away.

"You didn't say much after visiting with Ben last night," she continued.

"There wasn't much to say," I returned, unable to tell her my true feelings. "The kid's messed up in the head."

"He's lost both of his parents," she responded. "Tragically. I know that doesn't excuse him from what he did, but it has to play a part."

I placed the half-empty coffee cup on the counter to my left, brushed Gina's hand aside, and stepped away to face her.

"How can you say that?" I questioned heatedly. "Don't tell me you feel sorry for him?"

"I'm not saying that," she replied. "It's just.., losing both parents at such a young age certainly didn't help with whatever problems he was dealing with."

"No shit; he killed eight people, Gina. Eight! His problems were.., *are* much deeper than only his parents getting killed - one of which by his own hand, by the way."

She tightened her lips and gave me a disappointed look. Suddenly, I was that little boy, disappointing my parents, my big brother, all over again. I was upset but taking it out on the wrong person.

"Gina, I'm sor..."

"Oohh," she suddenly announced, leaning forward and grabbing her stomach.

"What is it?" I lunged at her, placing my hand on her back and bending over slightly with her. "Are you okay? Is it...?"

She put her hand against my stomach and gave a little shove as she stood upright, exhaling heavily.

"No, I'm good," she said. "She just gave me a really good kick."

"Are you sure? Here, sit down." I pulled a chair out from under the table and tugged at her arm to encourage her.

"Mick, stop," she said, smiling and shaking her head. "I'm fine. Really."

"Are you sure?" I asked again.

"Yes. But thank you for being that sweet man when I need you to be."

I gave her a sorrowful look as she placed her hand on her lower back.

"Gina I.. ,"

Just then, my ringing phone, which was on the table in front of us, interrupted my thoughts. We both glanced over and saw Frank's name prominently displayed on the screen. I watched Gina's shoulders drop in disappointment, followed by her expression.

"I don't have to answer that," I said, reaching for the "end call" button.

She stopped me by reaching around my face to place her hand on the side of my cheek, then gently turned my head to face hers.

"Yes, you do," she stated, nodding.

I could see it in her eyes. She was afraid. Not necessarily for the safety of herself, our little girl, or even the next poor victim of that sadistic maniac out there. No, she was afraid of what I'd become if I didn't put everything I had into taking that twisted fucker down. She knew I'd never forgive myself if I didn't do all I could. The guilt would slowly eat away at me until the man she married was no longer the man she lived with. I understood.

I silently nodded my reply and picked up the phone.

"Yeah, Lieu, this is Mick."

Gina drifted from my side as I listened to Frank's angry grumblings. A moment later, she pressed the coffee-filled tumbler against my chest and gave me a peck on the cheek, her subtle way of letting me know it was time to go to work; standing in our kitchen wasn't getting me any closer to catching the killer. I flashed an appreciative smile, grabbed my jacket from the back of the chair with my remaining two fingers, and then walked out the side door.

"I was working on something, Lieu," I responded. "I should have told you before I left, but I was a little heated."

He wasn't too happy I walked away from the crime scene last night, especially since the victim was someone he knew. Not to mention, my walking away only made him look bad. That wasn't like me – more like something Jimmy would have done. I suppose there were worse footsteps I could have followed.

I started my car, the phone still pressed tightly to my ear, while Frank continued to chew me out. Once the Bluetooth thankfully kicked in, I dropped the phone onto the passenger seat, saving my ear from any further damage by the Lieutenant's relentless screaming.

". . .half a mind to take you off this case! Do you understand me?"

"Loud and clear, Lieu," I replied (since the volume on my radio was turned up a few notches too high). I quickly rectified that.

"So, you mind telling me what the fuck was so important last night you had to storm out of there?"

"Can I tell you about it when I get in?"

"You can tell me about it *now*," he demanded.

I really didn't want to give him all the details over the phone. Maybe only a little tease. It was bigger than both of us. The FBI needed to be involved in this conversation.

"I felt it was important that I visit with Ben."

"What the Christ for," he yelled.

"He's the one who started this whole alphabet-killing mess," I answered. "I needed to talk to him about what he thought might be going on inside the killer's head."

"Did you get anything useful out of him?"

"I'll tell you all about it when I get in. I'll be there in ten minutes."

"No, you won't," he replied. "You're heading to Larson."

"What for?" I questioned.

"Larson PD tracked down one of those kids from the pictures in that Lynch boy's car. I want *you* over there, too. I don't want our department left out on any of the details that the kid might be able to provide. I contacted Captain Norris already; he knows you'll be along."

"What about our vic?"

"The FBI is all over that one like flies on shit. We need all our avenues covered. That means *you* are the lucky son of a bitch who gets to find out all you can about the previous victim."

"All right, Lieu; I'm on it. Text me the kid's name and address, would you?"

"Yeah."

I heard the phone click, and my stereo instantly kicked on. Like Jimmy, Frank didn't believe in saying goodbye. He'd get his point across, and that was that. There was no need to waste unnecessary breath on things that weren't pertinent to the case. A few seconds later, a text flashed across my screen.

Jason Polini - 17 Armitage Rd.

That was about fifteen minutes from my current location. It would give me just enough time to prepare myself for what I might possibly learn by questioning the kid. I hoped I wouldn't, but I knew better.

* * *

From the look of it, I pulled up to the property just in time. Sanchez and another uniformed officer were standing at the front door, presumably waiting for someone to answer. I saw Sanchez glance over his shoulder at me and nod as I exited my vehicle. He said something to the other officer while pointing at me, causing the other officer to turn in my direction and chuckle. Talk about stepping into an uncomfortable situation.

"Officer Sanchez," I said, nodding, trying to sound professional in front of his partner. "It looks like you just got here yourself."

"Oh yeah, we..."

He stopped in mid-sentence as the front door swung open and quickly turned forward to look professional himself.

"Hello, can I help you, officers?" a woman spoke, partially tucked behind the open door as if unsure we were actually police officers.

"Sorry to bother you, ma'am," Sanchez offered. "We were hoping to speak with Jason Polini. Does he live at this address?"

I saw enough of the woman's face to notice her eyes narrow in agitation.

"Yes, he lives here," she answered. "I'm his mother. What's this about? Has he done something?"

"Oh, no; not at all, ma'am," Sanchez replied as the mother stepped out from behind the door.

She was a petite woman, maybe in her late thirties, with blonde hair and dazzling green eyes. So much so that it was difficult to focus on anything else.

"We'd like to ask your son some questions if we may. About Matthew Lynch."

"Matthew Lynch?" she questioned. "Why does that name sound familiar?"

Sanchez looked at his partner, then at me as if he didn't know how to answer. I took the hint and stepped from the grass onto the bottom step.

"You might remember him from years ago," I jumped in. "We believe he might have babysat your son at some point."

"Oh, that's right," she responded. "Matty. Yes, he watched Jason for us quite a few times. Nice boy."

"Yes, well, I'm afraid there's been an incident, and we were hoping we could speak with your son about what he remembers about Matth.., uh, Matty."

"He's in his room; let me go get him. You can come on in."

She swung the door open wider and walked away. I gave Sanchez a look as if to say, she's not *un*attractive.

Sanchez nudged his partner. "Why don't you go back to the car and play with the radio or something, huh? We've got this."

The other officer stared me down for a moment, then shook his head begrudgingly and walked away.

"What was that all about Rubio?" I questioned, stepping through the door.

"The kid's a rook," he replied, following me inside. "He'll be fine."

"What did you say to him earlier?" I asked. "When I first got here?"

"I told him you were the fastest man alive and could totally beat him in a foot race."

I held back a grumble. "Fucker."

He snickered, then immediately forced a hard stop, clearing his throat as Mrs. Polini and her son came around the corner.

"I assured him he wasn't in any trouble," she began. "Don't make a liar out of me."

"No, ma'am," I replied. "No trouble."

"Well then, I'd still like to know what this is about," she requested, leading her son to the couch, where they both sat down rigidly on the edge of the cushions.

I looked at Sanchez and tilted my head, practically pleading with my eyes for him to start the conversation. He gave me a subtle nod, then looked at Jason, who was nervously staring at us, rubbing his hands back and forth across his thighs.

"Jason, I'm Officer Sanchez; this is Detective Dooley. Would it be okay if we asked you a few questions?"

The boy turned to his mother and then back to us and nodded.

"How old are you, son?"

"I'm eighteen," the boy answered.

"That's a nice age," Sanchez stated. "I want to ask you some things about someone you might recall from some time ago. Do you remember Matthew Lynch?"

I watched Jason's eyes widen before he dropped his stare to the floor and nodded.

"Do you remember how old you were when he used to babysit you?"

He shrugged his shoulders, never looking up. "Maybe ten or eleven."

"And how about when you last saw him?"

"I don't know," he said quietly, nervously scratching both of his knees.

"He was thirteen," the mother chimed in. "He came to his father and me and told us he didn't need anyone watching him anymore since he'd become a teenager." She reached over and grabbed his left hand, preventing him from fidgeting.

"If it's okay with you, ma'am, I'd like to ask some tougher questions now," Sanchez said.

"Tougher questions?" she asked, looking confused. She turned to her son, whose chin was still buried in his chest. "Jason, do you know what this is about?"

The boy didn't respond, keeping his eyes down and shaking his head.

"What other questions?" the mother asked.

"We'd like to ask Jason if we can."

"Jason," the mother rattled the boy's hand, "the officer is talking to you. Can he ask you some questions?"

He still didn't look up. Instead, he closed his eyes tightly, exhaled heavily from his nose, and gave a guarded nod.

"Jason," Sanchez began, "did Matty, um.., did he..,"

Sanchez stumbled for the words, turning to me for assistance. How did I know I was going to get stuck with the shitty part?

"It's of a sensitive nature, ma'am," I jumped in. "I'm afraid there's no easy way to ask. Jason, did Matthew ever do anything to you that might have been.., maybe a little inappropriate?"

"Wait, what?" Mrs. Polini expressed, suddenly looking distraught. "What are you saying?"

"I'm afraid we have reason to believe that Matthew might have done things... sexually inappropriate things... to some of the kids he babysat."

"No, that can't be," she said, shaking her head, a glint of fear in her eyes. She looked at her son, his head still drooped. "Tell them that isn't true. Tell them that never happened to you."

She said, "Tell *them*," but what she really meant was, "Tell *me*." The boy remained silent as a tear dripped from his cheek and splashed onto his mother's hand. That was the start of the floodgates opening as the liquid poured from Mrs. Polini's eyes. She leaned in and held her son in a tight embrace, screaming "No" and "Why didn't you tell me" while rubbing the back of his head. Sanchez and I waited until most of the tears subsided, but we had more questions to ask, and it wasn't going to get any easier.

Over the next thirty minutes or so, we continued with the difficult questions. Since the horrible secret was out, Jason suddenly felt compelled to spill all the painful details of what he'd been through under Matthew's care. Through the worst of it, his mother held his hand in hers while the other wiped away the continuous stream of tears that rolled down her face. What the boy endured was despicable, and over those thirty minutes, I watched Sanchez's expression sour to something I hadn't seen before. It was time to stop; we'd heard enough.

I sent Sanchez outside to get some air while I apologized to the Polinis for having put them through a difficult situation. It wasn't fair something like that happened to Jason, and I couldn't help but feel we had somehow just destroyed this family's life by bringing it to light when, in reality, Matthew Lynch had destroyed it years earlier.

By the time I stepped outside, Sanchez was pacing back and forth on the lawn, rubbing his temples, no doubt trying to erase the images from his head.

"You all right?" I asked, stepping down from the stairs.

He looked up at me with rage and bitter hatred in his eyes. "Are you kidding me right now?" he barked, throwing his arm out and pointing to the house. "Did you hear what that Lynch fucker did to that boy? It's disgusting."

"Take it easy, Rubio. And lower your voice, would you? We don't need them hearing this shit."

"Take it easy?" he seethed. "Take it easy? Think of all those kids in those pictures, man. What we just heard.., that was every one of them. Even if it was only one kid, that mother fucking pedophile got what he deserved. I'm glad that crazy psycho did him in."

"Guys," the rookie officer's voice bellowed, trying to gain our attention as he strode across the lawn in our direction.

I threw my arm out, rudely displaying my palm to the rookie, "Hold on, kid," before getting back in Sanchez's face. "You need to calm the fuck down," I stated through gritted teeth while grabbing his arm to pull him away from the house. "What happened to that kid in there was awful, but we can't be taking the side of a ruthless killer either."

"Guys," the rookie's voice called out again.

"I said, wait." A little too harshly, at that. "You need to get yourself straightened out, you hear me, Sanchez? The last thing you want is your captain finding out about you flying off the handle like this."

"Guys!" the rookie shouted that time.

"What the fuck is it, Prelendo?" Sanchez hollered.

"Captain Norris just radioed. They found another body. It looks like The Letter Man's M.O."

Well shit! When it rains, it sure does pour.

Chapter 12

O

After Sanchez had gotten off the call with his captain and blurted, *"Here we go again,"* he and Prelendo hopped in their cruiser, ready to take off. I don't think he was too happy with me after what went on outside the Polini residence, and I wasn't pushing the subject. Instead, I quietly stewed about the incident while I followed them to our next nightmare. I had no idea it was going to lead us back . . . here.

The words slipped out of my mouth as I stepped from my vehicle. "You've got to be shitting me."

"Weird, right?" Sanchez said, glancing at me as I joined the two officers at the lip of the grass.

I bit the inside of my cheek, shaking my head, staring out at the distant police presence congregating around the body while a few officers scoured the nearby landscape.

"Let's get this over with," I insisted.

Sanchez nodded his response as the three of us stepped forward into the sea of headstones at Our Lady of

Mercy Cemetery. Like it wasn't bad enough that I just buried a friend here three weeks earlier, now I had to deal with a murder scene on the same hallowed grounds. If I didn't know any better, I'd start to think Larson was becoming as bad as Southbridge. But, since I *did* know better, I quickly brushed that thought aside. No amount of crime could compare to the filth, corruption, and disgusting misdeeds of the pestilence-riddled streets of my lovely city.

As we weaved our way around the plots of the dead on our way to the killer's most recent victim, my attention shifted to the right, where several rows away, I could still see the recently compacted soil of Karen's burial site. A chill ran through me, knowing I was passing by one of The Letter Man's victims on my way to possibly another; this one, presumably number five.

"You all right, buddy?" Sanchez asked, noticing my sudden uneasiness. At least *he* appeared to be doing better.

I shook my head, "I won't be all right until that maniac is locked behind bars where he belongs."

"I hear you," Sanchez replied as we approached those already on the scene, including Lieutenant Frangione of the state police and Special Agents Lowe and Hayes. The city's coroner was also present, finishing up her analysis and declaring the body deceased, as was Shane, Larson's Chief Forensic Officer, swooping in to begin his examination. I tapped Agent Hayes on the shoulder to gain her attention.

"Detective Dooley," she stated, nodding her head. "I didn't expect to see you here."

"That makes two of us," I replied. "Officer Sanchez and I were questioning one of Matthew Lynch's molestation victims when we got the call."

"So it's true then?" she questioned. "About Lynch being a pedophile?"

I gave her a look that defined my grief, "All too."

She dropped her head and closed her eyes, exhaling deeply from her nose to convey her disgust before looking back at me. "At least we're learning more about the killer's motivations."

"Right," I added. "So what's the story here?"

"I think we're about to find out," she replied as the coroner approached to relay her findings.

"Well," the dark-haired woman began, still looking over her shoulder at the victim, "as murders go, this was a pretty clean one."

"Was that meant to be a joke?" Agent Lowe jumped in.

I knew where he was coming from. The vic was lying on his back, his lower half buried in a pile of dirt.

"Relax, Gunner," the coroner stated, shooting him an annoyed glare. "That's not how I meant it."

I leaned in and whispered to Agent Hayes. "Did she just call him by his first name?"

She tilted her head to my ear, "Angela and Gunner used to be an item."

"Ah, so he annoys *everybody*," I joked quietly.

"The obvious cause of death was strangulation," the coroner continued, "but we'll learn more from a full autopsy. Based on the ligature marks around the victim's neck, the killer used a thick, braided rope. It's not a typical choice unless we were talking about an old-fashioned hanging."

"Why is that?" I questioned.

Gunner quickly turned to me as if to steal the coroner's thunder, "More surface area. The thinner the line, such as braided twine or standard nylon cording, the easier it is to cut off the airways. Unfortunately for our victim here, it looks like the killer wanted him to struggle and to suffer slowly."

"That about sums it up," the coroner agreed. "I'm sure the medical examiner will give you a more in-depth report. I'm just here to declare the man's death."

"Thank you, Miss Fohmer," Hayes said.

"No problem," she replied. "I'll leave you to the fun stuff."

The coroner walked away, leaving us with Shane to offer more answers about what we were looking at. Miss Fohmer was right; compared to the other victims, this one was pretty mild. The brown-haired man was lying on his back, his hands folded over his abdomen, posed similarly to someone in a casket. A large hole beside the body ensured we knew where the mound of dirt covering his hips and legs was from, his shoes the only things still visible, sticking up out of the pile.

"Well," the forensic officer began, "I suppose we'll have to drag him out if we want any identification on the man."

"We know who this piece of shit is," Lieutenant Frangione spoke up, causing the Feds to look at him in curiosity. "Isn't that right, Sanchez?"

I peered at Sanchez and watched as he slowly shifted his eyes downward and nodded.

"Yeah," he confirmed quietly, "that's him, all right."

"Will someone tell me what the hell is going on here?" Agent Lowe bellowed.

"The man's name is Oliver Giorde," Frangione stated. "He was a serial rapist, convicted on three counts of aggravated sexual assault and rape, though we knew there were more victims that refused to step forward. The state police worked closely with the Larson PD to get the scumbag off the street. The son of a bitch served only twelve years before getting out on parole last year."

"You seem a bit heated, Lieutenant," Agent Hayes stated.

I saw Sanchez wince and dip his head to his chest.

"My daughter was one of the rape victims," Frangione seethed. "You'll excuse me if I don't shed a tear over this bastard's corpse."

He turned his head and spit at the ground near Oliver, almost hitting Shane. Hayes immediately glared at her partner and then back to the lieutenant.

"I'm sorry about your daughter, Lieutenant, but you realize this puts a wrinkle in the case."

"Yeah, yeah," he griped. "I know how this works. I'll excuse myself." He begrudgingly turned and started walking away.

"And you'll make yourself available for questioning when we return," Agent Lowe stated loudly.

"You're gonna treat me like I'm a goddamn suspect?" we heard him grumble. "Fuck you!"

We all stood motionless for a minute, watching him walk away before Shane grabbed our attention again.

"Lacerations on his wrists suggest he was bound for a time."

"That makes sense," Agent Lowe blurted. "The Killer's last message alluded to having Oliver held captive."

"And he's missing an ear, right?" I questioned.

"Both," Shane replied. "But how did you know?"

"He left us a parting gift with the last victim," I answered.

Just then, Sanchez let out an exasperated cry. "Oh, shit!"

"What is it, Rubio?" I questioned.

"I've been staring at that fucking gravestone," he pointed above where Oliver's head lay, "wondering where I recognized that name from. Samantha Cushing – she was one of the rape victims. She killed herself a few months after this guy was convicted."

"This isn't just a random location, then," I said toward Agent Hayes. "The killer put him here specifically to make a statement."

"We're going to need an address for Samantha's family members," Agent Lowe added. "We'll start with her immediate family and work our way out. We'll also need the name of the third rape victim."

"Agreed," Hayes said. "What can you tell us about the time of death?" she asked, looking back to the forensic officer.

"Hard to say, exactly. Sometime within the last twenty-four hours."

"I'm still confused," I jumped in. "If this is the work of our 'Letter Man,' why doesn't this guy have an O cut into him somewhere?"

"Oh, he does," said Shane excitedly. "The coroner found it before you three arrived. Only, it's not cut into him." He pulled the upper flaps of the man's button-down shirt apart, revealing his chest. "More like stapled."

Yup, he was a creative fucker. It looked like the killer used a hand stapler to form the letter O into the victim's chest. There must have been at least forty staples.

"Oh, hello," Shane stated, reaching his hand into the dead man's shirt pocket. "What have we here?"

Even before he pulled it out, we all knew what it was. The folded piece of paper in his emerging fingers confirmed it. He unraveled the note and began to read aloud.

THE WRETCHED SHALL FALL BEFORE ME. ⬤ WAS NO EXCEPTION. HE ENJOYED LISTENING TO HIS VICTIMS' SCREAMS AS HE VIOLENTLY RAPED THEM, SO FOR THAT, I TOOK HIS EARS. THEN I TOOK HIS LIFE. THIS MONSTER WILL NEVER HARM ANOTHER INNOCENT SOUL AGAIN. HE'LL BE TOO BUSY PUSHING UP DAISIES. IF THE LAW WON'T PUNISH THE WICKED, MY VENGEANCE WILL. PRAY FOR AN END IF YOU THINK IT WILL HELP. IT WON'T. YOU CAN HUNT ME, BUT YOU'LL NEVER CATCH ME. MY WORK WILL CONTINUE. OH, AND SPEAKING OF DAISIES . . .

α

"Mother fucker!" Agent Lowe raged, showing emotion for the first time. "He's taunting us."

"He's been doing that from the start," Sanchez stated.

"Yeah, well, now he's got the FBI on his ass," Agent Lowe said. "This lunatic thinks he's smart, but his days have just become numbered."

I looked at Agent Hayes and then back to Agent Lowe. "Special Agent Hayes doesn't like us to use the word 'lunatic.'"

"Fuck you, Dooley," was his retort. "You think you're funny?"

"Hey guys," Shane interrupted, "If you can hold that thought for a moment, I think there's something else."

We turned and gave him our full attention.

"These smudges around the victim's mouth seem a bit strange. It's like the killer was fumbling around there for some reason."

He reached forward and peeled Oliver's lips open with his fingers.

"Oh. Huh, that explains it."

"Explains what?" yapped Agent Lowe, still heated.

"The daisies comment," he replied. "His mouth is stuffed with them."

Hayes glanced over at me, "Eleven of them, I presume?"

Shane began easing them out, one at a time, laying them on the ground beside the body.

"Only ten," he answered.

"Ten?" I questioned confusedly.

"Oh, never mind; I missed one under the tongue."

I rolled my eyes and shook my head. I never thought I'd miss Vera and Barry as much as I did then.

"Can we get the body to the Medical Examiner for a full workup?" Agent Hayes inquired.

"Sure thing," Shane responded. "Can one of you give me a hand pulling him out from under the dirt?"

We all looked at each other and came to the same conclusion. Sanchez delivered the bad news.

"Prelendo, it's all you."

The rookie shook his head in discontent as he stepped forward. "Fuck."

I thought I saw Sanchez smirk. I think I felt one on my face as well.

Shane and the rookie each grabbed under an armpit and leveraged themselves.

"Okay, we're going to lift and pull. Ready?"

Prelendo nodded.

"And, go."

As the plan called for, they lifted Oliver's torso from the ground, but when they pulled his body from under the dirt mound, only his upper legs pulled free; his lower legs remained, cut off at the knees.

"Holy fuck!" I let out, turning away from the scene, fearing I'd get sick. That was when I saw it.

Up on the road, parked in front of Sanchez's cruiser, was the lime-green Hyundai that had been at Karen's funeral. The fucker was here again, watching what was going on. Without thinking, my focus wholly on the suspicious vehicle, I took off across the cemetery, heading for my car. I heard a voice cry out from behind me, "Where the fuck are you going," but I couldn't stop to answer. The driver of the green car quickly sped away, noticing my imminent arrival. My thoughts landed on, *oh no, you don't, mother fucker; you're not getting away from me.*

As I got to my car, my cell phone rang. Instinctively, I hit the "answer" button.

"Not now, Sanchez; I'm gonna get this fucker."

"Mick," a woman's voice returned. "This is Rosa."

Rosa? What the Hell was Gina's sister calling me for?

"I'm at Cooley General with Gina. She's gone into labor."

Chapter 13

Life After Death

I burst through the door in a panic, unsure of where I was supposed to go and hoping I wasn't too late. I ran to the reception station, my thoughts scrambled and in a haze.

"I'm having a baby!" I excitedly stated to the nurse behind the desk. "I mean, my wife is. *We* are. We're having a baby!"

The woman offered a reassuring smile to keep from giggling at the nonsense coming from my mouth.

"Congratulations, sir. What's your wife's name?"

"It's Gina Dooley," I replied. "Italian, dark curly hair." I didn't realize what I was saying until after the words came out. The nurse looked up from her monitor and gave me a perplexed stare like I was a nut. I shook my head and smiled nervously. "Sorry, I'm a police officer. It's a bad habit. This is our first kid."

107

"I never would have guessed," she responded playfully. "Your wife is on the second floor, Mr. Dooley. They're prepping her now."

I'm sure she said more, but as soon as I heard Gina was on the second floor, I was off to the elevator like a streak. I must have appeared rude, but I think she understood.

The elevator ride was the longest I'd ever taken. A woman and her young son were along for the trip. The boy held a balloon with a picture of a Teddy bear hugging a red heart with the words "Get well" at the top. I flashed him a friendly smile, but he nervously tucked himself partially behind his mother's leg, staring around it with one eye. I looked up at the mother uncomfortably, thinking I had upset the boy, then turned my stare forward to my reflection in the elevator doors. Seeing my reaction, the woman offered a kind response.

"He's anxious to see his father."

I nodded. "My wife." After a second or two of silence, I added, "She's not sick or anything."

Thankfully, the doors opened before I said more. There was no telling what kind of gibberish would fly out. I quickly exited; the other two occupants stayed behind.

As I turned the corner to make my way to the nurses' station, Rosa was already standing at the desk, coffee cup in hand, most likely complaining to the nurse about me. When she saw me approaching, she loudly stated, "Oh, there he is now."

Rosa and I never had the best relationship; I don't think she ever cared for me, but I was relieved to see her, thankful that I wasn't alone. She'd given me the details on my way over. She and Gina had plans for what was supposed to be a sister's day out at the spa, a rare opportunity for relaxation before Gina's due date. That all went sideways when Gina's water broke in Rosa's car.

"I'm not too late, am I?" I anxiously asked the nurse.

"No, Mr. Dooley," the nurse affirmed. "But her contractions are about five minutes apart, so it won't be long now. Will you be joining your wife for the delivery?"

I felt my stomach drop. I always knew this was coming; Gina and I discussed it. Now that it was time, I needed to hold it together.

"Mick," Rosa spoke up, snapping me from my stupor. "She asked you a question."

"Oh, uh, yeah," I said, shaking it off. "Yeah. I mean, yes. I will."

"Well then, let's get you ready, shall we?"

The nurse walked from around the desk and continued by me.

"Follow me, please."

Like a lost puppy, I did so, leaving Rosa behind. But I did hear her call out to me.

"Good luck, Mick."

In the eleven years I'd known her, that may have been the nicest thing she'd ever said to me.

After getting cleaned up at the prep sink, the nurse escorted me into the delivery room, where the doctor and two other nurses were already present. I took my place in a chair beside Gina's bed, her eyes staying focused on mine the entire time while I clasped her hand to give her comfort. Or maybe it was to comfort me. She smiled that beautiful smile of hers as sweat trickled down her forehead.

"Hi, baby," she said, winking. "I'm sorry you didn't get much notice; this girl wants out."

"No," I responded quietly, smiling and squeezing her hand tighter. "No sorries." I brushed a stray curl out of her eyes with my other hand. "We know *she's* ready; are you?"

I watched as she nodded slightly and bit her lower lip.

"Are *you*?" she replied, a look of worry in her eyes.

"Oh, baby, baby," I responded with excitement. "Am I ever!" I exclaimed.

Gina chuckled softly, her dimples on full display.

"I'm glad you could make it," she said, staring into my eyes.

"I wouldn't have missed it for the world," I replied, just before another contraction gripped her and she screamed. I felt her nails dig into the back of my hand, but I shrugged it off. If she had to deal with pain during this ordeal, I could do no less. I'm sure mine was insignificant in comparison.

The doctor swiveled in his seat, "Well, I think this one is about ready to come out," he said from behind his mask. "You're almost fully dilated. Now, in a bit, you will feel the contractions change. That's perfectly normal. When that happens, let me know, and breathe through it. Until then, you're doing great; keep up the good work. It won't be long now. If you can, I'd like you to try and relax for just a bit."

"I will," I announced, letting out a heavy breath.

I heard a nurse giggle as the doctor's eyes shifted to me curiously.

I shook my head and winced. "You were... talking to her, weren't you?" I questioned, realizing how silly I must have sounded.

He nodded. "I was. But you go ahead and try to relax also, Mr. Dooley. Everything's going to be just fine."

He gave me a wink. Even wearing a mask, I could tell he was flashing a huge smile. I glanced over at Gina, slightly embarrassed, wondering what she must think of me. If it was anything but love and understanding, I didn't recognize it. I could tell she was about to speak when another contraction hit, causing her body to jerk and stiffen while she let out another high-pitched scream. I hated seeing her in such agony.

When the pain subsided and her body calmed, the doctor patted her on the knee.

"Well, you sound about ready," he began. "Let me check your dilation progress." A few seconds later, he popped his head back up. "Okay, I think we're going to get started now. Gina, try not to push until I tell you, okay? Just relax and continue breathing - deep, calm breaths. Mr. Dooley, please go ahead and talk with your wife and help guide her."

I think he noticed my eyes had been more focused on his actions than on Gina. It was a subtle nudge on his part. He knew what he was doing.

"Okay, we're ready," he stated. "Here we go, now."

My mind went blank after those words. The room went silent. Everything around me ceased to exist. I was no longer interested in what the doctor was doing, catering only to Gina's needs. I breathed with her. I encouraged her. I held her head up at times. I felt myself push with her. And through it all, I held her hand.

I had no idea how long it took – it was as if time stood still. And when I felt a sudden change in Gina's body, and she let out a hefty sigh as her head hit the pillow, a chill ran through me. A single sound echoed in my ear, alerting me of another's presence.

Our baby girl's cries captured my heart.

I suddenly became light-headed, trying to stay in the moment. One of the nurses held our little girl in a linen cloth at the foot of the bed and quickly flashed her to us before stepping forward and laying her onto Gina's chest. I covered my mouth in awe as my eyes began to water.

The doctor stood from his seat and wiped the moisture from his brow with his sleeve.

"Congratulations. You have yourselves a beautiful, healthy baby girl. Would you like to cut the cord, Mr. Dooley?"

A lump formed in my throat as I watched the nurse place a metal clamp on the umbilical.

"Oh, uh, I..," I stumbled for the words.

"It's all right, Mr. Dooley," the nurse spoke, "I'll guide you through it."

I looked at Gina; she smiled and nodded. That was all the encouragement I needed.

The process was quicker and easier than I expected. When it was through, the nurse gently scooped up our little girl and brought her to a nearby station to clean her up. In less than two minutes, the beautiful, freshly washed, and wrapped Stella Mae, named after Gina's grandmother, was relinquished into her mother's waiting arms. We were parents for the first time, and I couldn't have been happier. Unfortunately, I had to take it all in while I could; we both knew the happiness wouldn't last. The Letter Man was still out there, and as long as he was, I couldn't rest easy. I'd never feel my family was safe.

Chapter 14
Secrets

It had been three days since I walked through the doors of my second home, the comforting smell of burnt coffee and stale donuts in the air mixed with a hint of spearmint-flavored gum (that did its best to mask the stench of cigarette breath from those officers who'd snuck a drag or two in the parking lot). I was taken a bit by surprise when I walked into the room to the roar of applause and saw a large banner hung from the ceiling with the word "congratulations" written on it in colorful letters. It was even more surprising to see Special Agent Lowe among the participants. He didn't strike me as a man who'd allow himself even a moment's rest to partake in such unprofessional activities. I didn't think he had it in him.

"Way to go, Dick Tracy," Vera blurted loudly. "I saw the pics your wife posted online. Your little swimmers did good. She's a cutie."

"Thanks, Vera," I said, smiling from ear to ear.

"And I'm not just saying that to be polite," she continued, "like I do to most people whose babies are ugly as fuck."

I cringed at the remark, as did most others in attendance. That was Vera for you. She said what she wanted, no matter what, and was unfiltered. If she *hadn't* said something cringe-worthy, I would have thought something was wrong with her. I had to admit, though, it made me feel good to know that my baby was cuter than most others she'd seen.

Once the clapping died down, I nodded my grateful approval to everyone and thanked them. I'd decided to keep the facade going; they didn't need to know how much I hated leaving Gina and Stella that morning, although I'm sure the other parents were well aware. I knew there was nothing to worry about; Rosa said she'd be over to help with things, but being a new father, I think worrying was a prerequisite for the job. Now that I was back at the station, where I could focus on other things, my worries shifted in a much darker direction.

"All right, everyone," Captain Redfern announced, "the fun's over. Let's get back to it." He then turned toward me and nodded, "Good to have you back, Dooley; sorry it wasn't longer." Then he walked off in the direction of his office.

I could have stayed away, taking the time allowed as a new father, but it didn't feel right with a killer still lurking out there. We needed every resource we could put into it. That included me getting my butt back into the station. Now that I'd made my dramatic entrance, where everyone tried their best to embarrass me - and succeeded – things could settle down and get back to normal.

Never one to pass up an opportunity to voice her dissatisfaction, Vera stormed past me on her way to the stairs, mumbling under her breath.

"I only came up here because I thought there'd be cake. Cheapskates couldn't even do that right. How do they expect a woman of my size to retain my glorious booty?"

All I could do was shake my head and smile, knowing I was where I needed to be.

As the remaining stragglers splintered off to carry on with their assigned duties, Frank peeked out from his doorway and pointed in my direction, signaling for me to join him in his office. On my way over, Special Agent Hayes intercepted me to shake my hand and to personally congratulate me.

"Congratulations, Mick," she expressed. "Stella is gorgeous."

"Thank you, Mar . . , um, Agent Hayes."

I was comforted that she smiled at my slip. Then, her face became playfully serious.

"It's quite all right, Detective Dooley," she stated in an exaggerated, masculine tone to convey a lighthearted message. I understood the hint and smiled.

"Listen," I began, "I'd like it if you could join me in the Lieutenant's office. There's something I need to talk with both of you about."

She paused, giving me a curious look.

"Well then, please," she said, extending her arm toward Frank's open door, "after you."

With her acceptance, I marched into Frank's office like a lion, full of confidence, hoping I wouldn't limp out like a lamb. Hayes followed me in, to Frank's surprise.

"What, I need the FBI present to speak with one of my detectives now?" he grumbled.

"I know you've been under a lot of pressure, Lieutenant," Hayes responded with a raised eyebrow. "I'll let that one slide."

"I asked her to join us, Lieu."

"Oh," Lieutenant Garrett squeaked out, his eyes narrowed in discomfiture. "I apologize, Miss Hayes."

She shot him a half-hearted grin as she nodded.

"All right, Dooley, you've got my ear," the Lieutenant stated, pointing to the empty chair in front of his desk. "So, what's this about then?"

I glanced at the chair and then at Hayes, offering her first dibs. She put up her hand and shook her head. Maybe she thought she wouldn't be there long. That was fine with me; I'd gladly sit. It would make it harder for them to chew on my ass for what I was about to tell them.

"You might recall I visited with Ben about a week ago."

Frank sat back in his chair, crossed his arms, and nodded.

"I do," he responded.

Hayes had a different reaction as she shot Frank an annoyed glare.

"Wait," she stopped me from continuing, "I don't recall hearing about this."

"He mentioned it to me in passing," Frank jumped in, taking the heat. "I didn't want to say anything until I had the details, which, from the sound of it, is what we're about to get."

I looked up at Hayes, her eyes searing a hole in my corneas.

"It was the night I stormed away from the Osterlander scene. An idea struck me, and I followed through on it."

"And that idea was ..?" she questioned.

"I thought it would be a good idea if we could get inside the killer's head. You know, see what makes him tick. I thought Ben might be able to help with that."

"The FBI has professional profilers for that, Detective," she stated angrily.

"I know," I replied uncomfortably, not expecting the hostility in her voice. "I'm not taking anything away from them, but in the end, it's all just guesswork, isn't it?"

"There's a little more to it than 'guesswork,'" she replied defensively.

"Of course," I responded. "But the fact remains, we have the man who started the whole thing incarcerated only twenty-five miles away, and he's willing to help. Why not utilize what we've got?"

"HA!" Frank chimed in. "Willing to help? You think we could even trust that little shit?"

"I do," I answered. "I've been giving it some thought the past few days. Someone else is out there stealing the kid's thunder. I think he wants to catch this guy as much as we do."

Frank glanced at Hayes, shrugging his shoulders, "I don't know; maybe Mick's onto something. What do you think, Agent Hayes?"

I watched as Hayes curled her lips inward, exhaling from her nose as she pondered the proposal. She then shifted her eyes to me inquisitively.

"How do we know Ben and this 'Letter Man' aren't working together? Has anyone checked the prison logs to see if Ben's had any visitors?"

"I've already checked," I answered. "I've been the only visitor the kid has had in almost a year."

"What about phone calls or mail?" she argued.

"The warden told me Ben's never been interested in making phone calls, and the only mail he gets is hate mail. I'm telling you, there's nothing; he only wants to help."

"I've been around long enough to know criminals don't offer their services out of the goodness of their hearts," she responded. "He must be looking for a deal. He's not going to get one."

I shook my head. "He's not looking for a deal; he knows he's not getting out of there."

"Then what?" Frank asked, leaning forward. "Don't tell me the kid's suddenly looking for a spot in Heaven. 'Cause that ain't happening, either."

I felt my palms becoming sweaty. My eyes shifted from Frank to Hayes and back to Frank again.

"He wants to read the killer's notes."

"What the Christ?" Frank barked, throwing his hands up in the air. "That kid has some balls. Fuck no. Let the kid get his jollies off the old-fashioned way. Hell, I'll even send him the magazines. That's *my* answer."

I expected that. What I didn't expect was what came next.

"Now, hold on a second, Lieutenant," Agent Hayes stated. "That's not a bad idea. Ben's a smart kid, and he *did* write similar letters. Perhaps he'd pick up on something we've overlooked. And it wouldn't be too difficult for us to arrange to have Mick bring a set of copies to him."

How did I know that was coming? Time to drop the bombshell.

"He wants to see the originals," I jumped in.

"What?" she questioned.

"He said he wants to see the originals, or it's no deal."

"What the fuck's the difference?" Frank hollered.

"I don't know, Lieu. He's a demented prick with screws loose in the head."

"So, we just give him copies and tell him they're the originals," Hayes added.

I shook my head, "He'll know they're copies, and then we're fucked."

"We're fucked anyway," Frank yelled. "Jesus Christ."

"I don't understand the fascination with the originals," Agent Hayes said, "but if we've gathered everything from them that we can, I don't see the harm. The problem is that Southbridge only has two originals; Larson has the rest. It'll take a bit of arm twisting, but I think I can convince Captain Norris to be agreeable."

"And if he isn't," I asked.

"Well then, I guess I'll pull rank on him and threaten him with hindering a federal investigation. Let's hope it doesn't come to that."

"And what about Agent Lowe?" Frank questioned.

Hayes walked to the door and looked at her partner from between the slats in the window blinds.

"He'll never go for it," she said quietly. Then she spun around to face us. "Which is why we're not going to tell him."

Frank pointed his finger at her, jabbing it back and forth as if he were impatiently pressing an elevator button, "I knew I liked you, Hayes."

"Oh good; that will come in handy when I'm relieved of my duties. Again."

Frank and I looked at each other, confused.

"Again?" Frank belted. "What's that about?"

"Nothing," Hayes replied unconvincingly. "Just something from my past I wouldn't care to discuss."

"Well then, I won't say anything to Lowe if you won't," I assured her.

"Wait a minute," Frank bellowed. "What about the note left in blood on Karen's wall?"

"He said he'd accept a picture of that," I replied.

"Oh, *that* one he's okay with?" Frank snorted. "Fucker!"

I shrugged my shoulders and shook my head. "We obviously can't bring the wall."

"So that's it then?" Frank questioned. "We're doing this?"

Hayes nodded. "Let's see where it takes us. Who knows; maybe Ben can redeem a little bit of himself."

"This has gotta stay in this office," Frank stated. "If anyone else catches wind, it'll find its way to Lowe." He winked at Agent Hayes. "We've got your back, Hayes."

"It's not my back I'm worried about," Hayes remarked. "But if there's nothing else, gentlemen, I'd best be heading out. It looks like I'm taking a trip to Larson this morning. I'll think of something to tell Agent Lowe."

Hayes composed herself and calmly walked out of the office, closing the door behind her.

"That Hayes is an all right lady," Frank said, staring at the closed door.

"Yeah, she is," I agreed. "Did they find anything out with the cameras outside Nancy's building?"

"They found out they were goddamn non-working pieces of shit."

"Nothing seems to want to go right for us in this case," I said.

"That's why this bullshit with Ben better pan out."

I nodded.

"Can I go now?" I questioned.

"No, I called you in here for a different reason. But hold on a second."

He held up his index finger to halt me and then picked up the phone.

"Vera, do you have the Lydon Foster and the Osterlander notes handy? Good. I'm going to send Mick down there to grab them from you. No, he won't get lost making his way down there. Oh, for the love of.., no, Vera, I'm not sending him to get cake first, Jesus Christ. Just have it ready, will you? Yeah."

As usual, he hung up without saying goodbye.

"So, what did you call me in here for?" I asked.

Frank dropped his head and began wiping his hand back and forth across his forehead as if he were struggling with something.

"How's the wife and kid?" he asked, maintaining his downward stare.

"They're good," I replied to the top of his head. "We're still getting used to having a newborn around, but it's an experience for sure."

"Good, good," Frank mumbled as if he hadn't heard a word I'd said. Then, the office became silent while I watched him relocate his hand to rub the back of his neck while his gaze remained on his desk. It was clear to see he was wrestling with something but didn't know how to approach the subject.

"Is everything all right, Lieutenant?"

"What?" he questioned, looking up at me, his hand still massaging the back of his neck. "Oh, yeah. Fine. Sorry, Mick, I shouldn't have asked you in here."

"It's all right, Lieu, I can go," I stated, about to push myself up from my seated position.

"Wait," Frank halted me. "Stay. I need to get something off my chest, and I don't need to be talking with one of the precinct shrinks."

"What is it, Lieu?" I questioned, concerned. Whatever it was, it sounded serious.

He closed his eyes and shook his head. "Aw, Fuck," he stated in almost a whisper. "This stays between us, got it?"

I nodded, my eyes wide with anticipation of hearing the worst.

"It's my wife," he opened up.

"Oh," was all I could muster. I wasn't sure how to react. I was never one to interfere in someone else's personal life. "Is she okay, Frank?"

"Remember how I told you Nancy and my wife were friends?"

"Yeah."

"Well, the Feds dug up all kinds of shit on Ms. Osterlander. Embezzlement, fraud.., you name it. If it had something to do with money and finances, her grubby hands were all over it. She was swindling people out of their 401k earnings, for Christ's sake."

"So then, the killer was right," I said. "But what does this have to do with your wife?"

"I questioned her about it. You know, to see if she knew anything about Nancy's illegalities."

"And?"

"She said she didn't know anything about it."

"Okay, then what's the problem? I don't understand."

"The problem is, I don't believe her."

"Oh," I said, sitting upright in my chair, suddenly feeling more uncomfortable than I already had been. "Maybe you shouldn't be telling me this."

"Cut the shit, Mick. I'll handle things if they need to be handled. I wanted to ask you, though, just between you and me, how do you know when Gina's lying to you?"

"That's just it, Lieu.., Gina doesn't lie to me; she's got no reason to."

He pointed his finger at me, "That's horseshit! That's what they want you to think. Let me tell you something - everybody lies; it's just a matter of how big or small the lie is. You'll see what I'm talking about when you've been married as long as I've been."

"Okay," I said, throwing my hands up in front of my chest. "I don't think we need to discuss this."

"Fuck," he whispered under his breath while shaking his head. "I'm sorry, kid. I shouldn't have mentioned any of this to you."

"It's okay, Lieu," I said, pushing myself from the chair, assuming we were through. "I don't mind. It's just.., you should really be having this conversation with your wife."

"No shit," he grumbled.

I threw my thumb over my shoulder, "If we're through then, I should... go and grab the killer's notes from Vera." Nothing said *"awkward"* quite like the way I presented it.

He gave me a somewhat distraught look, curling his upper lip.

"Yeah, we're done here."

He flapped his hand as if to shoo me from his office. It wouldn't have taken that much effort on his part; I was already halfway out the door.

Things were weighing on the man. I'd sure hate to be in his shoes. Whether his wife knew something or not, his words lingered with me.

Everybody lies; it's just a matter of how big or small the lie is.

I never thought of it much, but I supposed he was right. I didn't want to think that way about Gina, though. I didn't want to believe she had it in her. I couldn't. Ben, on the other hand..,

One step at a time, Mick, I thought. First, I had to gather all the killer's notes. Then, we'd see how big or small the kid's lies were.

Chapter 15

Criminal Minds

Vera looked up from her monitor as Danny opened the door for me. She gave me a curious look as she slapped her hand on a clear plastic baggie at the front of her desk and slid it back toward herself. I heard the lab door click shut behind me as she pinched the bag between her two fingers and lifted it from the desk, dangling it like a carrot in front of me. I reached for it, but she quickly yanked it away from my outstretched hand, smirking at my failed attempt.

"Oh no, you don't," she said. "What's the magic word?"

I shot her an unamused look while keeping my arm extended and hand opened, thinking she'd catch my drift. Instead, she raised her eyebrows as if waiting for my response.

"Come on, Vera," I said, "the lieutenant sent me down here to get the notes."

"Yeah," she replied, "and now you're here. I'm still going to need the magic word."

I shook my head, slightly annoyed. She wasn't going to back down.., and she knew I couldn't take her. I had to be the one to cave if I wanted the evidence.

"Please," I said, rolling my eyes.

She scrunched her face and stared at me funny.

"No, shrimp dick," she responded, slapping the baggie into my palm. "It was cunnilingus."

I heard Danny snicker as he walked back to his station.

"Like I would have ever gotten that," I responded, giving Danny the evil eye for laughing at me and encouraging Vera.

"I should hope not," Vera replied, "but maybe your wife."

I turned my attention back to her. "You know what I meant."

"I did. But, um, hello. It's me. What did you think the magic word would be?"

"Good point," I replied, glancing down at the bag in my hand, focusing on the contents within.

"And these are the originals?" I questioned.

"They are. And I'd better get them back when you're done showing that fucking twat bag."

"What?" I expressed, surprised at her response and playing it off as if I didn't know what she was talking about.

"Don't give me that dumbass look," she jabbed. "Do you honestly think I don't know what you're doing with them? I wasn't born yesterday. It's all over your face. You're bringing them to Ben to appeal for his help."

"How..? How did you know?"

"What, do you think you're the first person to enlist the aid of a serial killer? That shit's been happening since the 70s. Haven't you ever heard of John Douglas?"

I shook my head.

"Why am I not surprised," she responded. "Anyway, it doesn't matter. I'm kind of an expert at this stuff, numbnuts."

I must have had a concerned look on my face – one that guilted her into wanting to offer relief.

"Don't sweat it; Danny and I won't say anything."

I glanced over at her lab assistant, and he shook his head.

"You'd better not," I said, trying to portray toughness where there wasn't any. "If Lowe finds out about this, it's all of our asses."

"Oh, you're doing it behind that jackass's back? Then I'm definitely on board."

I tilted my head, "I mean it, Vera; this doesn't leave here."

"Yeah, yeah. It's our little secret." She pointed to the door. "You got what you came for; now get the fuck out of here."

I nodded in agreement, shaking the bag up and down from my fingertips. "Thanks."

"Yeah. And remember, I want that back."

I opened the door and walked out, shouting behind me before it closed, "You'll get them back."

I spent the next couple of hours reviewing the files of everything I'd missed the past few days. I'd looked at everything from Nancy Osterlander's shady dealings to the

FBI's interrogation of Lieutenant Frangione of the state police.

Osterlander swindled dozens of trusting elderly folks out of their retirement funds, giving us more suspects who might have had the motivation to kill her. The FBI didn't suspect any of Osterlander's victims; most of them were too old to have committed the crimes we were faced with. It could have been any of the family members, however, though I failed to see how such motives could have led them to commit all of the other murders. Still, it was going to keep the department busy for a while with all the interviews. Detective Frazier and Special Agent Lowe were spearheading that initiative.

State Police Lieutenant Frangione was grilled by Lowe and Hayes until they were adequately satisfied with his innocence. The poor guy had to relive the horrible experience of his daughter's rape and then deal with being looked at as a suspect in a murder investigation. I understood their reasoning; if somebody raped my little girl, I'd want to kill the fucker. In the Fed's eyes, the fact that the rapist ended up dead less than a year after his release from prison made Frangione a plausible suspect and his interrogation necessary. I didn't see it that way. It felt more like it was out of desperation; they were looking for anything. I was happy to hear, though, that they didn't have to involve his family. Opening old wounds was never a good thing. Frangione was, however, removed from the investigation.

I looked to my left, the ziplocked bag on my desk taunting me. I picked it up and stared into the clear plastic, the notes within, each packaged in an individual bag of their own, staring back at me.

"What the hell are you doing, Ben?" I whispered to myself. "What is it you're after?"

My drifting thoughts would have to wait for an answer. Agent Hayes burst through the door, storming toward Frank's office like she was on a mission. She was, of course, but she didn't have to make it so conspicuous. Lowe was too busy in the makeshift "command center," still siphoning details about the Osterlander victims' family members to notice. As Hayes neared Frank's door, she glanced my way and subtly nodded her head sideways, requesting I join her. I jumped at the chance. Sitting alone with my troubled thoughts only frustrated me.

As I got up from my seat, I peered around the room to see if anyone had noticed my movements. Nope. Like everyone else in the room, I was a nobody, trying to make it through the day. In this instance, that was a good thing. There'd be nobody wondering what was going on.

I entered Frank's office and closed the door behind me. Agent Hayes was standing to my left holding a manila envelope – I presumed with the original notes we were waiting for. She looked a bit frazzled, as if getting the evidence wasn't as easy as she'd hoped it would've been.

"Is that them?" I questioned, pointing to the envelope.

"Let's have a look," Frank requested, reaching forward from behind his desk, his fingers and thumb snapping together like pincers, eager to receive the package.

Hayes handed it over. Frank immediately tore into the flap to check the contents.

"We've got twenty-four hours," Hayes said as I watched Frank pull one of the pieces of evidence from the envelope.

"What are you talking about?" I asked.

"What I'm talking about is Chief Sutton was very resistant to handing over Larson's evidence in an ongoing investigation. He demanded to know what it was all about before he would agree."

I looked at Frank, who was uncharacteristically quiet during our conversation, expecting his face to be the usual burning red color whenever he got upset. I wasn't sure he'd heard a word we said; his eyes were fixated on the photograph he'd removed from the evidence envelope. It was obviously that of the message written in blood on Karen's wall.

"And so you told him?" I responded, turning my attention back to Hayes.

"He threatened to confront Special Agent Lowe about his underhanded demands concerning the handling of sensitive evidence. When I told him Lowe had nothing to do with it and that he didn't even know I was there, Chief Sutton backed down a bit. He doesn't care much for Special Agent Lowe."

"I get the feeling it's not only Chief Sutton who feels that way," I jumped in.

"Yeah, well, in any case, he insisted I tell him what we were up to."

"So, he's on board with it, then," I responded, glancing at Frank again, whose somber features were still gripped by the picture.

"Not exactly," Hayes replied. "He was torn by the decision, but he agreed to let us 'borrow' the evidence as long as we got it back to him within twenty-four hours. Otherwise, he'd be obligated to contact Lowe."

"Then, you're getting these over to Ben *today*," Frank chimed in, sliding the picture back into the envelope and handing it over to me.

"I'll contact the warden to let him know you're on your way," Hayes said.

I nodded and snatched the envelope from Frank's hand. "I'm on it," I said, reaching for the door. "I'll keep you posted."

* * *

I sat uncomfortably at the table, waiting for my guest to arrive. It wasn't so much the hard, wooden chair that made it uncomfortable as much as the guard in the corner, whose unwavering stare burned into me as if he didn't appreciate the babysitting watch duty with which he'd been tasked. I kept my eyes focused on the envelope in front of me. It helped me avoid his disdainful glare.

The envelope itself wasn't holding my attention. That honor went to Gina and Stella Mae. They were heavily in my thoughts as I traced my finger along the table's surface, writing Stella's name in imaginary cursive letters. Letters. How ironic that my mind should land on that subject just as I'm about to meet with The Alphabet Killer – the one responsible for unwittingly setting the latest homicidal maniac on his path.

Ben was a sadistic killer, begging for his father's affection. He believed his motives were righteous, helping the police rid the streets of criminals. He wanted his father to catch him, for him to earn the recognition he deserved. That's what Ben would have us believe, anyway. Jimmy received that recognition posthumously, and the city's residents were thankful yet sorrowful for his sacrifice. This latest nut job, however, isn't interested in helping the police. He has no interest in getting caught. His motives seem darker, as evidenced by the brutal nature of his killings. He enjoys his work and wants it to continue. I can't let that happen. I need to put an end to this. I need to put an end to *him*. That's the reason I'm here. The *only* reason I'm here.

Just then, my ears picked up on the sound of shuffling footsteps, Ben's chained ankles hindering his stride as he was escorted into the empty room by a second corrections officer. I noticed a smug look appear on his face after his eyes latched onto the envelope I brought with me. He was proud of himself and wasn't ashamed about flaunting it.

The officer forcibly sat Ben down in the chair across from where I sat. It was clear to me there was no love lost in their relationship. Ben smirked, raising his wrists over his shoulder for the officer to uncuff him.

"I don't think so, shithead," the officer responded before backing away and smiling at his buddy by the door. I'm guessing the warden didn't tell them they had to play nice while I was here.

Ben looked at me and shook his head, mumbling under his breath, "Asses." He threw his cuffed hands up onto the table and pointed to the envelope.

"Is that them?"

I nodded, "As promised."

He shot me an impressed look while nodding himself.

"I'm impressed, Mick. May I see them?"

I felt myself lick my lower lip, wondering if I should forget the whole thing and walk away. Who was I kidding? I already knew what the answer would be. I reached down and slid the envelope toward him. His eyes shifted to the table as he brought the back of his hand up to wipe the corner of his mouth, removing saliva that had gathered with his anticipated excitement. I felt my stomach turn.

As Ben opened the envelope and reached in, pulling the documents from their manila housing, I had to ask.

"Are you going to tell me why you needed the originals?"

He brought one of the baggies to his nose and breathed in deeply, closing his eyes as he did so as if he were sniffing an aged wine.

"It's the smell, Mick," he answered, opening his eyes while grinning. "I love me the smell of warranted death."

"Cut the shit, Ben."

He giggled at my response, the first sign of the Ben I once knew. Then, he shrugged his shoulders.

"I wanted to see how desperate you were," he said. "I'd say I received my answer. I also wanted to see if you had lied to me."

I gave him a nasty glance, curling my upper lip in disgust.

"Everybody lies," I said, repeating Frank's words. "It's just a matter of how big or small the lie is. The question is, were you lying about wanting to help?"

"I'll do what I can," he replied, pulling at the top of the first plastic bag to open it.

"Uh uh," I stated, snatching it from his hand before he succeeded. "The notes stay in the bags."

"What fun is that?" Ben questioned.

"I brought you the original notes; that was the deal. You can read them through the plastic."

Ben sneered but nodded his acceptance. I handed the bag back to him.

For several minutes, he shuffled from one note to the next, taking in the killer's words, until he landed on the picture taken of his mother's blood-smeared wall. The image captured a fraction of his mother's bloody body lying on the floor beneath the horrific declaration. It gave him pause. As much as Ben expressed his joy over his mother's death, somewhere inside, he still hurt. I couldn't help but think his uncaring demeanor was all denial, a façade. His face showed a different response. I think it ate at him to know his mother was dead. Good; let it eat away at him. It was all his doing.

"So, what do you think?" I asked, taking him from his reflective moment. "Do you see anything that stands out to you?"

He laid the picture down and slid it under one of the notes. I don't think he wanted me to notice.

"This guy is angry," he started. "Like, he's got some serious issues."

"We knew that already."

"No, I mean, this is personal. When I chose *my* people…"

"Victims!" I interrupted.

He smirked and gave me a subtle nod.

"Fine. I didn't choose my 'victims' because of something they had done to me. They were doing it to themselves. Their lives were heading down the toilet, and they were happy to speed things along by keeping up their destructive behaviors. They were all bad people, and they needed to die. It was never personal. But this..,"

He patted his palms on the pile of letters.

"Somebody did something to this guy that made him who he is. In *his* eyes, his victims aren't people. He uses words like 'human filth,' 'garbage,' and 'monster,' to describe them. He states their actions are 'wretched' and 'wicked,' but he doesn't see his own in that way. I was cleaning the streets to help my dad. This guy is doing it for himself. He wants everyone to understand his pain, his 'wrath.' He craves 'vengeance.' He's now gotten a taste of what it feels like. He'll keep on that path."

"Anything else?" I questioned.

"Without knowing the specific details of his kills, there's not much more I can help with. Maybe you can share a little with me."

"Go to hell," I replied.

"I thought I was already there," he said while I scooped up the documents and began stuffing them back into the envelope. "I will say this, Mick," he continued, "I'd be careful if I were you. This guy doesn't play nice, and he doesn't care much for the work you're doing."

"The work I'm doing?"

"He's blaming the law, the system, the lack of justice. So you see, Mick.., in the end, it's kind of *your* fault he's out there."

And that about did it for me. I raised my hand to get the guard's attention.

"Nice talking to you," I said sarcastically, getting up from my chair.

As the one guard started walking with me, I heard the other wrestle Ben to his feet.

"Mick!" Ben called out. "You know where to find me when you're ready to share all the gory details. I'll tell you everything you need to know about your 'Letter Man.'"

I didn't bother to look back. I didn't care to. There was nothing left to see.

Chapter 16

P

ive minutes. That's how long it was before all hell broke loose after I returned to the station. I had just dropped the evidence envelope onto Frank's desk and was in the middle of telling him about my grand visit with Ben when Special Agent Lowe hastily walked by, slapping his palm against the doorframe.

"Move it, gentlemen," he said, continuing his stride. "We've got ourselves a live one," his voice faded.

"What the fuck is he talking about?" Frank questioned, standing from behind his desk.

"I don't know," I replied, twisting in my chair to see other officers racing from their desks. Thankfully, Special Agent Hayes stopped in the open doorway to clue us in.

"Let's go, boys," she stated. "We think the killer struck again. Only, this time, he fucked up. The victim's alive."

"Holy shit!" I exclaimed, jumping from my seat so quickly that I almost knocked it over. Frank quickly

136

swerved around his desk to join me as we followed closely behind Hayes, joining the crowd of officers heading for the exit. I'd never seen such a mass exodus. Everyone wanted in on this one.

"What the hell does she mean, 'we think'?" Frank questioned.

I shrugged my shoulders.

"Hayes," I called out, trying to keep pace with her, "where are we going?"

She was too focused to stop or look back, but she'd heard me, as evidenced by her voice echoing off the glass door ahead of her.

"The Vinmore Apartments."

A chill ran through me, and I felt my stomach flop. The Vinmore Apartment building was where we finally caught Ben. It's also where he shot his father. I hadn't been back there since. I'd hoped there'd never have been a need to. Now, apparently, The Letter Man has forced my hand.

Shit.

I rode with Frank, which only heightened my uneasiness. He could see my discomfort and tried calming me down by staying positive.

"Sounds like we finally caught a break, huh?" he said. "We're gonna get this fucker."

Frank was on the rooftop that night, too. I knew he felt the same as me, but he did a better job of disguising his emotions. He was built for this job; I was barely growing into it.

"Yeah," I replied, keeping my eyes focused through the passenger side window. "Let's hope so."

A minute of silence followed while the buildings streaked by my view, my troubled thoughts taking me back to that night, the moment forever frozen in my brain.

"Please, Ben, I need you, son. Your mother needs you. Give me the gun. Please. Give me the gun."

Those were the last words I remember Jimmy saying before he lunged forward and grabbed the gun to prevent Ben from shooting himself. It was reckless, but that was Jimmy. It was also selfless, a reaction stemming from love. That was Jimmy, too, though he never would have admitted it had he lived.

"So, finish what you were telling me about the kid," Frank spoke, perhaps feeling the silence was more uncomfortable than where we were headed.

"There's not much to say," I replied. "He studied the killer's notes, then he made a few comments about the guy being angry."

"Angry?"

"Vengeful or some shit. Ben said the killer's motivations are different than what his were. There's something personal about them."

"Well, that's just fucking great! Someone's out there killing people because they got their poor feelings hurt. Boo frickin' hoo. His days are numbered now, the son of a bitch. We've got him," he nodded nervously, almost as if trying to convince himself. "Yeah, we've got him."

The remainder of the ride was silent except for Frank tapping his fingers anxiously against the steering wheel, occasionally letting out a whispered, "*We've got him.*" I nodded positively each time the words slipped from his lips, trying to reassure him that he was right. I think it was his way of coping with the idea that he didn't really believe it. And he wouldn't until the killer was in custody. I was on the same doubtful page.

We pulled up to the Vinmore Apartments, an empty ambulance already on site against the curb along the front of the building. An eerie feeling of dread washed over me, the familiar scene a carbon copy of that from two years earlier. Almost all the players were the same: me, Frank, Hayes, a few of the uniformed officers. It was as if we were reliving that night. Stepping from the vehicle, even the weight of the thick air itself felt the same. I looked at Frank; he somberly nodded. That was when I knew it was as difficult for him as it was for me. He and Jimmy didn't always see eye to eye on things, and their relationship seemed a bit strained for about a year or so before Jimmy's death, but he always had great respect for the man. Now, as we followed the FBI up the walkway to the entrance, trying to suppress the guilt for not having been able to save a fellow officer - a friend - it was hitting hard.

Special Agent Lowe took charge, directing the uniformed officers in their duties. He allowed two to enter after me and Frank. The others gathered on the property's front lawn, probably badmouthing the hard-nosed agent. I didn't blame them. Funny thing, though - I didn't blame Agent Lowe, either. We didn't need everyone huddled inside, disturbing the crime scene.

Unlike the last time we were here, the hallway corridor wasn't devoid of life. The first-floor tenants congregated outside their doors, whispering amongst themselves and pointing to the staircase leading to the second floor. As we climbed the stairs, we could hear the EMTs above, working diligently, their voices partially drowned out by the sound of mumbling on-lookers and a woman's hysterical cries. Lowe belted out an order to the officers behind us, requesting they keep the second-floor tenants back and under control while the four of us assessed the situation. By the time we reached the first landing, the two officers hurried past us; I imagined a sense of morbid curiosity was the true motivation for their rushed pace.

Once on the second floor, the signs of a horrific crime were plainly visible, including gawking neighbors with their cellphones in hand, taking videos to meet the demands of their many followers on social media. The two uniformed officers were doing their best to make room for us.

The EMTs had just finished strapping the victim to a gurney and were getting him ready for transport. A young woman, thin, with dirty-blonde hair, was sitting on the floor against an open door, apartment 2B, her knees bent up as she hugged them against her chest. Her arms were lined with bruises, she had a black eye and a swollen cheek, and her lower lip had a gash in it. She was trembling as tears streamed from her eyes, her stare focused on the man strapped to the gurney. Hayes immediately gravitated to the woman, squatting beside her to check on her while Lowe harrassed the EMTs.

"What's the story here?" he questioned, preventing them from wheeling the bleeding man away. "Is he alive?"

"He's alive but barely conscious," one of them responded. "He's sustained three stab wounds to the mid-section and his left external carotid artery has been severed. He's lost a lot of blood. Now, if you don't mind, we've got to get this man to the hospital."

"Can he talk?" Agent Lowe grunted, pushing his limits as they wheeled the man to the edge of the stairway.

"He won't live long enough to if he doesn't get into surgery soon," one griped back, showing his annoyance at the overbearing agent.

"Goddammit!" I heard Lowe's voice cry out and then slowly die down as I watched the paramedics struggle to get the gurney down the stairs. Two men from the first floor rushed up to the landing to aid them, proving there *were* good people left in this city. My thoughts drifted away for a moment. All the noises and voices in the hallway around me became muted and indistinguishable to my ears like I was underwater. I found myself in a daze, feeling numb, staring at a David Hasselhoff doormat at the foot of apartment 2A, unable to tear my eyes away from his cheerful smile until I heard Agent Lowe raise his voice again.

"Christ! Did anyone see *anything?*" he shouted, throwing his arms into the air in frustration at the gaping residents. "Fuck!"

Agent Hayes quickly jumped to her feet and dashed to her partner.

"Special Agent Lowe," she stated fervently, "you're out of line. I'm going to need you to step away."

She glanced in my direction with a stern look in her eyes, pointed at me, and then swung her arm toward the injured woman in the doorway, pulling me back into the moment. Without hesitation, I rushed to the battered woman, all the while listening to Hayes' footsteps leading Lowe down to the landing below while Frank stood quietly over my shoulder.

Lowe's behavior was uncharacteristic. I understood where he was coming from. This case had become more than he - than any of us expected. And every time we caught a break, the carpet was yanked out from under us. Not all was lost, however; we still had the woman. She appeared to be somehow involved in this, her bloody hands indicating she was either present from the start or she tried to stop the victim's bleeding. Either way offered us an opportunity. Still, if someone as calm and controlled as Agent Lowe could suddenly lose it, what chance did I have of walking away from this unscathed?

"Ma'am, are you all right?" I asked, trying to get her to look at me, a glaze forming over her inattentive stare. "Ma'am," I tried again, placing my hand gently on her shoulder. Something awoke in her; she tilted her head to me. "Can you tell us what happened?"

The woman's bottom lip quivered. She turned her head into the apartment and then back to me.

"I... I,"

"It's okay, miss," Frank spoke from above. "Take your time."

"There.., there was a man," she said, still trembling.

"Yes, a man," I responded, nodding. "Did he do those things to that gentleman?"

She didn't say anything, only nodding her response.

"Is that man still here?"

She shook her head, placing her chin on her bent knee.

Frank tapped my shoulder, "Maybe we should get her into the apartment." He nodded his head sideways at the curious onlookers still waving their phones. I nodded.

"What's your name?" I asked the woman.

"Charlene," she replied.

"Can you stand, Charlene?"

She nodded.

"May we help you into your apartment?"

She looked at me, then at Frank, as if judging our characters, then shifted her glare to her nosy neighbors. Succumbing to our suggestion, she extended her arms for us to grab hold.

"Here we go," Frank said, reaching under her left arm while I held her right. "Easy does it."

We shimmied our way through the doorway, easing the woman to the nearest piece of furniture - a loveseat. She sat down and dropped her arms to her lap, her blood-stained hands still balled into fists. We didn't shut the door behind us, expecting Hayes and Lowe to be along momentarily.

"Do you know the man who was stabbed?" I asked.

"Yes," she answered, "he's my boyfriend."

"Does he live here with you?"

"Yes," she nodded. Then, she scrunched her face and shook her head. "I mean, no. Well, sometimes."

I gave Frank a perplexed look, wondering if the shock of what had happened was causing her confusion.

"What's your boyfriend's name?" Frank asked.

"Peter."

I felt an instant chill. That fit the killer's pattern. P was the next letter on his list.

"Does Peter have a last name?" Frank continued his questioning.

"It's Petrulovich. Peter Petrulovich."

"Charlene, you said a man did that to Peter," I stated, getting back on point. "Did he also do *that* to you?" I motioned toward her battered face. She dropped her chin to her chest, embarrassed, and then her eyes slowly rolled forward to meet mine as she shook her head before immediately looking away.

"Oh," was all I managed to get out, just then understanding the woman's domestic situation. I looked at Frank for guidance. He shook his head, his unspoken words telling me not to pursue the subject. I felt my shoulders drop to match what my heart had done seconds earlier. My thoughts went to Gina, and I wondered how any man could physically abuse a woman. There was too much of that shit in the world. But Frank was right; I had to stick to the case.

"Charlene, can you tell us what happened?"

She kept her eyes averted as she began.

"Peter and I had just gotten into a fight. It wasn't a big deal or anything."

Why did they always do that? It sickened me. Even after being beaten, she was still defending him.

"He said he was going out to get some smokes," she continued. "I heard him raise his voice out in the hall. Like he was yelling at somebody, you know?"

"Did you happen to hear what he said?"

"Something like, 'C'mon, man; what the fuck do you want now?' Then I heard a commotion, and Peter screamed. I ran to the door to see what was going on, and when I opened it, a man was squatting over Peter's body, stabbing him in the chest. As soon as he realized I was there, he jumped to his feet and ran down the stairs."

"Did you get a look at the man? Can you describe him for us?"

"No," she shook her head. "His back was to me, and he was wearing one of those rain things - a black poncho with a hood."

I glanced at Frank, wondering if he thought the same as me. There'd been no rain. The killer wore that getup specifically to disguise himself. He knew going into an apartment building was risky. There was a chance there'd be people around. And whoever this guy was, it sounded like he and the victim had a previous run-in.

"I screamed for help," she continued, "while trying to stop the bleeding. There was so much blood. Finally, a woman from 2C came out. She saw what was going on and called 911."

Just then, Agents Hayes and Lowe appeared in the doorway. Charlene's eyes widened, nervous about their sudden entrance. Frank turned and walked over to Lowe to feed him some information, most likely to keep him from saying something stupid. Hayes calmly joined me. I quickly introduced them to ease Charlene's discomfort.

"Charlene, this is Special Agent Hayes with the FBI. The other gentleman is Special Agent Lowe."

"We spoke in the hall," Agent Hayes reminded me. "My offer still stands," she said to the woman. "I don't mind bringing you to the hospital."

"I don't want to go," Charlene replied, reaching up with her left hand to rub her swollen cheek.

Hayes offered a sympathetic nod. "I understand."

I felt Frank and Agent Lowe's presence crowding me; they'd finished their chat and decided to join us. Agent Lowe started right in.

"I'm very sorry about this whole ordeal, miss, but I need to speak with my colleague for a moment."

That was a surprise to Hayes. I noticed she shot her partner a curious look. He nodded his head sideways, suggesting she join him only a few feet away. If his goal was to be discreet about something, he didn't understand the concept. We couldn't help overhearing.

"What the hell is this?" he questioned – and not too quietly, doing an awful job of keeping the conversation to themselves. "This looks like a random incident. Why was this called in as one of ours? We don't even know if this is our guy."

"It is," Charlene blurted.

In unison, we all turned our attention to the woman.

"Excuse me?" Agent Lowe questioned.

Charlene's eyes shifted between the four of us.

"The one you're looking for," she responded, a sense of confidence in her voice. "You were wondering if it was *him* – The Letter Man. It's all that's ever on the news these days. It was him."

"Did he tell you that?" Agent Lowe asked, doubtful of the woman's response.

She shook her head, choosing to remain silent, perhaps feeling nervous about Agent Lowe's unbelieving glare.

"Then how can you possibly know something like that?"

Charlene averted her eyes, staring down at her right hand, still held in a tight fist. She looked up at me as if determining my belief in her words. She must have deemed me less cynical than my hard-nosed compatriot since she turned her trembling fist upward and slowly opened her hand.

I thought I heard Agent Hayes let out a gasp. Or it might have been me. I wasn't sure.

In the woman's palm sat a crumpled wad of paper, stained with blood and rolled into a tight ball. We all knew what it must have been. She'd held it in her hand the entire time. Agent Lowe wasn't pleased.

"If that's what I think it is," he raised his voice, "you've not only been holding onto evidence, but you've corrupted it as well."

"Calm down, Agent Lowe," Hayes said, putting her hand up to silence him.

"Don't tell me to..,"

"With all due respect, Agent," she interrupted, "you're teetering on that line. This isn't the Spanish Inquisition. If I feel your actions are detrimental or negatively impactful to this case, I'll tell you whatever needs to be said. Now pull yourself together, or I'll have no choice but to have you removed from the case."

Hayes was finally displaying the nerve of the woman I remembered. But while the two agents bickered, Frank tapped my arm to gain my attention. He was dangling a pair of latex gloves for me to put on. I let the two Feds stare each other down, each trying to gain dominance over the other until they heard me snap the fitted glove against my wrist. They turned in time to see me remove the red-steeped ball from Charlene's hand.

"He wore gloves, too," she said as I unraveled the tight ball. "Like those, only blue."

"Blue gloves," I repeated, looking at Hayes as she pulled a pair of matching whites from her pocket. "Okay. Got it."

I turned back to the blood-blotched paper and began reading the ink-smeared message to myself while Frank's head peeked over my shoulder to read along. When I was through, my eyes swept over the top of the paper to see Charlene staring intently at me.

"Did you read this?" I asked.

She nodded.

It was a little more clear now as to why Charlene had no interest in being at the hospital with her "boyfriend." It wasn't because of the beatings. Abuse victims often stayed in their relationships through the worst of it, either out of fear or from their misguided belief that the violence was somehow from a place of love. Charlene had just learned love played no part in it. I handed the note to Agent Hayes. She and Lowe scanned it carefully.

WHY DO THEY DO THESE THINGS? THEY MUST KNOW I'M WATCHING THEM, YET THEY CONTINUE THEIR WICKED WAYS. IT'S PUTRID VERMIN LIKE THIS WHO ARE TO BLAME FOR MY WRATH. THE WEAK PREY UPON THE INNOCENT. P WAS NO DIFFERENT. HE WAS A WEAK LITTLE MAN WHO BEAT WOMEN TO MAKE HIMSELF FEEL BETTER ABOUT HIS MISERABLE LIFE. THIS WOMAN WAS NOT HIS ONLY PUNCHING BAG: HE HAD SEVERAL OTHERS — ALL OF THEM UNKNOWN TO EACH OTHER. BUT I KNEW OF THEM. I'VE BEEN WATCHING P FOR SOME TIME NOW, JUST AS I'VE BEEN WATCHING OTHERS. BUT I'VE SEEN ENOUGH. THIS PUNY, PATHETIC PARASITE OF A MAN HAS BEATEN HIS FINAL VICTIM JUST AS HIS HEART HAS BEATEN ITS FINAL BEAT. THERE WILL BE NO REMORSE FOR THE FALLEN. THEY WILL ALL MEET THEIR END THE WAY THEY'VE LIVED THEIR WRETCHED LIVES — IN NASTY, HORRIBLE WAYS. THAT, OFFICERS, I PROMISE YOU. YOU SEEK JUSTICE, BUT MINE IS THE ONLY TRUE PATH. THE LETTER MAN HAS SPOKEN.

α

I let out a heavy breath and thought hard about asking my next question. Charlene had been through enough, her face displaying the hardship she'd endured for who knew how long. But if this maniac was to be stopped, the hard questions needed to be asked.

"Did you know of the other women?"

She dropped her head to her chest. "No."

"Do you know anyone who might have wanted to do this – someone who didn't like Peter?"

She shrugged her shoulders.

"He... didn't let me leave the apartment much."

"Do you have a job?" Hayes jumped in.

"I didn't need to work," Charlene answered, shaking her head. "Peter said he'd take care of me. He paid my bills, my rent. He didn't want me working."

"So, Peter had money?" Frank joined in.

"Yeah," she said. "Peter always had money. He didn't like me asking questions about it, though. And I was taken care of, so as long as I didn't mess up..,"

"I bet," Frank griped.

"I know this has been hard for you, Charlene," Agent Hayes said, stepping forward, "but is there anything else you can tell us about the man who did this? Was there anything that stood out to you?"

The woman closed her eyes tightly and brought her hand up to squeeze the bridge of her nose, trying to recall the slightest details. She shook her head in frustration.

"No," she replied. Then she snapped her head up, "No, wait. There was something else. As he ran down the stairs, he yelled something."

"Do you remember what it was?" I asked.

"Umm..," she struggled, tapping her fist against her forehead. Then she stopped and looked at me. "Oh, it was, 'The dead walk among us.'"

"The dead walk among us?" Agent Lowe blurted. "What kind of bullshit is that?"

"Maybe he's trying to tell us his future victims are all living on borrowed time," I stated, though I had no idea where it came from.

"Perhaps," Hayes responded. "Perhaps not."

"You thinking something else?" Frank questioned.

I watched as she squeezed her lips together to prevent herself from saying what she wanted. She shook her head instead.

"Did you need anything else from me?" Charlene asked. "That's everything I know; I swear."

Agent Lowe huffed and hastily removed himself from the apartment, dissatisfied with the results. Frank followed behind to keep the man from exploding out in the hallway.

"I think we have all we need for now," I said, reaching into my pocket to rummage for a business card. "If you think of anything else – anything at all, don't hesitate to call."

Hayes beat me to it, thrusting her arm forward and flashing her card to the woman.

"You can call my direct line," she said. "Anytime."

Charlene nodded and took the card. Then she looked at me, "I'll take yours too."

"Right, okay," I responded, fishing the card from my pocket.

As she reached for it, she smiled and asked, "Are you single?"

Shocked at the woman's shameless question, I instinctively pulled my card back.

"Oh, um," I lost my words for a moment. "I'm married." I held my left hand up and pointed to my wedding band, its shape barely noticeable through the latex glove.

Charlene's shoulders dropped. "You can keep your card then," she said snidely.

Hayes' eyes widened at the woman's response. "Right, well, thank you for your time. We'll get out of your way."

She grabbed my arm and yanked it back as she headed for the door. I still wasn't sure what just happened. Did Charlene just hit on me? She just watched her boyfriend get stabbed, for Christ's sake. What's wrong with people?

Shaking my head in disgust, I closed the door behind me. Joining the others, I frustratingly asked, "What now?"

Agent Lowe was the first to bark.

"We need to get to the hospital to question Mr. Petrulovich. Lieutenant Garrett - you and Special Agent Hayes question the other tenants; maybe somebody heard or saw something. Detective Dooley – you're with me; we're taking a trip to Cooley General."

Frank looked at me, knowing my feelings about the stoic Agent.

"You all right with that?" he questioned as if he had a say in the outcome.

"I'm fine," I nodded.

"Then let's get on with it," Lowe ordered, walking toward the stairs, his thoughts focused on one thing.

As I slowly followed, looking back at Frank and Agent Hayes, my thoughts, too, were focused on one thing.

What did I get myself into? And is it too late to back out?

Chapter 17

The Long Wait

The silence was more than I could handle. I wondered if Agent Lowe was as uncomfortable as I was, but his expressionless appearance told me nothing. The man was cold, then heated, calm, then fierce. I had no idea what to expect on the ride; I kept waiting for him to blow up. What I didn't expect was the deafening silence. I needed the noise. I'd even accept him calling me a massive fuck-up who was mishandling the case; it'd be something, and I'd be less nervous. At least I'd know what he was thinking. But the silence.., I couldn't stand it anymore; I had to say something.

"That was pretty messed up back there, huh?"

I glanced over at him, his focus never shifting from the road. I turned my attention back to the front after a few silent seconds ticked by. I felt my eyes twitching, wondering if I'd done something wrong to get on the man's bad side. That would, however, suggest he had a *good* side. I wasn't convinced of that yet. But then, after a few more tense moments, during which the thoughts in my brain were screaming at me, Lowe replied.

"What do you make of our perp?"

My thoughts immediately jumped to Ben's words.

"He's angry," I said, looking at Lowe's forward stare.

"No shit, Detective. Is that all your gut is telling you?"

Actually, my gut was telling me riding with Lowe was a mistake.

"What do you think this prick's motives are," he continued, "besides spelling out every fucking letter of the alphabet?"

I thought about it for a second before responding.

"It's personal. Somebody did something to this guy, and he's taking it out on others."

"Yeah. I have that same feeling. I'm glad we're on the same page. That scumbag Petrulovich better have something for us."

"He will," I responded. "I think he knew the killer. At least, that's what I suspect based on Charlene's comments. She heard Peter out in the hall, saying something like, '*C'mon, man. What do you want now?*'"

"When were you planning on sharing this little tidbit of information?"

"I thought I just did."

I watched as Agent Lowe's nostrils flared. I don't think he liked my little quip. That was fair; I could have worded it differently.

"I know you don't care for me, Detective, and that's fine. I'm not here to make friends. What I *am* here for is to get a homicidal maniac off the street. If I have to ruffle a few feathers to do it - so be it. I need to make sure everyone is in this together. What I *don't* need is some smart-mouthed detective who's still wet behind the ears, treating this as some game. And I won't tolerate the disrespect."

I was shocked by the agent's words. And perhaps, a bit angered. Where was it coming from? It didn't matter; I wasn't about to sit back and take it.

"You're a real piece of work, you know that, Special Agent Asshole?"

He turned his eyes to me, the first reaction I'd seen from him since getting into the vehicle.

"That's right; I said it. You're an asshole. Do you think this is all a game to me? I lost a friend to that son of a bitch. What did you lose; a little respect from your fellow asshole agents in Washington because you haven't solved the case yet? Boo hoo, you arrogant piece of shit. I shouldn't have *had* to share the information with you. You should have been in the apartment with us instead of throwing your little temper tantrum out in the hallway like a goddamn baby."

"You'd better watch yourself, Dooley," he responded.

"Fuck you," I replied, letting all the frustration out at once. "I've got a wife and kid who live in this city. Do you think I enjoy going home each night to see the disappointment on my wife's face – the fear – when she learns the killer is still out there? If you think I'm not taking this seriously, fuck you."

That shut him up. I don't think he knew what to say. He just scowled and turned back to concentrate on the road. He learned I wasn't going to be a pushover. Honestly, I wasn't sure until just then if I had it in me. I surprised the hell out of myself.

The rest of the ride ended as it had started: in silence.

Even when we arrived at the hospital, when exiting the vehicle, neither of us spoke a word. I think we were both too stubborn to say anything after my outburst. I let Agent Blowhard lead the way so he could recover some of his dignity from the car floor. Also because, technically, he was the one in charge.

I had to hand it to him, though; as much of a jerk as he was, he was a commanding person who knew his job well. He took control of a situation at the drop of a hat. He demonstrated that the moment we stepped into the hospital's lobby.

"I'm Special Agent Lowe with the FBI," he stated, flashing his badge to the front desk nurse. "A man was brought in with multiple stab wounds to his stomach and chest. We need to speak with him."

The nurse looked nervous, unsure of what to do. She'd probably never been pressed for information from a Federal Agent before.

"Yes, I know the person you're referring to; I saw him brought in about half an hour ago. If you'd like to sit in the waiting room, I'll have a doctor come out and speak with you."

"I know how this works," Lowe replied. "If we go to the waiting room, we fall into a black hole. We'll wait here, thanks."

The nurse gave us an annoyed look before turning to a second nurse seated beside her. The second nurse didn't look any less annoyed but gave her nod of approval - which was all Lowe needed to see. The first nurse got on the phone, her eyes shifting back and forth between us the entire time while she communicated Lowe's request to the doctor on the other end of the line.

"Yes, of course," the nurse ended her conversation. "Thank you, Doctor." She hung up and swung her head to her right. "If you wouldn't mind stepping off to the side, Doctor Singh will be right out to speak with you."

Agent Lowe walked to the side of the desk without saying a word. He was all business without an ounce of gratitude. I nodded and flashed a grateful smile, saying, "Thank you," as I walked away. The nurse appreciated my gesture, smiling and nodding back.

"You know, manners can go a long way," I said, joining Lowe.

He glanced at me quickly and then resumed his stoic stance. "In our line of work, we don't have time for manners."

I shrugged my left shoulder. "You live in a darker world than I care to live in."

"Look around you, Detective. Your world looks just as dark as mine."

I rolled my eyes as I looked away from him, hoping to avoid another pissing contest. The sad part was I *had* looked around me. The man wasn't wrong. This city seemed to get darker and dirtier every year. And like an infection, it was spreading. Larson had since fallen prey to the rampant crime festering in this city. Where would the most unsavory of criminals creep next?

Whatever negativity I felt, the answer would have to wait. Doctor Singh arrived.

"Gentlemen," he greeted with a heavy Indian accent.

He obviously didn't know Agent Lowe. "*Gentlemen*" was a bit generous.

"You're here for the stab victim?" he questioned.

"That's right," Agent Lowe answered.

"Please come with me," the doctor requested, turning and walking toward the open hallway.

Once we were away from the nurses' station and other visitors, the doctor stopped and turned his attention to us.

"The patient is currently in surgery. He sustained quite a bit of damage to his internal organs. It's a little touch-and-go right now. You're looking at a few hours. And if he makes it through, you'd be looking at a few more hours before he'd be in any shape to speak."

"He'd *better* make it," Lowe blurted.

"The surgeon and his team are doing everything they can, sir," Doctor Singh replied. "I assure you. In the meantime, you're welcome to wait as long as you'd like. I know it's not what you wanted to hear, but it's all I have for you at this time."

"Goddammit!" Lowe bellowed, turning away from the doctor.

My response was a little more tame.

"Thank you, Doctor. Please have someone notify us the moment he's out of surgery."

"Of course."

He gave me a nod, then looked at Lowe, whose back was still turned in frustration. When the doctor looked back at me, I shrugged my shoulders, unsure how to rationalize the agent's behavior. Doctor Singh flashed an understanding smile before walking away.

"Well, I assume we're staying," I said. "Come on; I'll buy you a coffee, and then we can find a seat."

He shot me a stern look before conceding.

I tried to convince Agent Lowe that the idea of a waiting room was that you actually sat down. Instead, he spent most of his time standing, staring out the front window into the parking lot. When he wasn't silently brooding, he was on the phone with Agent Hayes, updating her on our current situation, which hadn't changed over the previous three hours and seven phone calls. I had already made my one phone call to Gina to let her know about my late-night activities. After that, I took advantage of the cushioned sofa, thinking about the latest victim and the note the killer left behind.

Charlene's words kept coming back to me; *"C'mon, man; what do you want now?"* It was clear to me Peter knew his attacker. Or at least, they'd had a prior run-in. The perp knew of Peter's alleged activities. He said he'd been watching him. For how long and for what purpose? Was it because he knew Peter was beating women, or was that learned after he'd started watching him? I thought these were all great questions, ones I'd never learn the answers to until we caught the sick bastard.

I tried to think of more relevant questions as I stared out into the hospital's main corridor, the nurses' station becoming bombarded by a steady flow of incoming visitors anxiously waiting to sit with a friend or loved one recovering from surgery. I looked around the room. Who did Peter have? Two law-enforcement officials, ready to breathe down his neck. Life wasn't always fair.

After almost four hours of watching the constant traffic of doctors, nurses, CNAs, and even those among the cleaning staff parading past the waiting room doorway, I had to step out. I thought pacing the hallways might be a better use of my time. After twenty minutes of wandering the halls, watching medical staff entering and exiting patient rooms, it finally registered in my tiny brain. Charlene's comment smacked me between the eyes.

"He wore gloves, too. Like those, only blue."

I'd seen it over and over right in front of me and hadn't connected the dots. So many of the hospital's staff were wearing blue gloves. Not white. Not green.

Blue.

I pulled out my phone, frantically pressing buttons as if I'd stumbled upon some great revelation that only I knew about. I couldn't explain my reasoning for dialing Barry instead of simply walking to the nearest desk to ask an employee, but that's what I did. I think it was more instinctual than anything else. Whatever the reason, Barry was the one I trusted to give me answers.

"Hey, Barry," I began, "it's Mick Dooley. What? No, you don't have to worry about that; I'm not calling to ask you over for dinner."

Christ, had news of Gina's awful cooking spread to *everyone* I knew?

"I wanted to ask you something. I've seen you handling bodies and watched you perform a couple of autopsies. Okay, fine. I *started* to watch you perform the autopsies. You can't hold the last one over my head. I told you already, it was because of something I ate. That's not what I'm trying to get at. If I remember correctly, you wore blue gloves, right? Is there a significance? I mean, why blue instead of white?"

As much as I needed an answer, I was almost sorry I asked. Barry was long-winded in his explanation about blue gloves being well-suited in the medical field because they were far enough away from red on the color spectrum to help doctors see better in the operating room. They also revealed punctures and small tears more easily than non-colored gloves. I think he was just excited that someone was interested in what he did for a living. I wasn't; I just needed the low-down on the gloves.

"Thanks, Barry. I'm going to have to let you go. Someone's calling. Yeah, no problem. Bye."

Nobody was calling, but I'd just made my way back to the waiting room doorway, and I saw someone approaching who appeared to be a doctor, and his stare was locked on mine. I grabbed Lowe's attention.

"Are you the officers who are here for the stab victim?"

"We are," Agent Lowe asserted himself. "How soon will we be able to speak with him?"

"I'm the patient's surgeon. May I speak with you gentlemen out in the hall?" the doctor requested, extending his arm toward the open doorway.

I noticed Lowe give me an annoyed glance as he huffed his answer before walking past the doctor's extended arm. I followed suit, keeping my eyes on the doctor as I walked by. He showed no emotion.

Once out in the hall, where we were away from the listening ears of those still in the waiting room, Agent Lowe became his usual self, speaking up as if everything revolved around him.

"So what's this about, Doc?" he began. "Can we talk to him or not?"

"I'm afraid the wounds were too extensive," the surgeon answered. "We did everything we could. Unfortunately, there was just too much internal damage. The patient suffered a myocardial infarction. He didn't make it. I'm very sorry."

"Fuck!" Lowe blurted. "Goddammit!"

"I understand your frustration," the surgeon stated, "but please.., for the sake of the other patients' families."

That was the nice way of telling Lowe to *"shut the fuck up!"*

"Do you know if the patient had any next of kin?" the doctor asked.

"Who the hell knows?" Lowe fumed. "Christ."

"Um, no, we don't," I replied as Lowe stormed away, rubbing his forehead. "He has a.., *had* a girlfriend. Maybe she knows. We'll try to find out what we can."

"Thank you. And again, I'm very sorry."

"Yeah." I looked over at Lowe standing by the exit, staring out into the parking lot, his hands on his hips in frustration. "I think we're all feeling that way. Thank you, Doctor."

We both gave a mutual nod and walked our separate ways. The man just had a patient die on his table, and yet, I couldn't help thinking he was somehow the lucky one. He didn't have Special Agent Lowe to deal with.

"We were that fucking close," Lowe said as I made it to his side. "He got away with another one, the fucker. Now we're right back to square one."

"Maybe not *right* back," I said. "It may not be much - or maybe nothing at all - but I learned blue gloves are commonly used in the medical field."

"Blue gloves?" Lowe raged. "Is that the way your head works? We lose the best opportunity we've had to catch this guy, and you're talking to me about blue gloves? What the fuck, Dooley? You think this guy couldn't have just bought a pair of blue gloves, for fuck's sake?"

"Hey, I don't know. I'm trying here. What else have we got?"

"Right," Lowe stated, stepping closer to the exit so the sliding doors activated. "What the fuck else have we got?" His tone was both sarcastic and aggravated as he stepped out into the cool air, leaving me behind. I pondered the idea of calling someone else for a ride. A smarter man would have. That wasn't me. I watched Agent Lowe trodding slowly to his vehicle. He was a broken man - as if he felt the entire case hinged upon Peter's words. And now, he had nothing.

I decided it best if I rode back with him. I thought he was a strong man, the way he presented himself when he first barged into the station all those weeks back. Now, I saw him for who he was. He was human like the rest of us. More so than I gave him credit for. I couldn't let him ride back alone.

Plus, I knew a decent bar along the way.

Chapter 18

The Seeker

I stared at Stella Mae, sleeping so tenderly in her crib. She was such a precious thing. This child - so innocent, so pure, and so unaware of the cruel world she'd been born into. I'd do everything I could to make it better for her, but there was only so much I could do when I found myself bringing the stench of the rotting city home with me each night. I never noticed it before, and Gina never mentioned it. Now, with the smell of a newborn permeating my senses, it made *my* stink stand out like a sore thumb, the way the grunge and grime clung to me like a cold, clammy sweat. Sadly, I knew it would get worse before it got better.

I felt Gina's hand brush against my back, unaware she'd entered the room. I was so caught up in my thoughts and our beautiful girl that the rest of the world melted away.

"Hey, you," she whispered, resting her chin on my shoulder as I hunched over the crib's railing. "You're going to be late for work."

I shook my head while continuing to gaze at Stella's plump cheeks. "I don't care. You and Stella – that's all I care about."

She peeled her head from my shoulder, reached her hand around my chin, and lightly turned me to face her.

"That's not true," she said, an understanding smile on her lips.

I couldn't argue with her; I knew she was right.

"You care about so much and so many," she added. "That's one of the reasons why I fell in love with you."

"Oh, *that* was one of the reasons?" I joked, rolling my eyes.

"Well, that and your huge..," she brushed her palm across the front of my pants and raised her left eyebrow teasingly, "pension."

I pushed myself upright, giving Gina a playfully mean glare.

"Jerk."

"Hmm, and yet you married me anyway," she responded, smiling. "Imagine that."

"Imagine that," I replied, wrapping my arms around her lower back to pull her closer to me.

"Hey, don't get any ideas in front of the baby," she said, putting her arms in front of her chest between us.

"She's sleeping," I replied.

"And I'd like to keep it that way a little longer."

I flashed an exaggerated frown; it didn't faze her stance.

"Besides," she continued, "if we started anything now, you'd be three minutes *later* to work." She winked.

"Ouch," I said, dropping my shoulders in frustration and my arms from her back. "Uncalled for."

"Come on," she said, grabbing my hand and giving a slight tug, leading me toward the door. "Let's let her sleep."

My eyes grew wide, and I nodded incessantly like a young, excited child, a huge grin on my face.

"Bedroom?" I asked.

She rolled her eyes and shook her head.

"Kitchen."

My shoulders dropped again, denied for the second time in less than a minute. I suppose it was just as well; I had to remain focused if I was going to get through the day.

Gina led the way to the kitchen, where she had my lunch and a tumbler of coffee waiting for me.

She's such a great woman.

"You go out there and do some good today," she said, holding the coffee and brown bag in each hand.

For the "three minutes" remark, I left her holding onto them a little longer while I took my time slipping my jacket on. That was about the extent of my spitefulness. I took them both from her and gave her a peck on the cheek.

"Thanks, hon."

I started for the door when Gina called to me.

"Mick."

I turned, offering an inquiring glance, expecting another of her clever quips.

"If you get the chance," she started, her face stone-cold serious, "catch that fucker."

My mouth opened in surprise, but no words came out. Instead, I clamped it shut, squeezed my lips together, and nodded. I love that woman.

I didn't tell her my agenda for the day, and she wouldn't want me to. There wasn't going to be much catching of bad guys for me. After last week's disappointment, where the killer's latest victim died on the operating table before we could learn anything, we were closer to catching a cold than we were to catching that sadistic son of a bitch. So no, I'd decided I wasn't heading into the station this morning. I was working the case differently.

Lieutenant Garrett and Agent Hayes were already on board. And why not? We had another note from the freak. It couldn't hurt to hear what Ben thought of this guy's most recent love letter. I didn't, however, mention the other part to them. I didn't want to give them any opportunity to say "no." My way was better. It would be easier to claim naivety or inexperience if I got caught. Not to mention, I was giving them a way out if Agent Lowe ever caught wind of this. Plausible deniability. They could thank me later.

Speaking of thanking..,

I dialed Officer Sanchez on my car's Bluetooth. I'd been meaning to get in touch with him since I ditched him at the cemetery the day Gina went into labor. He sent us a congratulatory card and a bouquet for Gina, but I hadn't responded yet. He must think I'm still upset with him over how he reacted at that boy Jason's house. I wasn't. I just got distracted by things. Between the dead body at the cemetery and that suspicious character in the damn green car, I hadn't even given his behavior a second thought. And why shouldn't he have been upset? It was absolutely disgusting what Matthew Lynch did to that boy – and possibly others. I may have been too harsh on him.

"Hello," Rubio's voice boomed over the speakers.

"Hey, Sanchez, it's me," I replied.

"Well, if it isn't Mick 'Flash' Dooley."

"I see you're still holding onto the speed jokes," I responded.

"Oh, I hold onto everything, my man, especially if I can hold it over somebody's head," he chuckled. "So, how's it going with you? How's Gina and the kid?"

"They're great! They're both great."

"Good, good. Don't blink, man. Before you know it, your little girl's going to be a teenager, and you'll be wondering where the years went."

"That's what I've heard. Listen, I wanted to thank you for the card. And Gina loved the flowers, by the way."

"No sweat, buddy. I'm glad she liked them. I wasn't sure what to get; they were the first flowers I'd bought anybody since my wife.., well, the woman at the store helped me out."

"You did great," I replied. "Tulips are one of Gina's favorites."

"I got lucky with that one, I guess."

"Yeah. I also wanted to apologize about that day we talked to the kid. Things got a little heated, and I had no right to jump down your throat like I did."

"Don't sweat it, Mick," Sanchez countered. "You had *every* right to. I could have handled it better. Emotions were high that day – for the both of us. I've since talked with two other boys from the pictures. They both confirmed that they had been abused by the victim. I managed to hold it together better with those two. It helped that I brought along a specialist, an officer trained in dealing with situations involving crimes against children. They both denied killing Lynch and provided alibis, but neither were sad to hear of his murder."

"Fuck!" I couldn't help but let out. "That means every one of those boys in the pictures was probably sexually abused by the victim."

"That's what I figure, too."

And *this* is the world Stella Mae has to grow up in? Fuck that! Gina was right to send me off to work. As she said, I *did* care. I cared enough to want to clean up the streets. And that's what I intended to do.

"Remember at the cemetery," I questioned, "when I ran off?"

"Yeah, of course," Sanchez answered.

"I don't know if you noticed, but that guy with the green car was there again. That's who I was running after. I wanted to catch him before he got away."

"Oh, shit. Really? No, I didn't notice."

"He was at Karen's funeral, and then he was there again when we were investigating Oliver's death. I don't have a good feeling about that."

"What are you thinking?"

"What I'm thinking is, what if he was at the other crime scenes, too, and we just didn't notice?"

"That's a lot of thinking," he responded.

"Yeah, I know. I'm not saying it means anything. Just do me a favor, huh? When you're out there, keep your eyes peeled for a lime-green Hyundai. You know, just in case he was there for a reason, and it wasn't a good one."

"You got it."

"Thanks. I'm going to have to let you go, though. I've got a few more calls to make."

"Okay, speedy. Take it easy."

"You too."

We hung up, and I felt relieved that things were still okay between us. I was surprised I hadn't heard about the other boys, though. I thought the Larson PD would have shared that information with us. Then again, Southbridge wasn't sharing everything either - like my clandestine visits with The Alphabet Killer. As much as the two departments wanted to work as one, we were still working the case separately. That was the FBI's job to sort out. Mine was to focus on my task. Right now, that meant getting to BrentRidge Penitentiary.

After a few lengthy calls back to the station, I arrived at my destination. Hayes had already made the arrangements for me. It helped that the warden was a reasonable man and wanted to help us.

As before, I was escorted to the visitor's hall by a robust corrections officer (I think they grew them unnaturally big in these parts). As we entered the room, I could see something wasn't right. Ben was already present, waiting for me at the center table, but the left side of his face was swollen and bruised, he had a black eye, and his lower lip was cut.

"What happened to you?" I asked, taking my seat across from him.

"He had a little accident," a second officer standing by the far door announced. "Isn't that right, Haddick?"

Ben turned his head slightly to acknowledge the intimidating officer, then turned his battered face back to me.

"Yeah," Ben snarled. "A little accident."

He licked the cut on his lower lip, staring at me through cold eyes.

"He'd better hope an accident doesn't happen to *him*," Ben mumbled.

"What did you say, Haddick?" the guard questioned, stepping forward behind Ben. "What the fuck did you say to me?"

I threw my hand up, "Whoa! Hold on. Let's calm down. He was talking to *me*."

"Talking to you, huh?" the guard hissed. "Well, you better tell him to watch his fucking mouth. Got it?"

I stared at the large man, "Got it."

He backed away and took his position at the far door while the guard who escorted me retreated to the door we entered from.

"Tough crowd," I said to Ben quietly so as not to raise the ire of the already heated officer.

"You don't know the half of it," he replied.

"It's good that you're making friends," I stated sarcastically.

He ignored my comment, glancing down at the envelope I had placed on the table.

"What do you have for me?" he questioned.

I slid the envelope across to him, where he eagerly tore into it to retrieve its contents. After reviewing it, he shifted his eyes up from the paper.

"'*The only true path*,' huh?"

"What can I say," I responded, "he's a demented fuck."

"Not demented," Ben answered. "Hell-bent."

"Right. What was it you told me last time? '*He craves vengeance.*'"

"Believe me, or don't believe me, Mick. It makes no difference. But remember, you're the one out there with him. You're the one who has to live with the consequences. And your guilt."

"I'll believe you when you start giving me useful information."

"You gotta give useful information to get useful information." The right side of his mouth lifted to a half-smile. I assumed his left would have completed the other half had it not been for the bashing it took.

I drew in a heavy breath, knowing what I had to do. I slowly released it, looking into Ben's eyes, wondering what I was about to give up. Was it only the details of the crime scenes and that of the victims? Or was I giving up a piece of me that I could never get back? Whichever it was going to be, I started at the beginning.

Chapter 19

The Killing Kind

The words stuck in my head as I drove back to the precinct.

"The others were just collateral damage."

What was I supposed to take from that? Was Ben messing with me? Did I make a mistake thinking he would offer insight into The Letter Man killings? There had to be something more. Ben was smart and calculated. That's how he evaded capture for as long as he did. He had no reason to play mind games with me. There had to be something more in his cryptic messages. It was clear he didn't like what the new guy stood for. Even Ben knew they weren't the same. In his narcissistic view, imitation *wasn't* the sincerest form of flattery. The Letter Man wasn't merely copying Ben, he was tarnishing The Alphabet Killer's name, diminishing the effect The Alphabet Killer's presence had on the community. Who would remember him and all he did if The Letter Man was stealing all his glory? For that, I believed Ben *did* want to help. And in some small way, I think he *was* helping.

172

There were things he pointed out about the notes we hadn't considered. I only wish he could have been more specific. But how could I expect that of him? He wasn't involved in the case. He only had what details I provided him. It pained me to share what we knew, but it was the only way Ben would open up. So, I did what I felt was necessary. I let it all out, starting with the graphic details of his mother's death.

"Tell me again about her fingers and toes?" Ben requested.

"Why?" I questioned. *"Is there something we missed?"*

He looked at me with his usual deadpan stare, "No, I just liked hearing about her digits being removed."

"You're a sick bastard," I said through clenched teeth. "If that's the way this is going to be..,"

"No, no, I'm.., I'm sorry, Mick." He nodded as if to signify his sincerity. "Tell me more."

I silently stared into his eyes; he offered a practiced apologetic glare. It didn't make things right, but I still needed him. At least he showed he was putting the effort in, as rehearsed as it may have been. I threw my hand up onto the table and pointed at him sternly to let him know I wasn't fucking around.

"Show some fucking respect," I said through clenched teeth.

"I will," he replied, sitting a little straighter in his chair and folding his hands on the table. "Please continue."

And so, I did. Victim after victim, crime scene after brutal crime scene - I laid out all the gory details for him.

"What was with the long wait?" Ben questioned.

"What do you mean?"

"He sent the first letter over a year and a half ago. He knew who his first victim was going to be. Why did he wait so long to start?"

"How should I know?" I replied. "Maybe he was full of shit and didn't really know who would be first."

"He knew," Ben retorted. "I knew."

"I'm still not happy about that."

"So you've made clear," Ben continued. "No, he took that time to plan each kill. He was gathering his victims. By the time he started, he knew who was going to die by his hand. The question is, which one was his intended victim?"

"What the hell are you talking about?" I questioned. "They've all been his victims."

"Have they? Or was there only one he was after? I told you before he wasn't like me. The start of his killing spree, or his planning anyway, was in direct response to something. He was out for vengeance. The others were just collateral damage."

"Collateral damage, huh?"

He shrugged his shoulders. "If you find out who he was after - you find his motive, and you can narrow down your suspect field."

"Just like that?" I questioned sarcastically.

"Just like that."

"Well, you've read the letters, you've heard what he did to the victims..,"

"You want to know which of the deceased was his intended victim," Ben responded, smirking.

"I didn't come here for the wholesome conversations," I returned.

"I can't be certain," he replied. *"It wasn't my mother, that much I know."*

"How do you know that?"

"Her death was to give me a present." He flashed a grin. *"Okay, probably not. He killed her to make a statement – to set you back on your heels, keep you distracted from the real target. It's all right there in his messages. His first letter, the one you and that putz Ritchie brought to me, stated that K would be his first victim and that he had plans for others. He reiterated that fact, written on the wall with my mother's blood. She was the first of his handiwork but wouldn't be the last. Also, 'The best is yet to come' was a dead giveaway. No pun intended. Why would he save his best for someone else if she was the one he was after? Plus, the man had to practice for his grand finale. Every rookie knows that. Hell, look how sloppy I was with that fat bastard Bruce."*

"Okay, enough," I ceded, *"that all makes sense, but what of his other victims?"*

"That's where things get tricky."

"How so?"

"Because of the brutal nature of the killings. It's hard to determine which had a more personal touch."

"Personal touch?" I said, disgusted at the comment.

"What would you call it when someone dismembers his victims? Not to mention, he was holding onto some of them for a later kill. That's pretty fucking personal."

The kid had a point. The Letter Man wasn't just killing people; he was torturing them - making them suffer. That was more personal than shooting them from a distance or stabbing them in the neck and walking away.

"Remember, these weren't random victims. He knew in advance who was to die and what he was going to do to them. He planned for it."

"Only if you're right about that," I interrupted.

Ben smiled, "I am. He took the time to set up the scene. He neatly placed body parts in a row, he posed Lydon, he sat at Nancy's desk and wrote his little note. You don't do that on a whim. It takes a special kind of person to do the things he's been doing?"

"And what kind of person is that?" I asked.

He stared at me in silence, letting the seconds tick by.

"The killing kind," he answered. "If I were you, I'd focus on victims L through O."

"What about Peter?" I asked.

"What about him? He was the exception, not the rule. The killer knew he wouldn't have the same kind of time as the others. Even if the girlfriend wasn't home, an apartment hallway isn't private enough. Maybe it was an impulse kill. Maybe The Letter Man became impatient, or something set him off. Either way, the killer has demonstrated he likes to take his time with his victims. With Peter, he knew he didn't have that kind of time."

"Well, there was something else," I jumped in, interrupting Ben's speech. "The girlfriend told us the killer yelled something as he ran off."

"Which was..?"

"He said, 'The dead walk among us.'"

Ben's eyes shifted down to the table. He appeared to be giving the words serious thought.

"Interesting," he replied.

"What's so interesting about that?"

"That he would say anything at all. 'The dead walk among us.' There wasn't a mention of anything like that in any of his notes. Are you sure it's the same killer?"

"We have his note." I pointed to the paper in front of Ben. "Can't fake that."

"What about the girlfriend? Can she be trusted?"

"Can you be trusted?" I threw back at him.

He licked his bottom lip, rubbing his tongue back and forth across the cut he'd received.

"Fair enough," he responded. "Then I take back what I said about Peter's murder being an impulse kill."

"Why is that?" I questioned.

"I'd say your killer wanted to be seen."

"Why the fuck would the killer want to be seen?" I questioned with irritation in my voice.

"I don't know, Mick," he returned with the same irritation. "Am I expected to have all the answers? Do some detective work. Think about it; why would somebody want to be seen?"

"Because they wanted to get caught," I returned. "Only - I don't think this guy wants to get caught."

"Well then, I guess the answer lies somewhere in between, doesn't it?" he responded.

"What does that mean?"

"You're a smart guy, Mick. I'm sure you'll figure it out."

I didn't get a chance to respond before the burly guard behind Ben stepped forward to tell me that my hour was up. I let out a frustrated breath. Not because there was still more to learn but because I was leaving with more questions than I arrived with.

The kid was smart. I couldn't help but think he knew more than what he wanted me to believe. But how much could he really know from just a handful of notes and descriptions of the crime scenes? He wasn't there. He didn't have the stench of the dead on his clothing. Maybe he was feeding me a barrel full of horse shit.

Or maybe his twisted mind worked differently.

I'm not sure I had what it took to understand what went on in a cold-blooded killer's head. I noticed how Ben kept questioning which of the victims *was* the killer's true target – past tense - as if the killer already succeeded in his task. He thought we should focus our attention on only four of the victims. If he was right about the killer being after only one target from the start, what made him think the target wasn't still out there? I know what Ben would say.

"He'd want to kill the victim sooner rather than later in case something went wrong; he wouldn't want to risk getting caught before he could seek his revenge."

But then, if that were true, why would he keep going? I heard Ben's voice, once again, provide the answer.

"He's gotten a taste for it. He likes it."

Holy shit! Maybe I *was* starting to understand what went on in the killer's head. What I didn't know was if that was a good thing or a bad thing.

And that thought scared me more than the killer himself.

Chapter 20
The Deep Chill

Things were better, weren't they? Wasn't that why I was allowed this small moment? I nodded to the man in the mirror along the far wall, his unbelieving eyes staring back. Yeah, sure, things were better. Yeah right. If I thought that was true, why did I feel the need to remind myself of that as I tossed back another shot before slamming the empty glass onto the oaken bar?

"Another, Scotty," I ordered, "before I haul your ass in for obstruction."

"Obstruction for what," the bartender questioned, pouring another 1.5 oz. of Jim Beam.

"For keeping me waiting with an empty glass," I replied.

"Hey, hey," Sanchez said, diverting his attention away from the scantily-clad woman at the pool table long enough to swivel around on his stool to face me. "Maybe you should slow it down, buddy."

"Oh, I'm sorry, Officer," I responded, placing my wrists together and extending my arms toward him, "are you going to arrest me?"

"Yup, I think you've had enough for one evening," he stated. He put his hand up to get the bartender's attention, then waved his fingers from side to side under his neck to signal that he was cutting me off.

"But I'm not done," I bellowed, downing the poured drink. "I've got a few more left in me."

"No, you're done," Sanchez returned, slapping two twenties down and sliding them to the backside of the bar.

"You're a party pooper," I complained, with about as much seriousness as I could while using the word "pooper."

"Yeah, well, you'll thank me in the morning," Sanchez responded. "As it is, Gina's probably going to have my ass for dragging you out tonight."

"Nah," I replied. "She knows I needed this. She's been on my case for a while about getting out. She said she couldn't stand watching me mope around the house like I was disinterested in her and the baby. That's ridiculous. I love her and Stella. If anything, she probably wanted me out of the house because she felt I was smothering them too much. She didn't want to deal with me."

"Well, you have been acting kinda funny lately."

"Funny how?"

"I don't know. Just funny. Different."

"Fuck you," I said a bit too loudly, poking my index finger into Sanchez's chest.

Sanchez quickly swept his gaze around, slightly embarrassed by my belligerent outburst, before eyeballing me.

"That's what I'm talking about," he said in a hushed tone, leaning in slightly. "What's gotten into you, man?"

"What's gotten into *me*?" I shot back.

"That's right," he remarked. "I mean, fuck, you should be feeling good. Things have finally quieted down. It's been over two months since The Letter Man killed his last victim. Maybe he's done. It's over. Things can get back to normal. Or, whatever, just fucking enjoy the downtime; it's not your problem."

"It'll never be normal," I interjected, my teeth clenched. "We didn't catch the son of a bitch; he's still out there; he'll strike again."

"You don't know that."

"Of course I do. Parasites like that don't just go away. It's only a matter of when and how."

"You need to relax, man," Sanchez replied, placing his hand on my shoulder. "Maybe the guy got hit by a bus or something. I don't know. My point is, there haven't been any more killings. Can't you just be happy about that?"

"I'll be happy when we put that fucker down like the rabid dog he is."

"I'm just saying, if we never hear from him again, would that be such a bad thing? Maybe that last guy - what was his name..?"

"Who?"

"The guy who died in the hospital. The one who was beating that Charlene chick."

"Peter," I answered. "Peter Petru... something."

"Yeah, him. Maybe that was who the killer was after all along, and now that he'd gotten him, he doesn't need to kill anymore."

"That wasn't who the killer was after," I replied.

"What do you mean? What makes you say that?"

"Because of the way The Letter Man has killed, he'd want it to be something more. He's a sadistic freak, and he's angry. He wouldn't settle for a quick stabbing in an apartment hallway when he could take his time torturing and mutilating instead. We've both seen what he's done before. There's no fucking way it was Peter. It had to be one of the earlier victims. Or, worse yet, he's still out there hunting, waiting for the right opportunity to strike. He's taunting us. He's taunting *me*. The fucker's probably watching me, for all I know."

"Now you're sounding paranoid."

"That's the kind of thing these crazy bastards do."

"Well, fuck," Sanchez commented. "It sounds like you got the guy all figured out. And you know what - you might have had me fooled into believing you knew what you were talking about if you weren't three sheets to the wind right now. Besides, this isn't even your case; it belongs to the Feds."

"Fuck off," I responded. "You're wrong. It *is* mine. I need to stop this guy for my wife and daughter's safety. And you know what else you're wrong about?" I questioned, my speech slurred. "Three sheets, my ass. I'm the whole goddamn sailboat. Now, if you'll excuse me..,"

I looked to my left and spotted the bartender at the other end of the bar.

"Scotty!" I announced, snapping my fingers in the air. "Get me and my fine Hispanic friend here another round."

"No, Mick," Sanchez said, pulling my arm down. "Your drinking night is over. Let's get you home."

He stood from his stool and tugged at my sleeve. I looked over at the bartender and threw my hands up in a questioning manner.

"Are you going to let this man drag one of your paying customers away?"

"*He* paid," Scotty replied, pointing at Sanchez.

"Oh, suddenly you've got all the answers. Well, I've got money too, shithead."

The bartender smirked, "What can I tell ya; he's a cop."

"I'm a cop too, asshole."

"Mick, that's enough!" Sanchez raised his voice. "Let's go."

He tugged at my arm again, more forcefully this time.

"Fuck it," I gave in. "I didn't want to drink in this lousy bar anyway."

I slapped the empty shot glass with my hand, sending it tumbling across the bar toward some patrons on my left.

The bartender shook his head in irritation.

"Rubio, get that drunk piece of shit out of my bar."

"I'm handling it," Sanchez replied.

I yanked my arm away from Sanchez's hand as I rose from my seat.

"I can manage," I snapped. "I'm happy to be getting out of this dump."

"Come on, then," Sanchez nodded sideways, encouraging me toward the door. "Let's get out of here."

He pointed to the door, practically shoving me forward. As I exited into the chilly night air, I heard him offer some apologies to those within before following me out into the parking lot.

"Why do you always have to do that?" I questioned heatedly, slogging across the slushy pavement.

"Do what?"

"What you just did – apologizing like that. Why do you always have to play the good guy, making me feel like I'm some asshole cop?"

"I'm not playing the good guy," he replied. "And right now, you *are* being an asshole."

"Shut the fuck up," I said, stumbling my way to his vehicle.

"Case in point. Now get in the car."

I slid myself into the cold leather seat, not happy with how the night was ending. I now understood why Gina wanted me out of the house for a while.

"Listen," I started in again as if I hadn't gotten my point across, "I'm just saying, we can't forget what the guy has done just because we haven't heard from him in a while."

"I never said '*forget*,'" he responded, pulling out of the parking lot.

"You might as well have," I argued. "You go about your days as if all is well – as if the guy never existed. Screw that. Some of us can't live our lives with blinders on."

"Is that what you think, man? Well, fuck you. I know it's probably the alcohol talking, but do you know what your problem is? You're not grateful for what you've got. You're too busy trying to make the world some perfect place to fit in with your expectations. Well, I hate to break the news to you, buddy, but the world will never be *that* perfect. There's grime everywhere, and there's dirt on everyone. How you deal with it is *your* problem."

"It doesn't faze you at all, does it," I asked, "knowing he's still out there?"

"Maybe he is; maybe he isn't. You said somebody caught him in the act last time. Maybe that was enough to chase him away - scare the guy straight."

"Don't be stupid; that was probably his plan," I mumbled.

"What the fuck are you talking about now?"

"Nothing."

"Listen, I just think you need to allow yourself to breathe a little. Not everything has to be *your* problem."

"Whose problem is it going to be then?" I questioned. "Yours?"

"Fuck that shit," Sanchez replied. "I've got enough of my own problems to deal with. I sure as shit don't want to deal with yours too."

I shook my head in agitation, staring out the side window, watching the houses pass by in streaks. I wondered if the same worries weighed upon the residents' shoulders as much as the heavy burden I'd placed upon my own. I couldn't help but think they were the lucky ones. They could forget, move on, and pretend they were safe. I wanted that, too – to be oblivious to the evil in the real world and no longer carry the burden, the fear. But I did, and that wouldn't change.

I knew Sanchez was right. I should appreciate the fact there haven't been any more killings. The problem was - I wasn't built like that. I became a cop to stop people like that goddamn maniac. As long as he was out there, I couldn't rest. The victims, the families affected by their deaths – they needed justice. *Karen* needed justice. No matter what Sanchez said or tried to convince me of, I *was* who I *was*.

We pulled up along the grass in front of my house, neither speaking a word as I opened my door. I could see the kitchen light was on, and I hoped it was out of courtesy instead of Gina staying awake out of some feeling of obligation or anger. I bent over and peered at Sanchez through the open door.

"You're a lousy therapist, you know that?"

"Yeah, well, you're a lousy drunk," he retorted.

"I can't disagree with you there," I replied.

"Hey," Sanchez shouted before I closed the door, "are we still on for next month?"

"Yeah, we're still on."

"All right. Tell Gina I said hello. And apologize to her for me, would you?"

"For what?"

"For bringing you home in this condition."

"Yeah, yeah." I nodded and closed the door just as snow flurries began falling upon my face. As Sanchez drove off into the distance, I looked up at the night sky, letting the white flakes tickle my nose as I inhaled heavily to calm my thoughts before heading inside. Whatever kind of ass I may have been this night, I wasn't bringing that home to Gina. She didn't deserve that.

I slowly strode up the driveway, wondering if it was the ice or the alcohol that was making it difficult to make it to the side door. I'd wager it was a little of both, though I leaned more toward the alcohol.

When I stepped inside, Gina was standing by the counter, raising and lowering a tea bag into a mug of hot water. It was something she always did instead of letting the bag naturally steep. The tea itself, though, was something she only drank when she was nervous.

"Hey," I said in almost a whisper, "you didn't have to wait up for me."

She let out a fake, half-hearted chuckle, "If only that were the reason."

"What's going on; is something wrong? Is Stella okay?"

"I managed to get her to stop crying and fall asleep only fifteen minutes ago," Gina said, looking as though she were battling to hold back tears.

"Oh, hey," I said softly, wrapping my arm around her shoulder and pulling her into me. "She's sleeping now; it's going to be all right."

"Is it?" she questioned. "I don't even know what I'm doing half the time. We've got this baby girl, and she needs so much attention, and I'm trying to keep it together, but I go back to work in a few weeks, and I can't even get her to stop crying. Maybe I'm just not cut out to be a mother. Babies can sense that kind of thing, you know."

"Hey, you need to stop that," I said, consoling her. "That's ridiculous. You're a great mother. Stella knows that, and she loves you. We both knew being parents wasn't going to be easy. Nobody figures it out at first. But we've got this. We're going to get through the tough times. And don't worry about when it's time for you to go back to work. We'll figure it out. Together. We always do."

"I can't do it alone, Mick," she expressed, squeezing her cheek into my chest.

"You're not alone," I responded. "I'm right here."

"You're here, but you haven't been you. I need *this* Mick right here; the one you are right now. Not the other Mick that's been so distant lately. Ever since the murders stopped, it's like me and Stella have become secondary in your life."

She peeled herself away from my chest, her cheeks rosy red and damp from the tears that streamed down and seeped into my shirt.

"Come on, hon," I tried to reassure, "that's crazy. You and Stella mean everything to me."

"Then why can't you just be happy that it's over? You act like you need there to be more death for your life to have purpose. *We* should be your purpose, Mick, not some demented psychopath. It's been months. Why can't you just let it go?"

I felt something rip into my heart.

"Gina, I..,"

"I can't do this right now, Mick," she interrupted, dropping her head and pressing her palm against my chest to keep me from getting closer to her. "I need to get some sleep, and you need to shower. You smell like a distillery."

I felt my mouth open, desperately wanting to say something to keep her with me, but nothing came out. She turned and slowly made her way to the bedroom, leaving me alone to reflect upon all that she'd said. And not just *her* words, but Rubio's too. They both were trying to tell me. It was true, I haven't been myself.

I glanced over at the counter, the mug of tea untouched, and thought about Gina and the baby and what they meant to me. The answer was easy: more than life itself. Yet here I was, concerned more with the death of others, obsessed with catching a killer who, for all I knew, was dead himself. Sanchez was right; I needed to be more grateful that the killings had stopped. The fear, the worry

– it was over. My family was safe, and that was what mattered most.

I poured the tea into the sink, blankly staring at the steaming liquid as it swirled down the drain, a visual representation of what would become my life if I didn't get things back on track. Gina and Stella were my world; nothing else.

I turned the kitchen light off and fumbled my way into the living room, the floor swaying a bit under my feet. I couldn't get ready for bed just yet, an overwhelming array of crazy thoughts dancing in my head. Instead, I found myself peering out the front window, staring into the calm night, watching the snowflakes flutter down, bathing in the streetlight's warm glow on their way to crashing against the cold pavement below. It was such a serene moment that had suddenly washed over me, one in direct conflict with the bitter turmoil swirling around my brain moments earlier. In the deafening silence of the night, a single thought clawed its way to the forefront of my mind, fighting for dominance and screaming louder than all the others.

Fuck The Letter Man.

I'd be an idiot not to listen.

Chapter 21

Time to Kill

My head was hurting. Bad. It served me right. I hadn't been out drinking in a long time, and I took the one opportunity I had to overdo it. I knew Sanchez had been looking forward to it. Unfortunately, things didn't play out as either of us had hoped. That was on me. I'd have to find a way to smooth things over with him. But only after I found a way to relieve this pounding headache first. It didn't help that the detective bureau was bustling. Phones were ringing off the hook, detectives were springing from their seats in search of coffee, and Frank was belting out orders like.., well.., Frank. The place was finally starting to feel normal again. But loud.

The Letter Man case hadn't been dropped or forgotten; it simply took a backseat to more recent ones. If things didn't change, it would soon end up in storage marked "Ongoing" or "Unsolved." Special Agent Lowe had been called back to the Pierre field office two weeks earlier to work alongside the NSA on a national security case. Special Agent Hayes requested to stay a little longer so she could wrap things up on The Letter Man case in a nice, shiny bow. I wasn't convinced that was her only reason; she seemed driven about something.

The State Police were doing most of the heavy lifting, following up on whatever leads presented themselves. They shook down Victor Ramos for answers, claiming that Lyden Foster's death looked like a Columbian cartel hit. They knew that wasn't the case, but since Lyden had been one of Victor's drug pushers, it gave them the excuse they needed to dig deeper into Ramos' operations. They'd also tracked down ten of the thirteen boys sexually abused by Matthew Lynch. Nothing had come from any of it, though, except the knowledge of the disgusting things Lynch did to each of them.

Frank was keeping an eye on his wife's financials while he sorted out whatever trust issues he had. I didn't feel good about it, but I also hadn't said anything to Hayes about his concerns regarding his wife and the Osterlander case. I figured that was for him to bring up if the situation called for it. I shouldn't even know about it, but for some reason, Frank insisted on keeping me involved. I think it was his way of relieving stress. Sure, pile it on me; I can take it.

Hayes kept to herself, for the most part, re-examining the evidence that both the Southbridge and Larson PD had collected on The Letter Man case. She almost seemed obsessed. If I hadn't known better, I would have thought she was taking this case personally. Maybe she felt catching the killer was her only way back into the good graces of the Bureau's top dogs. I'd even caught her a few times making phone calls that, for some reason, felt secretive, the way she'd immediately hush up when I'd walk into her loaner office or the way she'd abruptly hang up as if she didn't want anyone to hear what she was talking about. I'm sure it wasn't anything with which I needed to concern myself. It just felt uncomfortable at times. Why the fuck should I care what information she was passing off to others at the FBI? The case felt dead.

For me, it *was*.

I had another case to focus on. A wave of drugstore robberies that had recently hit the surrounding areas inevitably spilled into Southbridge. Four perps, wearing Donald Trump masks, were caught on camera robbing Hannigan's Pharmacy at gunpoint. It was the second such robbery in as many days, and the eighth overall, attributed to the masked felons. The previous seven incidences were rather tame, with the robbers grabbing the money and running, but the latest one resulted in an innocent customer getting hospitalized from injuries sustained by one of the gunmen. I always knew Southbridge brought out the best in people. Camera footage showed the attack was unprovoked. The armed thugs were becoming more brazen. It was only a matter of time before one of their hold-ups ended in a homicide.

We did manage to catch a break, though, if that's what you'd call it. When hearing sirens approaching, one of the robbers panicked and yelled the name Jerome to his asshole buddy - the one beating on the male shopper. The four quickly fled the scene without realizing "Jerome" had left something behind. During the physical altercation, the hat he'd been wearing was knocked off his head. In his haste to get away before the police arrived, he'd forgotten about it. The hat, and whatever hair or scalp DNA lingering within, was a nice gift for us to be able to present to Vera and her sidekick lab rat, Danny.

I thought I'd check in with "The Dragon" to see if she'd found anything useful from the punk's cap. Anything was better than sitting on my thumbs, waiting for something to drop onto my lap. Not to mention, some of the other detectives still whispered their thoughts on The Letter Man case, and I couldn't be around that; it reminded me of our . . , of *my* failure.

I got up from my desk – which used to be Jimmy's before my promotion to detective. It sat vacant for over a year until I moved upstairs to the Detective Bureau. Nobody else dared disturb it. I told Frank I'd be honored to sit at Jimmy's old desk. He allowed it, knowing our relationship. Others weren't as welcoming.

I slinked downstairs, hoping to avoid detection by Frank on my way past his office. He looked too engrossed in a phone conversation to notice me. That was a good thing. He probably would have called me into his office to unload more details about his wife's spending habits.

As I landed on the lower floor at the bottom of the stairs, Vera already had her finger on the trigger to unlock the lab door, her other hand waving me in. I figured that reaction was better than her usual eye roll when she saw me coming. Maybe I was finally growing on her - like mold.

I heard the click as I approached the glass door but still entered cautiously. Vera wasn't called "The Dragon" for nothing.

"I hope you don't mind me barging in like this," I stated, thinking it wise to take the passive approach.

"I knew you'd be down here sooner or later," Vera replied. "I was just telling Danny I haven't seen a dick in a while, then poof, you appear. It's like a sign from above."

"The heavens, huh?" I questioned. "I didn't realize you were the religious sort."

"What? Fuck no, Tweedle Dumb. And that's dumb with a B, mind you. I meant literally from above - like upstairs, jackhole. It was only a matter of time before one of you attention-seekers came calling for my help."

"What can I say," I responded, "I know where the real brains of the operation are situated."

"Yeah," she replied, "funny how you only know that when you need something."

"That only proves it; you're right again."

"Hmph," she let out, nodding her head. "You're here to learn what I've got on that dumb schmuck 'Jerome,' aintcha?"

"I was hoping you had something, yeah."

"Well I was hoping *you* had something for me, too, but you're probably still happily married.

"Vera."

"Just kidding. I was hoping you'd have something on The Letter Man to bring to Mama, but I don't see that you've brought anything in here with you."

"You know the case has gone cold, Vera," I replied. "Let Agent Hayes and the State Police keep their noses to the ground on that one. I'm sure they'll find the guy's corpse somewhere and trace it back to the killings. Case closed."

"Oh, no, you don't," she responded, wagging her finger back and forth. "You don't get to come down here and shatter my dreams. You may be a Sensitive Sally Pants about the whole thing, but some of us want more bite than to find out the guy just up and died on us. That would be a disappointment."

"A disappointment?"

"Damn straight. It wouldn't be right if that twatbag got off that easy. Where's the justice in that? He needs to get what's coming to him."

"For a moment, I thought you were rooting for him."

"Hey, I may enjoy studying up on these scumbags, but it doesn't mean I condone that shit."

"Well, for what it's worth, Vera, it's been months without a peep. I'll take that kind of 'disappointment' over another dead body, any day."

She stared at me with a blank look on her face, followed by an awkward silence. My comfort level dropped a few degrees to match the sudden chill in the air. I looked away from her gaze to notice Danny's eyes also upon me, but at least he had the decency to quickly turn away, pretending he hadn't been paying attention to our conversation the entire time. When my eyes veered back to Vera's, she gave me a squinted glare like I was in for an earful.

"You know what your problem is, Mick?" she began, letting me know my assumption was correct. "You keep thinking you're something you're not."

"Oh, really?" I replied. "And what's that?"

"A normal guy," she responded. "But here's the thing - you're not normal; you're a cop. And not just any cop, but a detective on the Southbridge police force. You grew up in this shithole city. You knew what these streets were like. And yet you enrolled in the academy, anyway. You knew what you were getting into the moment you earned that badge. You can stand there, trying to convince yourself you're all happy and shit about that psycho killer not being on the prowl anymore, but don't come down here trying to convince *me* of that garbage. You're insulting my intelligence. You want that freak out there just as much as I do so you can take the fucker down. Now, if you feel I've got any of that wrong, and I'm just talking out of my fat ass, then you're not the detective – or the man – I thought you were."

Vera's words gutted me. Not because I took offense to anything she said - but because she was right. If I wasn't in this job to rid the city of bastards like The Letter Man, then I wasn't a worthy enough detective to sit at the same desk Jimmy had for all those years. What would he have thought of me if he knew I was so willing to give up on a case like that only to let those around me handle it instead? I could feel the blood in my veins beginning to boil. Whether it was her intention or not, Vera awakened a spark in me I had tried to suppress in favor of being a family man. Ever since The Letter Man killings began, I'd struggled between being the best detective I could be and being the husband.., and now father I *needed* to be. Why did there have to be a choice? Why couldn't I be both? That was something Jimmy hadn't quite figured out. I loved the man like a brother, but I'd be damned if I was going to travel down the same lonely path he had.

I unclenched my teeth, ready to respond to Vera's comments with a confident and determined statement, when my phone rang, causing me to stiffen and swallow my words down. I pulled the phone from my pocket while continuing to stare at Vera. I wasn't about to avert my gaze after what she'd just put me through (whether she realized it or not).

"Yeah, this is Mick," I answered with a bit more force than necessary.

"Where the fuck are you?" Frank's voice boomed from the phone's speaker loud enough for Danny to hear it from across the room.

"I'm with Vera in the lab, Lieu. What's going on?"

"Get your ass up here," he demanded. "Now!"

He hung up before I could question him further, though I knew better than to do that, anyhow. Something was stuck in his craw, and I didn't want to push my luck.

Vera relaxed her taut face, flashing a more sympathetic look. Who was I kidding? I've never seen Vera show sympathy. It was more probable she'd just let out a fart.

"Looks like you're off the hook," I stated. "No need to feed me details about the four dirtbag perps."

"So then, you don't want me to tell you we got a hit on that twerp Jerome?" Vera replied.

I felt my shoulders drop as I let out a breath. Intrigued, I had to respond.

"Okay, hit me with it."

"His name is Jerome Kenshaw. He lives over on the west side and has a rap sheet longer than my last boyfriend's sex pistol. Of course, if you knew my last boyfriend, you'd know that wasn't much of an accomplishment. He was more of a Snub-nose .38 Special than a Colt Peacemaker. I used to call him Pinky Dick. Let me know if you need me to explain any part of that to you."

"No, I got it, Vera. Thanks. Why didn't you tell me about Jerome from the start?"

"And miss out on an opportunity to fuck with you?" she replied. "Fat chance."

"Just get the information up to Lieutenant Garrett, would you?"

"What do you think I was doing before you came down here, fuzznuts?"

"Right," I said, nodding while turning to make my leave.

As I started out the door, I saw Danny flash me a smile and a quick, friendly wave as if we were buddies. I didn't know him that well. He was always so quiet and mostly kept to himself. Too bad his reserved nature hadn't rubbed off on Vera. Speaking of which . . , before closing the door, I captured her attention once again.

"You know, Vera, I've been meaning to ask you, have you always had a strange fascination with male genitalia?"

"What? Is that wrong?" she answered with a crooked grin. "I'm still waiting to get a shot with yours, big boy."

I let out a slight chuckle and eased the door shut. That Vera was a quick-witted one. In a way, I envied her. She knew how to make the best out of a humorless job. As I ascended the stairs, I couldn't help but think how all humor had ceased to exist on the upper floor long ago. If Frank was calling me up there to tell me one more time how he thought his wife might be squirreling away money into some secret bank account, I swear to Christ, I was going to lose my shit.

When I turned the corner from the staircase and saw Agent Hayes in Frank's office, her arms folded about her chest and her facial features reminiscent of the cold, calculating robot she had been two years earlier, I knew it was something more serious. Frank's eyes locked onto mine as I entered his office.

"Shut the door," he barked.

"Am I in some sort of trouble?" I asked, pushing the door closed. I don't know why my mind went there, but the way Frank was snarling, it was a reasonable question.

"We just received this," he responded, his fingertips sliding an envelope across his desk toward me.

I let out a heavy breath through my nose. "Shit. Is that what I think it is?"

"Read it," Hayes answered.

Reluctantly, my fingers fidgeted with the torn opening of the envelope and pulled out the folded paper from within. My heart was beating through my chest. At first, I thought it was because I was nervous. Then I realized it was something more; it was adrenaline. I was excited. I unfolded the flaps and began to read.

I AM NOT PLEASED. I DIDN'T GET TO FINISH WHAT I STARTED ON MY LAST VICTIM. THOUGH THE OUTCOME WAS THE SAME, I HAD BIGGER PLANS FOR P. THAT BITCH STOPPED MY FUN BEFORE THE GRAND FINALE. DIDN'T SHE REALIZE IT WAS ALL FOR HER? THE UNGRATEFUL COW. THAT BEHAVIOR ANGERS ME. MY RAGE IS WITHOUT LIMITS. I WILL NOT BE DENIED MY PREY. HEED MY WORDS: YOU'VE NOT WITNESSED THE EXTENT OF MY WRATH. BUT YOU WILL. OR SHOULD I SAY, Q WILL. I AM NO LONGER PLAYING GAMES. THE REST WILL NOW PAY.

A

I lowered the paper onto Frank's desk, my focus shifting between him and Hayes, taking note of their unspoken fears. I cleared my throat and peered down at the note.

"We knew it was only a matter of time," I said.

"Well, no fucking shit, genius," Frank retorted. "You got any other words of wisdom you'd care to share?"

I lifted my head and glared at my lieutenant with a look that made his focus waver.

"The A," I answered.

"What about it," Frank shrugged.

"In all of The Letter Man's previous notes, his signature was the lowercase version of the Greek letter Alpha. This one is uppercase."

"I noticed that as well," Hayes said.

"Is that supposed to mean something?" Frank questioned. "You thinking this is some kind of copycat?"

I looked at Frank and then turned my stare to Agent Hayes.

"No, it's not a copycat; this is him. If the capital A is what I think it means, then we're in for a world of shit."

Chapter 22

Q

That "world of shit" I mentioned rolled in like a freight train. Frank and Hayes weren't convinced the little love letter we received was from our homicidal maniac. I knew better. It had to be him. He knew what went on in the apartment building with Peter and Charlene. And now that I was standing in the aftermath of the twisted fuck's latest kill, there was no denying it. Frank and Hayes would believe it now.

"What the fuck is going on here, Mick?" Sanchez questioned, slumped over and holding his hand to his mouth like he was about to hurl. "Shit, fuck! How does somebody even do something like this?"

"My first guess would be with a machete," Chief Forensic Officer Shane answered. He was looking up from the severed foot to address the rhetorical question while some Larson crime lab techs snapped pictures of the gruesome scene we'd walked in on.

Newly assigned Detective Murcur from the Larson Detective Bureau stood over the forensic officer, taking notes of every little detail. Sanchez's rookie partner was outside, pacing back and forth across the parking lot, probably reconsidering his career path. As for me, I was only here because Agent Hayes insisted I accompany her.

We'd heard it was bad; we had no idea it was *this* bad.

"Do we know if this is Quinn?" I asked.

Detective Murcur nodded. "Quinn Welker. Twenty-six years old. We found his wallet in a pair of pants in the bedroom."

"What can you tell us?" Hayes asked, directing her question toward Shane, who was squatting over the victim, the crime scene seemingly having little effect on either of them.

"I can tell you the killer's a real sicko," he began. "Okay, let's see," he continued, standing up and pointing around the room like he was mapping out a mental diagram in his head, piecing together the series of events that took place. "A naked victim, clothes in the bedroom, a damp towel on the floor by the bathroom door... I believe the victim had just gotten out of the shower when he was surprised by the killer. The killer then forced him to sit in that chair." He pointed to a turned-over chair in the center of the room. "His arms were bound behind the chair like this." He demonstrated the action by swinging his arms behind his back. "And his mouth was duct taped shut, as you can see. Based on the arterial spray, I'd say this was where the killer took his first strike at the victim. It wasn't a clean cut as you'll notice from the torn flesh on the left side of his neck. It didn't kill him instantly, but it caused him to fall to his right, tipping over the chair. Or maybe the sick bastard knocked him over. We can't know with any certainty. There are some severe gouge marks on the floor beneath the chair legs that would suggest the victim struggled to free himself from his bonds. But this is where things get a little crazy."

"As if that's not already crazy enough?" I voiced to Hayes, though I'm sure it was loud enough for everyone around me to hear it.

"The killer cut Quinn loose," Shane continued. "We know this because his bonds were a clean cut. The killer knew his victim was as good as dead; he was going to bleed out."

"Then why cut him loose at all?" I asked.

"That's the point, isn't it, Detective? I think he wanted to watch him squirm. The trail of bloody handprints indicates the victim crawled his way about ten feet before collapsing, probably unable to drag himself any farther due to lack of blood. Or maybe that was when the killer cut off the victim's right hand. That would've also stopped him from crawling away. Shock would have set in around that time, as well. That was probably the best thing that could have happened to the victim. Quinn wouldn't have felt what was happening. His conscious brain would have flipped a switch, a sort of protective response. The lucky bastard didn't have to feel what came next."

From where I stood, what came next was a horrific nightmare. If how everything was laid out for us on the floor like a goddamn exhibit was any indication, his left hand was next to be severed, followed by his feet. Then, his arms. Then, his legs. And finally, his head, duct-taped mouth and all. Nine body parts lined up in a nice, tidy row. It was the killer's usual statement. Nine letters of the alphabet remained– nine victims to follow.

"Where's the torso?" Hayes questioned.

"The guy threw it in the tub," Detective Murcur replied, throwing his thumb over his shoulder.

"I gotta get out of here," Sanchez announced. "I think I'm going to be sick."

He pushed his way by me in a hurry, heading for the door, the poor bastard. He and his partner didn't sign up for this shit. It was supposed to be a routine arrest.

Thanks to Vera's lab work, the Southbridge PD picked up that drugstore-thieving asshole punk Jerome Kenshaw on charges of robbery and aggravated assault. The son of a bitch made us work for it, but we managed to get him to roll on one of his posse, Quinn Welker, a Larson resident. We contacted the Larson PD, and a warrant was issued for the scumbag's arrest. Sanchez and the rook were the lucky ones assigned to take him into custody.

This mess was what they stumbled into.

Agent Hayes marched to the nearest wall and placed her palm on it while staring at the floor.

"What the fuck is *she* doing?" Murcur questioned.

"Sshhh!" she replied, giving him a nasty look.

He looked at me for guidance, but I had no idea what was happening. All I could do was shrug my shoulders.

"The walls are thin in this building," she stated, giving us the answer we sought. "I can hear the woman next door. Even with the victim unable to yell for help, you'd think someone in one of the adjoining apartments would have heard something."

"Sanchez said the radio was playing pretty loud when they arrived," Murcur responded, pointing to a stereo against the far wall.

"I'm guessing it was off when our Mr. Welker hopped into the shower," Shane jumped in.

"Why the fuck would you guess that?" Murcur questioned.

Shane shot the detective an agitated glare before answering. "My theory is that the killer turned it on, which is what alerted the victim to someone in his apartment. Smart. Quinn came running out of the bathroom, still wet, only to find the killer waiting for him. You know the rest."

"No, I don't know the rest," I stated as if it were my place to make such a remark. "I didn't see any sign of forced entry. Are you telling me the killer just walked in? What the fuck; does anyone lock their doors?"

"Did you happen to look around on your way over here?" Murcer asked in an annoyed tone. "This neighborhood isn't exactly paved with golden streets. Do you think Southbridge is the only city in the gutter? Larson's got its share of hapless indigents, too, Detective. And this right here is as poor as it gets. Why lock your door when you don't have shit to steal?"

"Come on," I argued. "The guy's got a nicer stereo than I've got, for crying out loud."

"Yeah? And if you dig deep enough, asshole, I bet you'll find that's stolen from Walmart or one of those rich snobs on the upper west side."

"Enough, gentlemen," Hayes barked. "Can we focus on what we know?"

"We know we've got a dead body, Agent," Murcur said, still annoyed. "That's about all we know,"

"And we know it's the same killer," I added.

"We don't know that, Detective," Hayes responded.

"*I* know it," I stated adamantly. "Quinn. Q - that was all I needed to know. It fits. The rest of this shit is him telling us how he's not fucking around anymore."

"If you're right, Detective," Hayes replied, "then where's the note?"

"It's here somewhere," I answered. "It has to be."

Shane raised his hand like he was back in school. "My crew and I can start digging around. If there's a note, we'll find it. But I'm going to need you to leave the crime scene." He glared at Detective Murcur, "*All* of you."

That little gesture spoke volumes about the type of person Murcur was. I thought it was just me, but nope, he's a jackass.

"That's fine," Hayes nodded. "We'll let you get to it. In the meantime, we can start questioning the other residents to see if anybody saw or heard anything. Murcur, call your boys back in here. We could use their help. I want to question as many folks as we can."

"You realize nobody's gonna talk," he responded.

"Yeah, I'm getting that fuzzy feeling."

As weird as it might have seemed, and maybe I was in the minority, it was good to see Hayes taking charge like that. She had become a different person when Special Agent Lowe was around. Now that he'd been called away, she could let her true self take charge. I knew it wouldn't last, though. Those idiots in Washington had no idea what kind of agent she was. With the killer's return, it was only a matter of time before Lowe graced us with his presence again. Then she'd be back to *taking* orders instead of *giving* them, and *I'd* be back to rolling my eyes at everything that came out of his mouth. It didn't seem right, but it was what we'd be stuck with.

Once Sanchez and the rookie, Prelendo, joined us from their hiatus, we each splintered off to different doors to begin our questioning. Hayes and I took the near-side apartments; Sanchez and Prelendo took the opposite. I wonder if Murcur felt left out, forced to check with the tenants around the corner. That was fine with me; someone had to do it, and it kept him out of my hair.

We hadn't even been at it for five minutes when Quinn's apartment door opened, and Shane peeked out.

"Guys, you're gonna want to see this."

Hayes jumped right to it, having just hit a dead end with the tenant in apartment 4. I wasn't quite finished yet with the meth head in apartment 6 that I was fortunate enough to be questioning. I noticed the rookie had already struck out at his chosen door, but he refused to follow Hayes' lead back into Quinn's apartment. I couldn't blame him; you didn't get used to seeing such gruesome scenes. I'd already seen more than I'd ever wanted and thought I'd gotten better at keeping it together, but even I was in no hurry to get back in there.

I could hear Sanchez behind me, trying to wrap things up with his interviewee, but it wasn't working as planned. The woman kept interrupting his questions, asking him when the police were going to start searching for her missing cat. She wasn't being very nice about it, either. If it were me, I would've told her we found her cat dead in the dumpster outside just to shut her up. Sanchez wasn't like that, though. He had to be more sensitive about it since he was the local law enforcement.

Murcur was also one of Larson's finest - and I use that term loosely - but something told me he would have had no qualms about giving the woman some of her nasty back. Apparently, the man also had good ears. He immediately sprinted from around the corner after Shane's announcement, wanting to be right behind Agent Hayes.

Well, I suppose it *was* his crime scene, after all. More power to you, buddy.

By the time I finished with my toothless tenant and stepped back into Quinn's apartment, Detective Murcur was standing beside one of the lab techs holding a bloody piece of paper, staring at it intensely, his jaw tightened. Hayes and Shane were stepping from the bathroom, the agent's expression dour, her eyes cold and dark. She glanced at me from across the room and subtly nodded, letting me know I was right; this was indeed the work of The Letter Man.

"Where did you find it?" I asked.

"It was in the tub under the torso," Shane replied. "We rolled it over, and there it was, along with a big, capital Q cut into the lower back."

I shook my head in disgust. "What's it say, Murcur?"

"Here, read it yourself." He extended his arm toward me, the blood-smeared paper drooping from his fingers.

I quickly patted my pockets in desperation.

"Shit! I don't have any gloves. I need some gloves."

Shane stepped forward, "Here you go, Detective," he said, pulling an extra pair from his jacket and holding them out for me.

I reached forward to snag them from him, "Thank y..," when I suddenly froze, my words incomplete. My brain latched onto an earlier conversation as I stared at the blue gloves in his hand. My eyes shifted inquisitively to Shane's innocuous stare, then back to the colored gloves he offered me.

"It's all right, Detective," he smiled, "go ahead; I always carry extra with me."

I apprehensively grabbed the gloves as I shook off the unnerving thoughts rolling around my head.

"Thank you," I nodded, finally weaving together a coherent response.

I slapped the gloves on as quickly as possible, trying to refocus my attention on the killer's crimson-drenched note. I gently eased the soaked paper from Murcur's fingertips, the threat of tearing the delicate paper a concern. I felt myself heavily swallow as I peered down at the ink-smeared message, the black mingling with the red. Though the words were difficult to read, the message was all too clear.

WELCOME BACK TO THE TERROR. I'M SURE YOU DIDN'T MIND THE QUIET WHILE IT LASTED. IT TOOK ME A WHILE TO FIND A Q WORTHY OF MY TALENTS. MY SILENCE HAS NOW ENDED. I THINK YOU'LL AGREE, IT WAS WORTH THE WAIT. DON'T SHED A TEAR FOR THIS PUTRID WASTE OF FLESH. HIS DEATH SERVES MORE OF A PURPOSE THAN HIS MEANINGLESS LIFE EVER DID.

IT'S A SHAME YOU SEE THESE VERMIN AS ONLY MISGUIDED CRIMINALS – ALWAYS SO EAGER TO SPARE THEIR WORTHLESS LIVES IN THE HOPES THEY CAN BE REDEEMED. YOUR HOPES ARE USELESSLY SQUANDERED. THESE FILTHY BOTTOM FEEDERS ARE A PESTILENCE — A PLAGUE ON THE GOOD CITIZENS OF MY CITY. THEY TAKE, AND THEY TAKE, AND THEY TAKE UNTIL ALL THAT IS LEFT BEHIND IS PAIN AND SUFFERING. I WILL NO LONGER TOLERATE SUCH BLATANT DISREGARD FOR THE INNOCENT LIVES DESTROYED BY THE CARRION WHO ARE LEFT TO WALK UNPUNISHED AMONG US. I AM HERE TO PUT AN END TO THEIR MISERABLE EXISTENCE.

I HAVE ENDURED TOO MUCH, ONLY TO WATCH TOO MANY OF THEIR KIND WALK FREE. THEY ARE ALL GHOSTS, LIVING ON BORROWED TIME. I WILL SEE THIS THROUGH TO THE END.

DON'T GET IN MY WAY.

A

I let the words sink in for a moment. The killer is becoming more unstable, letting his emotions guide him, and because of it, he's getting sloppy.

"He's a Larson resident," I said, looking up from the wet paper, the first hint of optimism in my voice in quite a while.

"You caught that too, huh?" Agent Hayes responded.

"What?" Detective Murcur questioned, puzzled at our presumption. "What makes you think that?"

"He wrote '*my city*,'" I pointed out. "Unless the killer suddenly forgot where he was when he killed Quinn, I'd say that means Larson is where he lives."

"It makes sense," Sanchez's voice echoed from the open doorway, the rookie standing in the hall behind him, looking over his shoulder. "His first victim was a Larson resident."

"Hey, aren't you supposed to be out there questioning the other tenants, Sanchez?" Murcur said heatedly. "Why don't you and your little play date get back to your duties and leave the detective work to the detectives."

"Hey, fuck you, Murcur," Sanchez snapped back. "I thought we were on the same team. Let's go, Prelendo," he tapped the rookie on the arm. "Let's let the cocksucker think he's something special."

Sanchez walked back into the hall while Prelendo stayed behind, shooting Murcur a nasty glance. Murcur paid no attention to the rookie's glare, instead turning his attention toward Agent Hayes. But *I* saw it. Prelendo was only waiting for Murcur to look away so he could flip him the bird. The rookie hadn't been with the force long enough to have the courage to do it to Murcur's face.

"This is all just speculation," Murcur continued. "This guy could be playing us."

"He could be," Hayes replied, "but so far, this is the only lead we've got."

"Then we've got squat," Murcur said. "Maybe we'll be able to get more from the note when Shane gets it back to the lab." He extended his open hand toward me, requesting I hand over the note. I was about to when Hayes jumped in.

"Actually, I'll be taking that piece of evidence with *me*," she stated, stepping forward and pinching the edge of the paper in her fingers. "I want *my* people to handle it."

"Now hold on a minute, Agent," Murcur argued. "You can't just..,"

Hayes whipped herself around to face him, promptly shutting down the detective's arrogant chatter.

"First of all, Detective," Hayes stated through gritted teeth, "it's *Special* Agent."

There she was, I thought, *the tough-as-nails agent.*

"And second," she continued, "let me remind you, this is a *federal* investigation. Any evidence collected is the property of the U.S. Government and its agencies. And although this is currently a joint effort between our departments, a single phone call can turn this into a full FBI takeover. So, Detective, *you* are only here out of courtesy on my part. Don't let me regret that."

"So that's how it's going to be, huh?" Murcur griped. "You're going to throw your little FBI badge in my face? We'll see what Chief Sutton has to say about this. After this little charade, you'll be lucky to get any cooperation from the Larson PD."

Murcur stormed past us, bumping my shoulder on the way by as if I had something to do with Hayes' call. He mustered a "*fucking bitch*" on his way out the door. I couldn't say as I blamed him. If she had done that in Southbridge, there would have been even more outrage. Even so, it was kind of cool to see.

Hayes turned to me with a sour look on her face. I responded by handing her the bloody paper. If experience taught me anything, I knew better than to get in her way. She nodded appreciatively at my compliance.

"I'll need this bagged," she ordered Shane. "Or are we going to have a problem, too?"

Shane shook his head. "No problem on my end; I hate that jerk. And I don't think you have anything to worry about; most of the department can't stand him."

"Good to know," she responded, "but I wasn't worried."

"Are you going to bring your people in here to take over?" Shane asked, sounding disappointed.

"No," Hayes replied. "You continue. Your team is more than capable of handling things. I'm going to step out for a moment to get some air. I expect the note bagged and ready for me when I return."

"Sure thing," Shane replied.

Hayes stared into my eyes before walking out. She wasn't happy about what she did, but I knew what it was about. Her eyes gave away her intentions. She wasn't trying to throw her weight around; she wanted the evidence with her in Southbridge. Smart. It made it that much easier for me to bring it to Ben.

I stood silent, staring at the awful scene on the floor, Quinn's body cut into pieces and displayed like some Bodyworks exhibit. What was wrong with the sick bastard? What was done to the killer to make him do this? I felt my hands begin to shake with anger.

"Is everything all right, Detective?" Shane asked me, shaking me from my thoughts, an out-of-place smile on his lips.

"What? Oh, yeah. I'm fine. I mean, you know, considering."

"Right," he answered, nodding. "I'm going to get back to it, then."

He turned from me and joined with one of his lab techs, occasionally glancing at me from across the room as if checking to see if I was still in the apartment. It became uncomfortable after the fourth or fifth time. I wondered if my presence was bothering him as much as his glares were bothering me. My eyes shifted down to my shaking hands, focusing on the dried blood stains all over the blue gloves I wore.

Huh.

The blue gloves.

Chapter 23

Boiling Point

We were supposed to be having a good time and enjoying a nice dinner at Rosa's house, but my mind was on the case. It was *always* on the case. I couldn't just forget what I'd seen earlier in the day - a man's body cut apart like it had been. How was I expected to put something like that out of my mind and have a good time?

Rosa wanted to see Stella Mae in the worst way. She could have dropped by anytime, but she knew Gina would have wanted to cook a big meal (those Italians love to cook), and she didn't want to add to Gina's load. Instead, she invited us over to her place for dinner. She should have known Gina would have jumped right into the kitchen to help as soon as we arrived – or should I say, to do all the work? From the moment we walked through the door, Rosa forgot all about her hosting duties and snatched up Stella and started dancing around the living room while Gina prepared the creamy Tuscan chicken penne. I'm sure it didn't bother Gina at all, but it bothered me – probably more than it should have. I'd be lying if I said it was because I didn't like that Gina was doing all the work when she should have been taking it easy. That was part of it, for sure, but it was also because I was looking forward to a good meal, and now that Gina was doing the cooking, my hopes were diminished. For all the stereotypes regarding Italian cooking, none of them hit my wife.

Rosa took her new-found freedom from the meal-prepping responsibilities to flaunt our daughter in front of us, complimenting her wardrobe and distracting Gina from realizing she was the designated cook for the evening.

"The bow on her head is adorable, guys," Rosa announced, fluffing the fabric of the pink accessory.

"Isn't it?" Gina replied over the half-wall of the kitchen. "Mick said it was ridiculous to go through the trouble."

"Mick!" Rosa cried, playfully slapping me on my upper arm.

"What the fuck, Rosa?" I snapped.

Stunned, Rosa instinctively turned Stella away from me as if I were going to jump out of my seat to attack her for such a malicious act of aggression.

I might have overreacted a bit. To be fair, I hadn't been paying attention to the conversation, so the slap caught me off guard.

Gina shuffled to the threshold between the kitchen and living room to stare out at me.

"What was *that*, Mick?" she questioned sternly.

"I'm sorry, hon; I was distracted." I turned to her sister. "Rosa, I'm sorry."

"Geez, Mick, warn me next time you're going to have a conniption," Rosa replied.

I guess that meant she accepted my apology.

"It's okay, baby," she continued, rubbing Stella's rose-colored cheeks. "Your daddy didn't mean to yell like that."

Great! Suddenly, I was the bad guy. I rolled my eyes.

"Mick, you know how I feel about the language around the baby," Gina added, still standing in the opening. "I don't want her to hear that."

"I know," I replied a bit louder. "I said I was sorry. Can we please move on?"

"What's gotten into you, Mick?" Gina asked.

I could have told her about what I'd seen: the horrible murder, the blood, the note – all of it, but I couldn't lay that on her shoulders. She didn't need to hear the details of that part of my life. It was easier to lock it away and use something else, *anything* else, as an excuse to explode.

"What's gotten into *me*?" I questioned. "Does anyone else see what's wrong here? Every time you two get together, you gang up on me."

"What? Where's this coming from?" Gina asked.

"Of course, *you* don't see it," I responded, standing from the couch. "You two always stick up for one another. I mean, you don't even care that you're here doing all of the cooking. Hell, Gina, we might as well have stayed home. It would have been the same."

"I wasn't going to let her do everything, Mick," Rosa chirped. "I just wanted to visit with Stella for a while."

"You don't need to apologize, Rosa," Gina stated. "Mick's out of line."

"There it is," I said heatedly. "*I'm* the one who's out of line. Again! It's always me."

"I don't know what this is all about, Mick," Gina said, stepping from the kitchen to take Stella off her sister's hands, "but it's gotta stop. You're scaring Stella."

"I'm not scaring Stella," I said, pointing to our little girl. "She's smiling, for crying out loud. Stop trying to make me out to be the villain."

That was the problem; they weren't trying to make me out to be anything. It all fell on my shoulders. Deep down, I knew it, but I had gone past that breaking point and couldn't turn back. Or I didn't *want* to. My outburst was my only release. I was frustrated. I was angry. It just came out at the wrong time and to the wrong people. Once I'd realized it, I didn't know how to let it go. I felt more ashamed than anything else, which only fueled my anger. Only – it wasn't them I was angry with. But here I was, unloading on those I cared about. That made me more ashamed, which made me more angry. It was a vicious cycle I couldn't break.

"Baby, whatever this is," Gina stated, swirling her hand in a circle in front of me, "I'm not having it. You need to go and work this out somewhere else."

Those words hit me harder than a Mack truck.

"But Gina..,"

"No, Mick, you need to go. We can talk about this later. Rosa will bring me and Stella home."

She turned to her sister, silently asking for approval.

"Y-yeah, of course," Rosa agreed, nodding. "I'll bring you home."

"There you go," Gina continued, turning back to me. "Now you don't have to worry about us. So, go on. You clearly don't want to be here. And right now, the way you're acting, I don't want you here either."

I just felt the sting of being slapped in the face without Gina laying a hand on me.

"Babe, can I just explain..,"

"I don't want to hear it, Mick," Gina spoke over me. "I get it; you're dealing with something. That doesn't mean you get to dump it all over us. Go and do whatever it is you need to do. Just don't do it here."

I opened my mouth to say something, but words hadn't always been my best friend when feeling this way. Not that words had ever been my expertise. I saw Gina's face and gave up trying. I shook my head in frustration. Not at Gina - not even at Rosa. I think they both knew that. In a way, I think Gina asked me to leave because she understood. The case had already dug its claws in deep and was slowly tearing me apart. She knew I couldn't relax and pretend everything was rainbows while a killer roamed free. She also knew that whatever unsettling thoughts gnawed at me, if I didn't resolve them soon, the same claws that had me in their unrelenting grip would tear our marriage apart.

I felt my shoulders drop as I sighed, looking at Stella Mae in her mother's arms, hugging Gina's neck, not a care in the world. I softly rubbed the back of her head and smiled.

"I'll go," I ceded, whispering as if I worried Stella would hear me and think I was leaving *her*. That was *never* happening.

As I turned for the door, Gina grabbed my shirt sleeve at the wrist.

"I'll bring some food home."

With my head hung low, I nodded. It was better to keep my saddened stare averted. It was all I could do. If I had looked into her eyes, the shame I felt would have caused me to break down. As it were, tears were already forming as I opened the door and solemnly walked out.

It was for the best. I needed to get out of there. My mind was not in a good place. Unfortunately, it wasn't getting any better on my way home. Night had fallen, and the worst of the city's darkness dwellers had come out to play. All along Booker Ave - or "Hooker Highway" as the locals called it - the mile-long strip of debauchery and destitution I'd found myself on, the bad element of Southbridge was alive and well this night.

The street was a well-known haven for prostitutes and degenerates alike. Everywhere I looked, The Letter Man stared back at me. Any one of the filthy lowlifes occupying space on the littered sidewalks, the back alleyways, the darkened street corners, or the piss-covered stoops of every rundown shop could have been the killer we were after. They watched me as I drove by, pointing at me and laughing at my ineptitude. They were free to kill again – to cut another person into bits and pieces while I remained tunnel-visioned, keeping my eyes on the road, ignoring the killer's blatant taunts.

The notes, the meticulous way he lined up body parts, counting down his victims - the way he was toying with us, I was seeing red. My hands gripped the steering wheel tighter, squeezing the blood from my knuckles.

Who the fuck was he? Was he the dealer on the corner up ahead, trying to act smooth like I hadn't just watched him pass a dime bag to that kid? Maybe he was that drunk, urinating on the side of Carlos' Convenience. Or maybe he was one of the numerous Johns along "Hooker Highway," taking on side jobs when he wasn't pimping out one of his whores. In this neighborhood, the suspects were many, and the victims were countless. And not only victims of The Letter Man but of themselves. I tried to convince myself that none of these people were as patient or as calculated as the killer. That was why I had to keep my focus forward - my eyes on the pavement. In my current frame of mind, my judgment could be too easily swayed by the sight of such depravity.

Perhaps if I had been more observant of my immediate surroundings, I would have noticed the 32-ounce beverage being hurled in my direction *before* it struck my windshield. Upon contact, the brown liquid exploded from the paper cup, splashing across my field of view.

"What the fuck!" I yelled, stomping on my brakes, my car coming to a screeching halt as I stared at the now-empty "Big Slurp" cup resting on my wipers, its contents smeared across the glass, mingling with the crusted remnants of dried bird droppings and the splattered remains of long-dead insects.

I jumped from my car in a fit of rage, spotting the punk kid who'd just made the biggest mistake of his life still standing on the sidewalk to my left. He flashed me a shit-eating grin, unafraid, as if he ruled these streets. Out here, he thought he could do anything he pleased without repercussions. Such self-importance, as if he thought I gave a damn about his worthless life. Perhaps, on another night, he would have been right.

Even as I stormed toward him with fire in my eyes, the twenty-something delinquent stood his ground.

"What you gonna do, pops?" he brazenly yelled, flipping me the finger. "Get your fucking ass back in your car, old man."

"You picked the wrong guy, you piece of shit," I said through clenched teeth as I approached.

"Oh, you wanna throw down, mother-fucker?" he said, putting his hands up in fists, acting cocky. "Come and get some, ghost."

Just as I got to the sidewalk, I lifted the lower flap of my shirt that had been concealing the badge clipped to my belt. "I'm a cop, you fucking dimwit asshole."

I heard myself announcing it, but it didn't quite register as I charged at the scumbag, slamming his body into the locked cage of the closed storefront behind him.

"Hey, man," he yelled, surprised by my actions. "What the fuck?" He put his open hands up in front of his chest. "I didn't know you were a cop, okay?"

"Shut the fuck up," I yelled, putting my finger in his face. "You ain't so bad now, are you, tough guy? Turn around and put your goddamn hands on the cage."

"But I was..,"

"I said, turn around, asshole." I grabbed him by the shoulder and spun him around, pushing his chest against the metal bars, my usual mild-mannered detective role taking a backseat to my previously harsher beat cop days.

"Ow! Fuck, man," he screamed - a wasted effort that fell on deaf ears.

"Spread your legs." I kicked his left ankle hard to get my point across. He understood.

I quickly patted him down, pulling his wallet from his back pocket and throwing it on the ground by his left foot.

"C'mon, man; what the fuck?" the punk questioned.

"I didn't say you could speak," I snapped, slapping the back of his head.

"Shit, man," he responded.

"Put your hands on the back of your head."

He hesitated. I pressed my palm into his upper back, pushing him harder into the security fence.

"I said put your fucking hands on your head, ass wipe."

"Okay, okay," he submitted, reaching around and clasping his fingers behind his head.

I reached for my belt, not thinking straight. I didn't have my cuffs on me; they were still in the car. Fuck.

I grabbed his right thumb and yanked, peeling his hand away from the other and folding his arm down by his lower back. I then grabbed his left hand, doing the same.

"Interlock your fingers, fucker."

He complied.

"Keep 'em that way and turn around," I ordered. "Put your back up against the fence."

"Take it easy, I'm doing it," he griped. "Fuck."

He turned as I directed, his face no longer showing the cocky expression he had when he thought I was Joe Victim.

"Why'd you call me a ghost, huh, Asshole?" I questioned, recalling the phrase from the killer's note.

"What?" he replied, looking confused.

"Ghost!" I shouted. "You called me a ghost. Why?"

He shrugged his shoulders. "I don't know, man. I say shit. What of it?"

"Did you call me a ghost because I'm white? Or maybe it was because you were going to kill me."

"Fuck, man; I was just trying to scare you."

I stared at him, my eyes narrowing in disdain.

"Are you him?" I asked, my teeth gritted.

"What? Him who?"

"I asked you a question, asshole," I said louder, slapping the side of his head.

"Hey, what the fuck, man?" he complained. "I don't know what you're talking about."

I glared at the punk, watching his every move - his shifting eyes and uncontrolled nervous twitching.

"Yeah, you *are* him, ain'tcha?" I nodded.

"I ain't nobody, man," he responded.

"You get off on doing that to people, don't you?" I questioned, curling my lip up in disgust.

"I told you, I didn't know you were a cop."

"I got you, you demented fuck."

I glanced to my left and then to my right, unconsciously looking for prying eyes. The darkened street was bare of stray wanderers. All the criminals of "Hooker Highway" were a few blocks back. All except this one — the worst of them all. His mistake.

"Yeah," I smiled, turning back to face the trash-talking hoodlum, "I got you."

I looked into his eyes and could only see The Letter Man staring back. At that moment, everything that had been building up inside me boiled up to the top. Mick, the good-natured cop, was no longer in control. I became someone else - some*thing* else.

My first punch knocked his head backward into the fencing, causing his body to recoil into my second punch, which knocked him to the ground. He screamed a few obscenities and tried to kick at me, but it was no use. I was on top of him in an instant, my body fueled by adrenaline, my fists by pure rage. Over and over, my fists slammed into his face until my knuckles were as bloody as his victims. I punished the freak for all that he'd done, the lives he'd taken, and I didn't stop until I knew it was over. It was finally over.

I'd done it; I stopped him. I put an end to..,

Suddenly, the glaze over my eyes dissipated, and I stared in horror at the outcome of my actions. I looked at my bloody hands as they began to shake.

"What have I done?" I spoke aloud.

My earlier words crashed into my skull like a freight train.

"Stop trying to make me out to be the villain."

I looked at the battered and beaten boy at my feet and realized..,

I *was* the villain.

"Shit! Fuck! Fuck! Shit!"

I looked around me for someone, anyone. It was quiet. My mind was racing a mile a minute. What did I do? What did I do?

Wobbly, I ran to my car and got on the radio.

"This is Detective Dooley, requesting an ambulance at 1273 Booker Avenue."

Chapter 24

Regrets

The one EMT was eyeballing me while his partner cinched the strap over the unconscious boy. They worked fast. They'd gotten him onto a gurney before even another officer arrived. While they wheeled him past me to the rear of the ambulance, the same EMT continued to stare.

"Any idea what happened here?" he asked. "Do you know who did this?"

I shook my head. "No. No idea." I didn't know why I said that. It just came out. *Everybody lies,* Frank's words echoed in my brain.

I watched as the EMT's eyes shifted downward to my scraped-up knuckles.

"No idea, huh?" he said, raising his eyes to meet mine.

"What?" I snapped argumentatively. "You got something to say?"

"Nope, nothing," he replied, shaking his head as he and his partner slid the gurney into the back of the ambulance. The partner jumped in the back with the beaten victim while the inquisitive one closed the doors and slapped his blue-latex-gloved palm (something I noticed right away) against the painted, white M beneath the rear window. "Hang tight in there, Evan," he hollered to his partner. He gave me a final glance before turning away toward the driver's side of the vehicle.

As he opened his door to get in, I had to ask. "Is he going to be okay?"

He gave me a nasty glare before rolling his eyes and sliding into his seat. I guess he felt I didn't deserve a response.

As I watched the ambulance pull away from the curb, a uniformed officer arrived in a black and white just ahead of them. Officer Reddin stepped from the vehicle, watching the ambulance pass by.

"Hey, Mick," he said, leaning one arm on the top of his door. "Everything all right here? What happened?"

"Everything's fine," I answered. "Some hoodlum got himself scraped up in a fight."

"That's it?" he responded. "I'm telling you, it's always something in this neighborhood."

"Yeah."

"Looks like *you're* having a night." I followed his pointed finger to the large beverage cup still on my windshield, the dried soft drink smeared across the glass.

I nodded. "Yeah."

"The fucking balls on some of these punk kids, huh? You're over here trying to help one of their own, and they go and do that to your car while you're distracted."

"Yeah."

"I'll tell you what, though; the bastard being taken away was lucky you were here."

"Yeah."

"He won't see it that way, though. Around here, we're the bad guys, and they're the helpless victims. The piece of shit probably got what was coming to him."

"Are you done here, Officer?" I shouted at him, irritated. "Christ!"

"Geez, I'm sorry, Mick," he responded. "I didn't know you were so sensitive about the riff-raff around here."

He gave me a look that matched the EMT's as he got back into his cruiser.

"Have yourself a nice night," he barked sarcastically before closing his door and peeling off.

I closed my eyes and bowed my head, feeling mentally drained. Without thinking, I wiped across my forehead with the back of my hand, and a jolt of pain shot through me, my knuckles offering the bitter reminder of my misdeeds.

"Ouch! Fuck!" I shook my hand to dull the stinging sensation and looked at the open wounds. I couldn't see anything but the boy's swollen face, and no matter how hard I tried, I couldn't let it go. That wasn't me back there. It *was*, but it *wasn't*. That was the goddamn Letter Man, gripping me in a stranglehold, dragging me down into his dark rabbit hole. I lost control. I knew better, and I *still* lost control. I couldn't let that happen again. I wouldn't. But I also couldn't act like nothing had happened. I knew what I needed to do.

"Shit."

*　*　*

I stared at the floor between my feet, my right leg bobbing up and down anxiously while I sat in the waiting area. A little girl sitting with an older gentleman across the room smiled at me when I glanced up. I couldn't even muster a returned smile; I didn't have the heart. I returned my eyes to the cold tile beneath me, hoping she wouldn't take offense.

I'd already sent a uniformed officer away. He showed up to take the victim's statement, but with the boy being unconscious, I told him I'd take care of it. There was no need for both of us to be here, waiting for who knows how long. The truth was far more despicable. I was ashamed of what I'd done and wasn't ready for anyone to know about it. Who would they.., *what* would they see when they looked at me?

My thoughts were scattered, jumping around faster than I could corral them. I could have killed that boy. Over what? A cup of soda thrown at my car? Is that what I'm becoming? Is that what this case is doing to me? Is that what happened to Jimmy? Is that why his life spiraled down the drain like so many detectives before him? Was that where I was headed? More importantly, was it too late to stop it?

I was so drenched in thoughts of self-loathing that I didn't hear the nurse approach – or call to me – until she tapped me on the shoulder to gain my attention. I instantly jumped to my feet.

"Detective Dooley?" the soft-spoken nurse questioned.

"Yes," I replied.

"I was told you were inquiring about the boy who was brought in earlier this evening - the assault victim?"

"Yes; can you tell me if he's going to be all right?"

"Well, he's banged up pretty good," she replied. "He'll be staying with us for a few days, but we expect he'll make a full recovery."

Hearing those words was like a wave of relief washing over me. I needed that.

"That's good to hear. Thank you."

"You're welcome, Detective."

She smiled and walked back to her station.

I let out a heavy sigh, thankful for the positive news. I turned my head back to the little girl, whose eyes were still upon me, and managed an unenthusiastic grin. I hope she wasn't expecting more, or she'd be just another person I've disappointed tonight.

Having heard the boy was going to be fine, at least in time, I slithered my way to the exit. I'd caused enough trouble this evening and hoped I could still redeem a portion of myself. I owed Gina an apology for how I'd been acting. I finally understood what she'd been trying to tell me. I only hoped it wasn't too late to find my way back.

The entire drive home, the boy's battered face, interspersed with Rosa's shocked glare and Gina's disappointed scowl, flashed before me like slides in a View-Master. One after another after another – view, skip, repeat. They only ceased when I pulled into the driveway and saw a light coming from the living room. All the pictures faded, and only Gina's face remained.

I had no idea what I was walking into, but I deserved anything and everything she planned to throw in my face. I hoped it was only words and not a frying pan.

I readied myself at the side door, calming my nerves before walking in. The last thing I wanted was to wake

Stella. The fact that Gina was awake was already bad enough. Waking our little girl would only make matters worse.

The knob twisted freely in my hand, a sign that she wasn't angry enough to make me struggle with my keys in the dark. I opened the door into the darkened kitchen, the soft glow of Gina's reading lamp illuminating through the threshold from the living room. I closed the door and immediately heard her place her book down on the small table beside her favorite chair. I slowly shuffled my way to the opening of the living room, my face showing the regret of a broken man. I expected little sympathy.

I stepped into the living room, peering at Gina, her arms crossed about her chest, and expected a hushed argument to begin. Instead, I received a sorrowful stare.

"I don't want us to be like this," she stated tenderly. "We can't. I know you're dealing with a lot, and I can't expect you to make it all disappear like it doesn't exist just because I wish it didn't. It's unfair of me to think you can do that. But it goes both ways, Mick. You can't be bringing that home to our little girl. I need to know that you're okay. Please tell me you're okay so we can move forward. And if you're not – if you need time by yourself to sort things out – we can make arrangements."

"I don't want to be like this either," I responded. "And I'm good now. I mean, I'm better. I'll *be* better."

"Promise?"

"I promise. You and Stella are everything to me."

She gave me a look of forgiveness, and I felt myself battling to prevent my eyes from watering.

"We'd better be," she said, curling her lips into a smile.

If I could have captured that moment and stored it away for times when I needed..,

"So, where have you been?" she asked.

,..I'd be pulling it out of storage right now.

I had no choice; I couldn't keep it from her. She needed to hear it from me before she heard it from someone else.

"I...I was at the hospital."

Gina sat forward in her chair, alarmed.

"What? Why? What's going on? Are you hurt?"

"No, it wasn't for me."

"Then why; who?" she questioned, still concerned.

"I did something tonight," I said, peeling my eyes from her in shame. "I...hurt someone."

"What? How?"

"It was after I left you and Rosa," I replied. "I was angry with myself, and I couldn't stop thinking about this case, what it was doing to me. It was in my head, and it was burning me up. Then, on the way home, some punk threw a drink at my windshield, and I lost it. I was so furious. I didn't know what I was doing until I had the kid on the ground, pounding on him."

"You beat up a kid?" she questioned, her voice raised.

I closed my eyes and nodded, unable to process my reasoning. The words hit me harder when coming from someone else.

"I mean, he was like in his early twenties."

"Like that makes a difference?"

"No, of course not. I was just..,"

"Babe, how much trouble are you in?"

"I'm not in any trouble. I mean, nobody knows about it. I didn't tell anybody."

"Mick!" she screeched softly. "That poor boy. You can't hide this. You have to tell someone. Tell Frank. He'll understand."

"I know, I know. I planned on telling him first thing in the morning. But..,"

"But what?"

"Gina, I could get in a lot of trouble."

"What kind of trouble?" she asked.

I shrugged my shoulders. "I'm not sure. It could be bad."

"Then you can't wait, Mick," she said louder. "You gotta call Frank *now*. Tell him what you did before it's worse. He'll know what to do."

The worst part was I knew she was right, but I was still looking for excuses.

"It's almost eleven o'clock," I argued. "He'll be sleeping."

"Then wake him up."

I wasn't going to win this argument. The truth was, deep down, I didn't *want* to. I needed to step up – to accept whatever was coming to me. It would only take a single phone call. But I was afraid. Not so much for myself - I could handle whatever the consequences. I was more worried about Gina and the baby. How much mud would I be dragging them through? The public wouldn't see it as the actions of only an overstressed, out-of-control cop. The family always took the heat right alongside. How could I do that to them? What was I thinking? I'd always done everything to protect them, but now, when the shit was about to hit the fan, they were going to get caught in the splatter. It wasn't fair, and it was all my fault. I was a piece of garbage.

"Mick!" Gina exclaimed again. She meant business.

My shoulders dropped, and I pulled my cell from my pocket. I pulled up Frank's number and stared at the screen for a few seconds before pressing the call button. Maybe I'd get lucky, and he'd sleep through it. That thought quickly faded when the ringing stopped, replaced with a terse, "This had better be important."

"Frank, it's Mick," I began. "Sorry to bother you. There's something I gotta tell you."

Chapter 25

Visiting Hours Are Over

Are the nights ever going to get easy again? Maybe in time. For now, I should expect many more restless nights. Although enough bourbon or scotch could help alleviate that predicament.

The night before, Frank kept me on the phone for over an hour, trying to sort out the details of what I'd done. As expected, he wasn't happy, but it was in my best interest to come clean, even at the expense of losing my job. He did his best to assure me that wouldn't happen. He'd dealt with a similar situation a few years back when Jimmy got a little rough with an uncooperative homicide suspect, an incident that ended in an unfortunate hospital stay for the suspected perp. I hadn't heard anything about that particular happening until Frank came clean with me about their little cover-up. He told me not to sweat it - nobody else knew about it, either. He knew how to protect his officers from IA nightmares. The difference was Jimmy beat a suspect everyone knew was a cold-blooded killer – a man later convicted and sentenced to twelve years in prison. I beat an innocent kid. Well, maybe not innocent, but far from deserving the punishment I dished out. And now, as I'd found myself in a closed-door meeting with Lieutenant Garrett, it wasn't going away.

"We're going to make this go away," Frank grunted, standing behind his desk and pointing his finger at me.

"Maybe it *shouldn't* go away, Lieutenant," I responded. "I put a kid in the hospital."

"You're right; maybe it shouldn't," he said. "But that's what's going to happen. There are more important things going on in this city than some punk getting roughed up by a cop. We've got a sadistic killer out there, and I'm not going to lose one of my detectives over it. And I wouldn't lose any sleep over it if I were you. I had the kid checked out. Roderick Bagoli. He's got a list of misdemeanors as long as my arm, including assault charges. The kid was obviously looking to start something. If it wasn't you driving by last night, it would have been somebody else. Who knows how that would have turned out? Hell, you probably did him a favor. For all we know, he was next on The Letter Man's list. But I'm telling you this right now - you *will* be spending time with the department shrink. The last thing we need right now is an officer losing his shit."

"But Lieutenant, I still don't think I should..,"

Special Agent Hayes' voice rang out from behind me as she barged through the door. "Don't think you should...what?"

Frank immediately jumped in.

"Jesus Christ! Doesn't anyone know how to knock around here? We were just discussing Mick bringing the killer's latest note to Ben to see what he has to say."

"Oh, and you don't think you should, Detective?" Hayes questioned.

I looked at Frank, who gave me an ever-so-subtle shake of his head. I wanted to come clean – to tell Hayes what I had done, but maybe Frank was right. If I said something now, Hayes would have no choice but to have me removed from the case. I'd be Internal Affairs' poster child for weeks, and the force would lose another resource. My focus needed to be on The Letter Man.

"I don't know," I replied, hiding my guilt. "I don't know if bringing any of this to Ben is helping."

"Where is this coming from?" Hayes asked. "After your last visit, you said Ben was finally opening up and giving you helpful information. Didn't he tell us it would be in our best interest to focus our efforts on victims L through O if we wanted to learn the killer's motives?"

"Yeah, but..,"

"'But' nothing, Detective," she interjected. "As far as I'm concerned, we use him as long as he's willing to help. I'd have my own agents in there grilling him if I thought it would get us any closer to catching the twisted fucker, but I know it wouldn't work. He trusts *you*. No, I think Lieutenant Garrett is right. Bring the Q note to Ben. Let's see what he has to say."

I looked at her sternly, wanting to put my foot down and refuse. It would be a wasted effort; she wouldn't budge from her stance. Frank was already going to bat for me over my previous night's screw-up; I couldn't ask him to do it twice in one day. I had no other choice.

"Fine," I answered. "But I'm not happy about it."

"Like the rest of us, Detective," Hayes responded, "you don't get paid to be happy, so get over yourself."

I glared at Frank, hoping he'd have something positive to say.

"Don't look at me," he said, raising his hands to his chest defensively, "I'm married. I haven't been happy in thirty-one years." He let out a disingenuous chuckle.

I should have known better than to expect more.

"Great!" Hayes responded. "I'll contact the warden to let him know you'll be coming."

"Yeah, great," I repeated sarcastically, stepping by her to remove myself from Frank's office.

* * *

It wasn't that I didn't appreciate Ben's insight into the murders. We were getting desperate, and anything beneficial he could provide might bring us one step closer to ending the killer's reign of terror. But after last night, I felt I was becoming someone else. I didn't know if I could stomach it anymore. The more time I spent with Ben, the more it seemed I was losing a part of myself. And, as I stared at the guard watching over me from his post at the doorway, I wondered how much *he* had lost, being among the inmates day in and day out.

I lowered my eyes to the plastic baggie on the table, the note within displaying more stains of red than its natural color. Though still legible, the lines of black ink bled across the paper, making the words more difficult to read. It didn't matter; the blood told enough of the story.

"Well, look who's returned," a voice came out of nowhere, causing me to look up. "And here I thought I said something to offend you."

Ben was escorted into the room by another guard I hadn't seen before. He painstakingly maneuvered his way over to my table, his ankles outfitted in the usual shackles, his wrists cuffed at his waist.

"Yeah, it's been a couple of months," I said, nodding. "You're looking better than when last I saw you."

"What can I say?" he responded, standing across from me. "I've worked things out with the hired help."

"Yeah, that last guy seemed a little hotheaded. Where is he?" Who was I to judge? I beat up a young man because of a soft drink.

"Oh, ah," Ben began, spinning to face his handler so the guard could uncuff his wrists, "he had a little accident."

I was sure I knew what he meant, but I didn't want to know badly enough to ask him. Yet another dark secret I'd choose to stow away and compartmentalize.

Once the cuffs were off, Ben slid into his seat, and the guard backed away, keeping his eyes trained on his ward. Ben immediately pointed to the sealed bag in front of me.

"Do you see what I see?" he softly sang to the familiar holiday tune. "You know, I wrote that in one of *my* notes. I thought it was clever at the time. Now it just sounds so.., trite."

"Yeah, whatever," I returned.

"I saw on the news that there'd been another slaying. I was wondering when you were going to bring me something. That must be the Q letter if I'm not mistaken."

I slid the bag across the table. "It's Q," I replied. "Same deal as before; the bag stays sealed."

He grinned. "Of course."

I watched his eyes travel back and forth across the paper, taking in the killer's words. When he was through, he placed the bag back on the table and slid it back to me, his face lacking its usual flippancy.

"You guys are fucked!" he stated, letting out a breath.

"Why do you say that?" I asked.

"The guy is pissed," he answered. "He graduated himself to the large Alpha letter. I feel like something's happened. What am I missing? What *aren't* you showing me?"

The kid was good. I purposely kept the other note tucked away in my pocket to see if he was as intuitive as he claimed to be. I guess he was. I pulled the second note out, the first we received after the killer's hiatus, and slammed it on the table.

"You little fucker; how did you know?"

"For one, you had a smug look on your face like this was a test. Second, I wouldn't suspect the killer – a man who's been in control from the start – to suddenly go from 0-300 without something setting him off."

He reached forward about three-quarters of the way to the ziplocked bag, froze, and looked up at me to see my eyes trained on his every movement. A cocky look returned to his face.

"May I?" he asked. "I mean, I'm assuming you took it out for a reason?"

I nodded, straight-faced.

He extended his reach the rest of the way and snagged the plastic evidence baggie from the table. After quickly scanning the words, he gently placed the note on the table and began rubbing his hand across the top of the plastic as if trying to iron out the many wrinkles along its surface.

"Well?" I questioned.

He raised his eyes to me, his expression deadpan. "He's lying."

"What do you mean?" I asked.

"He didn't have bigger plans for Peter. We've been over this before. He accomplished what he wanted; he was caught in the act. For what reason is something I'm sure you'll work out. I'll tell you this, though.., he's upset that his deeds are unappreciated. And for that, he's upping his game. I'd be careful if I were you."

"Why is that?"

"He wants to punish those most deserving for their crimes, but he's progressing. He's not afraid to hurt others – even innocent lives – to get what he wants."

"So you think his threat is real?"

"Get in his way and find out," Ben leered. "But you'd better have backup."

I grabbed the note from in front of him and stacked it on top of the first.

"I take it victim Q was in no condition to tell you a tale," he continued.

"The victim.., Quinn, was dismembered," I informed him. "His limbless torso was tossed in the tub, along with the note now decorated with his blood. The killer lined up all of Quinn's body parts, including his head, in a neat little formation for us to see."

"Well, that's a little much," Ben said.

"Tell me about it."

"So, where was the last victim?" he asked.

"In his apartment."

"Good to know. I meant, which city?"

"Larson."

"Then, that's where your killer's from."

"We figured that already," I remarked.

"Great job, Detective," he said mockingly, clapping his hands like he was at a golf tournament. "Did you also figure out his original intended target was a Larson resident? That should help narrow it down a little."

"What makes you so sure of that?" I questioned.

"Oh.., just a hunch."

"If you know something more..,"

"How could I possibly know more?" he answered smugly. "I only know and see what you and the news share with me."

"Then stop with the games, pretending you know more than you do."

"Am I playing games, Mick? I thought I was trying to help you. You should be more fucking appreciative. Now I understand where that other guy is coming from."

"I should have known coming here was a mistake," I remarked, scooping up the notes and putting them away in my pocket. "You're nothing but a waste of my time."

"Oh really? Maybe you should take a closer look at the victims – the ones I told you to focus on - and figure out which murder was different from the others."

"Different from the others, huh?"

"That's right. If what you've shared with me is accurate, then there's something about one of the deceased that the killer did differently from any of his other victims."

"They've *all* been different," I said.

"Well then," Ben said, his head tilted, "I don't think you're looking close enough."

"Cut the shit, Ben. Why don't you tell me what you think you know?"

"Hey, I told you," he responded with an arrogant grin, "I don't know anything. I mean, let's face it, if I were smart, I wouldn't have been caught."

"You know something?" I added. "You're right. You're not that smart. You insist on pushing away the one friend you've got. Well, I'll tell you what, you don't have to push anymore."

I stood from my seat, staring down at Ben.

"Coming here was a mistake from the start. You, this place.., it's not the best for one's frame of mind."

"Come on, Mick," Ben stated, a touch of nervousness in his voice, "sit down. I'm just playing."

"No, Ben. I mean it, I'm done. I have no reason to come back here."

"You've said that before."

"Well, I won't say it again."

"Mick..,"

"See ya, kid."

I nodded to the Corrections Officer who had escorted me in and turned toward the door behind me.

"Mick, come on," Ben pleaded.

I continued walking.

"Mick!" he yelled.

I didn't bother to look back. The guard caught up with me and led me out of the room. I heard a final fading comment as we headed down the hallway.

"You're all I've got left."

Was I supposed to feel bad? I didn't. Should I have stayed longer? I wouldn't. I meant what I said. For my sanity, for the sake of my family, I couldn't keep doing this. I gave the little prick a chance, and he blew it. There's plenty of regret to go around. It shouldn't only be me who feels it. Now he can live with some.

I'm sure Frank will understand. And if I have to, I'll *make* Hayes understand. All of this was *my* idea, after all. I gave the kid a shot; it didn't work out. Now, I'll have to do it my way.

It's time I became the detective I'm supposed to be.

Chapter 26

The Puzzle

When I returned to the station, I couldn't help but notice the second, large black SUV with government plates parked in the lot. That could only mean one thing, and it didn't bode well.

With word of the latest victim being broadcast on every news station and social media outlet, it was only a matter of time before Washington sent their obedient pet back here to Southbridge. I could only hope he was less rabid this time around.

I walked into the Detective Bureau to the sound of muffled arguing coming from the briefing room. Everyone was doing their best to pretend not to be listening, but their uncomfortable stares and uncharacteristic shuffling of papers around their desks told the tale. I saw Frank sitting in his office, his head hung down, his forehead perched between his thumb and index finger, while his other hand squeezed the phone to his ear. He was either being discreet about prying or the only one doing actual work. Whichever it was, I knew better than to inter-

243

rupt. I glanced over at Detective Frazier, whose desk was closest to the briefing room. He was rearranging the contents of his desk drawer. His actions would have been more convincing if he'd ever taken such initiative in the past. That, and the fact that I just watched him move a stapler back and forth several times inside the drawer before it finally landed back in its original location, was a clear sign of his eavesdropping. And since he'd have heard more than the others, he was my target.

"Yo, Frazier," I quietly voiced, stepping beside his desk. "What's going on?" I slung my chin sideways, signaling toward the briefing room.

"Special Agent 'stick up my ass' came back, thinking he was going to re-take the case," he explained. "Special Agent Hayes had a few choice words about that. They've been at it for the past fifteen minutes. Chief Copelli's in there, too, trying to smooth things over."

"Just what we needed," I responded sarcastically. "Gunner charging in here with both guns blazing. Is he even capable of checking his ego at the door?"

Frazier rolled his eyes just as the briefing room door flung open. Chief Copelli peeked his head out.

"Ah, Dooley," he barked, "you *are* here. Get your goddamn ass in here. And grab Lieutenant Garrett on your way. He's joining us as well."

"He's on the phone," I replied.

"I don't care if he's on the phone or on the shitter, for Christ's sake. Get him in here. Now!"

I responded with, "Yes sir," but it was to a closed door by the time the words came out.

"Sounds like you're in for it now, buddy-boy," Frazier harassed. "It was nice knowing you."

I shook my head at his comment and let out a slight huff. It wasn't like Chief Copelli to raise his voice. I wondered what it could be about. Did Frank come forward about my previous night's outburst? Fuck!

I walked to Frank's open door and knocked on the side casing to get his attention. He tilted his head up, displaying his usual annoyed expression.

"What?" he snapped.

"Chief Copelli is requesting you in the briefing room," I answered.

"Can't you see I'm on the phone, Dooley?"

"He made it clear that he didn't care, Lieu. He wants us both in there now."

"Jesus Christ!" he yelled. "What now?" He waved his hand to shoo me away. "I'll be right behind you."

I hoped that was true as I walked away. I did what I could, but Frank was often too stubborn to get out of his own way. He was a grown man; he could make his own decisions. If he wanted the Chief breathing down his neck, so be it.

I opened the briefing room door to the three occupants fiercely staring at me. I threw my thumb over my shoulder as I stepped inside.

"Lieutenant Garrett will be right in."

"I'm right here," the lieutenant's voice rang out from behind me, holding his arm out to prevent me from closing the door on him.

"Good," Chief Copelli stated as Frank slipped through the open door. He barely managed to get it closed before Chief Copelli laid into us.

"Would you two care to explain this business about delivering sensitive evidence about The Letter Man case to the Haddick boy?"

We both shot Agent Hayes a curious glare. She offered a cold stare in return.

Frank's upper lip twinged before he started in with an explanation.

"I thought it would..,"

"No!" I jumped in. "I appreciate Lieutenant Garrett stepping in like that, but it was *my* idea. I thought Ben could help us understand the killer's thought processes since he was the one who started the whole thing. He said he'd do what he could to help, but only if we provided him with the killer's notes. We'd gotten everything we could from them, so I figured it couldn't hurt."

"Oh, you figured it couldn't hurt, did you?" the Chief said. "And what about you?" he asked, turning to Frank. "What's *your* role in all of this?"

Frank's eyes narrowed, peering at Agent Hayes as if waiting for her to speak up. When she didn't, he turned his attention to Chief Copelli, whose arms were folded in front of his chest while the fingers of his right hand tapped impatiently on his left bicep.

"My role is as it has been through this entire investigation," Frank answered. "We're doing all we can to catch a sadistic killer. If one of my men comes to me with an idea that could lead us in the right direction, no matter how much it strays from the norm, I'm not going to turn my nose up at it. The way I see it, it's better than sitting here with our thumbs up our asses, waiting for the guy to strike again."

"Did it ever occur to either of you," Agent Lowe responded, "that Ben could be feeding information to someone on the outside?"

"He's not," I shot out.

"Maybe not directly," Lowe continued, "but who knows who he's telling inside those walls. Any one of those incarcerated felons could be slipping breadcrumbs to the murderer, and *you're* in there, delivering the whole goddamn loaf to him."

"I think you've been watching too many movies," I returned snarkily. "Ben's only reading the notes and providing his insight. Do you honestly think feeding the killer information about the grotesque details of his kills is going to help the killer? He already knows what he's done."

"I think you underestimate today's criminal, Detective," Lowe replied.

"All right, all right, gentlemen," Chief Copelli jumped in, stepping between me and the encroaching Agent Lowe. "Listen," he said, directing his comment at me, "I understand you did what you thought was right. We're all under a lot of pressure here, and having no solid leads doesn't help, but this extra-curricular activity stops now. If I didn't need every available officer on this, I'd have you both relegated to desk duty."

"It doesn't matter now, anyway," I spoke up. "I told Ben I wasn't going back."

"And why is that, Detective?" Lowe questioned.

"He was playing games - answering my questions with riddles."

"What kind of riddles?" Agent Hayes finally joined in, acting as if she hadn't known about my clandestine meetings with Ben. All my respect for her went out the window with that move. There was no need for her to cower down that way.

"I think I'd prefer to share those details with Chief Copelli when not in the presence of the FBI," I stated.

"Well, I think you've forgotten this is a federal investigation," Lowe took pleasure in reminding me. "So, I don't care what you prefer, Dooley. You'll be sharing those details with us right *now*."

As much as I wasn't on his most cherished list of officers, I looked to Chief Copelli for support. He wasn't offering any.

"Well, come on now, Detective," he said, "let's hear it."

"Ben told me if we wanted to understand the killer, we should be concentrating our efforts on victims L through O."

"And why is that?" Chief Copelli asked.

"He thinks one of them was the killer's original target. He then told me that one of those murders was different than the others, and when we figure out what that difference is, that's the person for whom we should be taking a closer look."

"They were *all* killed differently," Hayes chimed in.

"That's what *I* said; he said I wasn't looking close enough."

"Then he's full of shit," Lowe blurted.

"I said that too."

"Now, hold on a minute," Agent Hayes stated. "Let's assume for a moment Ben is onto something."

"Oh, come on, Agent Hayes," Lowe bellowed. "You're not actually feeding into that kid's bullshit."

"As much as I hate to admit it," Frank jumped in, "I'd have to agree with Agent Hayes. It can't hurt to take a closer look."

"You talked with the boy," Chief Copelli said, placing his hand on my shoulder, "what do you think? Could Ben know more than what he's letting on?"

I shrugged my shoulders, "I mean, he's a smart kid. There were times when it seemed he was genuinely trying to help, but then he'd make certain comments about the victims that sickened me. I don't know if he knows anything or if he was blowing smoke up my ass."

"What is your gut telling you, son?" the Chief asked.

I thought about those words. Jimmy used to tell me relying on his gut was sometimes better than doing actual police work. I tried listening to mine, thinking of what the kid told me and how he acted. He *did* seem to know things. Maybe *his* gut was like his old man's. If that were true, perhaps we should start listening.

"I think we should take a look," I conceded.

"That's good enough for me," the Chief accepted.

"Okay," Hayes began, "so let's think about how the victims were killed."

"Are we actually entertaining this idea?" Lowe complained.

"Humor us," Hayes replied, striding to an available whiteboard on a nearby wall.

"Lyden Foster was dismembered and posed," Frank quickly jumped in before Lowe could argue further.

Hayes jotted his response down on the board.

"Matthew Lynch was nailed to a tree and had an axe embedded in his skull," I stated, looking around at the others.

"Nancy had letter openers shoved into her eye sockets," Frank said, shaking his head in disgust.

"And Oliver was strangled with a rope," Hayes added, frantically compiling their thoughts into barely legible written words.

"All of the murders involved sharp weapons except for Oliver's," Frank said. "Could that be it?"

"Only one was dismembered," Lowe joined in.

"Actually, Oliver's legs were cut off," I responded.

"Wait, does that disqualify Oliver, then?" Frank asked.

"Fuck if I know."

"What else is there?" Hayes questioned, pausing with her hand raised against the board, ready to transcribe.

"Two were inside, two were outside," I answered.

"That doesn't help then, does it?" Frank said.

"I'm just throwing things out there. Ben said the killer did something differently with one victim compared to all the rest."

"*All* the rest?" Chief Copelli asked. "Or just the four?"

"I don't know; I think all of them."

"Two were sitting," Hayes added. "One standing, one lying down."

"Nancy was the only one that didn't have something cut off her," Frank said, grasping at straws.

"Peter didn't either," Hayes responded.

"Does he count?" Frank questioned. "The killer didn't finish."

"Ben thinks he did and that it was all for show."

"It could be anything," Lowe stated in aggravation. "We don't know what we're looking for, so we're seeing what we want to see."

"Wait, wait," I jumped in excitedly. "Ben seemed confident that the killer was after a Larson resident."

"If that were true, that would narrow it down to Matthew or Oliver," Hayes said.

"I'm telling you," Frank grumbled, "it's Oliver."

"But what about the legs?" I questioned.

"Shit. I forgot about that," he answered.

"What are we missing?" I questioned rhetorically, rubbing my forehead.

"Matthew was found naked," Hayes answered, "but then, so was Quinn."

"This is what the case has become?" Lowe snapped in frustration. "Oliver was the only one killed by strangulation. Matthew was the only one killed standing up. Is this really what we're investigating?"

"Wait a minute," I said, putting a finger up while I thought things through. "Ben said, 'Differently than all the others.' I can think of one thing, for sure, that was different for one victim than any of the others."

"What's that?" the Chief asked.

"Outside."

"We just went over this," Hayes said. "Both Matthew and Oliver were found outside."

"That's true," I nodded. "But only one was *killed* outside. All of the victims except Matthew were killed indoors - including Oliver. His body was later dumped at the cemetery."

"You think that could be it?" Hayes asked.

"He was out in the open, stripped naked with a tree branch stuck up his ass, in an area where any hiker could have come across him. The killer didn't only want him dead; he wanted to humiliate him."

"Punishment for molesting those boys," Frank agreed, nodding. "Seems plausible."

"If that's the case, then we have to get those boys and their parents in here for questioning," Hayes said. "Any one of them could be our killer."

"Did we track them all down?" Lowe asked.

"All but two of them," Hayes replied.

"Then we need to keep looking," Chief Copelli stated. "Lieutenant - contact the Larson PD. Explain the situation and ask them to bring in the Matthew Lynch victims and their families. Detective Dooley, you do the same with the Southbridge victims."

Agent Hayes interjected, "Special Agent Lowe and I will take another shot at locating the remaining two boys – see if we can dig something up."

"Good," Chielf Copelli said. "Maybe we're finally getting somewhere. Let's go, then."

He clapped his hands together like he was the coach of a little league team, psyching his players up before a game. Strangely, at least for me, it worked. I felt excited about where this was leading. Maybe it was because I contributed something positive for a change. That, and the fact I still had a job.

Just as I opened the door, Hayes called out, "Hang on." She was holding her phone in her hand, looking at the screen. "Chief Sutton is calling *now*."

I closed the door.

"This is Special Agent Hayes," she answered. "What? When? And you're sure..? Right. Got it. We're on our way."

She hung up and displayed a cold stare.

"Looking for the boys will have to wait," she said. "They just found another body."

Chapter 27

R

I hitched a ride with the Feds to the scene. I thought being in the back seat would be more comfortable than the front for the simple fact that the two agents would have no choice but to bicker with each other, leaving me out of it. I thought I'd gotten away with it, the way Agent Lowe started questioning Agent Hayes almost immediately.

"You think I don't know you had something to do with those secretive meetings with Ben?" he said to Hayes. "These yahoos wouldn't have thought of that on their own."

"I'm right here, asshole," I said.

He ignored my comment and continued. "You might as well come clean before the Deputy Director hears about it. You already know you're not his favorite person right now. You've been on his shit list since whatever that crap was you pulled a couple of years back; this might be the thing that pushes you over that cliff you've been dangling from."

"And how would the Deputy Director hear about it?" Hayes questioned.

Lowe turned to her and gave her a smirk, letting her know his intentions should she step out of line again. I didn't know what Hayes' issues with her bosses were or what she did to get on their bad side, but Lowe made it painfully clear that he would have no trouble using that ammunition against her. I'm sure that was payback for her earlier threats against him.

"How did you know?" she succumbed.

It was a simple enough question that somehow opened the door for Lowe to drag me into the conversation.

"You think these bozos would have the wherewithal to do anything on their own without getting someone's approval first?"

He stated that purposefully loud enough to provoke me. It worked.

"Hey, fuck you!" I shouted. "I was going to see Ben with or without someone's approval."

"If you think that murderous punk had any intention of helping with the case, then you're a lousy detective, Dooley." He shot me a glare in the rearview mirror.

"Well, you're a lousy agent," I retorted.

Wow, what a zinger, I thought. *That's the way to hit him where it hurts, Mick.*

"As far as I'm concerned," I continued, hoping to redeem myself from the lousy comeback, "that kid has given us more insight into the killer in only a few meetings than you have since you first strut into town with your boots and spurs."

"Can you two give it a rest?" Hayes yelled. "I feel like I'm babysitting, for crying out loud. What's done is done.

It's in the past. Special Agent Lowe – if you feel you need to report me to the Deputy Director, then do it; but do it *after* we catch this son of a bitch. Until then, can we please focus on our current situation?"

I heard Lowe let out a displeased huff before sinking into his seat. I was more vocal about it, replying with a pouty "fine" as I crossed my arms about my chest and stared out the side window. The rest of the trip remained silent. So much for the backseat being more comfortable.

Ours was the sixth vehicle to arrive at the intended destination, behind three cruisers, the Larson police forensic van, and a channel 33 news van, whose crew was setting up down the street. As I exited the SUV, I read the sign on the exterior of the building – DeMarkis Garage, 187 McKinstry Street, an out-of-the-way garage on a dead-end street. Parked in the small empty lot in front was a shiny, black Corvette – one of my favorite vehicles I'd never have an opportunity to own. Along the front face of the building were three large bay doors, one of them open. Inside, four uniformed officers were standing over Chief Forensic Officer Shane, who, himself, was crouching over a body lying under a partially dismantled Ford Mustang Shelby. Two others, wearing navy-colored CSI jackets, were slowly, methodically making their way around the vehicle from opposite directions.

As the agents and I walked by one of the parked cruisers, I noticed a bearded man in the back seat, glaring at us through beady eyes, his hands cuffed behind his back, and his heated breath steaming up the rear door window. Was it him? Was it finally over?

The three of us stepped into the garage to join with the others. I could feel the tension in the air as soon as we entered through the bay door as the Larson officers stared at us side-eyed before parting to give the agents a better look at the crime scene. It wasn't what we'd first thought.

From a distance, it appeared the body was lying under the car as if he were doing an oil change. Now that we were closer, we saw that wasn't the case. The vehicle's front driver's side tire was gone, and the man's abdomen was pinned under the wheel hub, crushed by the vehicle's weight, its rusted rotor digging into his flesh. His left pant leg below his knee was covered in blood, his shin crushed, only not by the Shelby. Lying on the concrete floor near the rear tire, flagged by a yellow A-frame evidence marker, a blood-spattered sledgehammer - the chosen weapon. Another evidence marker sat beside a jack stand ten feet to our left, dented and tipped on its side. A few feet farther, a third A-frame on the floor marked the location of a firearm. Smeared in blood on the driver's side door was the letter R. It was situated just above what appeared to be a bullet hole, no doubt fired from the same gun.

I glanced to the right of the Shelby, where, in the next bay, the body of a bright yellow Porche was half-stripped down to its frame. In front of the Shelby, parked perpendicular to it along the far wall, was a silver Pontiac GTO up on four jack stands, its tires removed. If I were a betting man, I'd say we stumbled upon some illicit activity. DeMarkis Garage looked more like a front for an illegal chop shop operation than a legitimate garage.

"What's the story on this one?" Agent Lowe questioned just as I heard another vehicle pulling up out front.

"He's dead if that's what you were wondering," Shane answered. "The victim's name is Ronan, if we're to believe the name patch on his shirt. Why wouldn't we, right? He's got no ID on him, but the garage *is* owned by Ronan De-Markis, along with his brother Salvatore. It looks like Ronan here was working under the car when the killer first took a sledgehammer to his leg. I'd say just for the fun of it. He then whacked the jack stand out from under the frame, dropping the car onto the unlucky bastard. The victim didn't die right away, probably wishing he had. While he was trapped and in excruciating pain, the killer would have taken several more swings at Ronan's leg to cause the kind of damage you're seeing."

"Jesus!" I gasped audibly. "But you caught the son of a bitch," I stated loudly with excitement, throwing my thumb over my shoulder at the parked cruiser outside the door.

"That's not the killer," a familiar voice cried out from behind us.

Detective Murcur took his sweet time strolling in.

"That's a two-bit car thief," he continued, "looking to score some easy cash. I've been on the case for months. Toby Dertich. He's a low-life cog in a much larger boost ring. I've been surveilling him for some time now, but he's always managed to elude me before I could find out the location of his drop-off point. I guess we're standing in it now."

"And I suppose he eluded you tonight, too, since you're just now getting here," I said snarkily.

"I had the day off, asshole," he replied. "We get those now and again. I came here out of the goodness of my heart. You're welcome."

He gave me a sarcastic grin.

Agent Hayes turned her body to face him, her arms crossed and a suspicious look in her eyes. "And what makes you think your car thief isn't the killer?" she questioned.

"Oh look," the detective responded with his lip curled, "the bitch is back."

Agent Lowe immediately stepped between Hayes and Murcur. I watched his nose wrinkle and his cheeks flare out as he tightened his jaw.

"What did you just say?" Lowe asked through clenched teeth.

Murcur replied, "I don't believe we've met. Who the fuck are you? Based on the matching stick up your ass, you must be another Washington blowhard."

"I'm Special Agent Gunner Lowe, smartass. I'm the one in charge of this investigation. You'd better watch yourself, Detective. If you ever disrespect one of my agents again, I'll have you working security at the local elementary school as their newest resource officer. There; now we've met, shithead. Any other comments you'd care to make?"

Murcur shook his head and sneered. "Not really."

"Good."

Lowe turned back to the four officers. "Now then, how did we end up here?"

One of the officers straightened up, raising his chin to speak. "We'd gotten a call to be on the lookout for a stolen Corvette. It was stolen only ten minutes earlier from the downtown parking garage. My partner and I happened to be patrolling this area and passed by what appeared to be the suspected vehicle turning down McKinstry. We turned around to get confirmation. By the time we got here, the vehicle was already parked out front. It was still running with no driver in sight, so we figured he must have gone inside. Just as we parked, the suspect burst from the garage door, panicked and sweaty, his face looking like he'd just seen a ghost. We apprehended him before he could get back to the 'Vette. He kept mumbling, going on about how he '*didn't have anything to do with it.*' When we told him we knew he'd stolen the car, he said he wasn't talking about that. He said, '*In there. I had nothing to do with that.*' We threw him in the backseat of the cruiser and then checked out what he was rambling on about. We had no idea we'd be walking into a homicide."

"Did anyone question Mr. Dertich out there?" Lowe asked.

"Yes, sir," the officer replied. "Considering the alternative charges, he didn't mind telling us he was scouring the downtown parking garage for over an hour, looking to lift a vehicle."

"And, of course, there's nobody to confirm that," Hayes stated.

"Nobody has to," Shane stated, standing from his position. "The body tells the story. Well, part of it. Your car thief tells the rest."

"How do you mean?" I asked, watching his team fan out to comb the rest of the garage.

"If you look here," Shane bent down and pulled up the lower portion of Ronan's shirt to expose his side, "you'll notice darkened patches on the victim's skin. That's blood pooling. In time, about two to four hours after death, those patches begin to join, creating larger purplish areas. That hasn't happened yet. The body's still flaccid and warm. I'd say he hasn't been dead for two hours."

"And exactly how does that absolve that scumbag out there?" I inquired a second time.

"Well," Shane continued, "assuming the gun and the bullet hole in the door played a part in this whole mess, we already checked him for gunshot residue; he's clean. We also checked his clothes for blood spatter. You can see how the blood spots came off the crushed leg in this direction. The killer would have been standing here, taking his swings at the leg. He would have been right in the path of the spray coming back at him. Mr. Dertich has no sign of blood on him at all. Now, you're probably asking yourself, '*What does that mean?*' Well, he would have had to change clothes, wash himself up, get to the parking garage downtown, steal the car, drive back here, and for what reason? To risk getting caught? He'd have known he wasn't getting paid. The timeframe doesn't work. He didn't kill anybody. Though if he'd gotten here ten, maybe fifteen minutes earlier than he had, he might have walked in on the killer."

"Then we'd have *two* dead bodies on our hands," Detective Murcur chimed in.

"I'm afraid we already do," one of Shane's men yelled out from across the garage, standing in front of the wheel-less GTO. He was peering into the rear passenger window while waving us over. "You're going to want to see this."

Chapter 28

S

They huddled around the open door like excited kids in front of the chimpanzee enclosure at the local zoo, hoping to be the first to catch a glimpse of something they hadn't seen before. I was content standing in the back. It was always those in front who were in the most danger of having monkey shit flung at them. Unfortunately, no matter how much you tried to avoid it, when enough shit was hurled in your direction, some of the splatter was bound to hit you.

"Dooley, get over here," Special Agent Lowe demanded. "And, Jesus Christ, will the rest of you officers back away and give us some breathing room? Somebody shut the bay door before the news crew outside gets any funny ideas. The last thing the public needs are images of a dead body being plastered all over the evening news."

The uniformed officers scattered, parting like the Red Sea under Moses' command, giving me a clear view of the dead body in the back seat. I didn't just get the splatter; the entire mound of feces hit me in the face.

Detective Murcur remained, as he was the Larson detective assigned to the case. Special Agents Lowe and Hayes were the leads on the investigation. They had no choice. Me? I shouldn't have even been here. But for some God-forsaken reason, Hayes thought it best if I tagged along. I was mentally prepared for one body. I hadn't prepared myself for a second.

The feeling came upon me in an instant. I felt my insides churn, and I became lightheaded. Instinctively, I bent over, propping one hand against the top of my knee to hold me up while the other went to my forehead to wipe away the cold, clammy sweat that had instantly formed.

"Oh, shit," Murcur blurted. "Just what we need, a detective with a weak stomach. If you're going to throw up, Dooley, do it somewhere else. I don't want any of that hitting my shoes."

"Shut the fuck up, Murcur," I managed to squeak out between the heavy breaths. "I'm fine; I just need a minute."

I took in a stunted breath, then exhaled, hoping nothing solid came out along with it.

"You going to be okay?" Hayes questioned, placing her hand gently on my upper back.

I nodded and stood upright. "Yeah, I'm good. It was just something I ate earlier; it's finally catching up with me."

"Uh huh," Murcur commented, rolling his eyes and flashing an unbelieving grin.

"So, what do we have?" I inquired, trying to prove my strong constitution while shifting the attention back to the homicide victim. It seemed to work, as all eyes turned to Shane for answers, who was standing on a step stool, leaning halfway into the backseat.

Shane responded, "Well, there's the obvious love letter attached to the lug wrench the killer used to impale our dead friend here."

He wasn't kidding. The victim was lying on his back, knees slightly bent, his head and upper back propped up against the far door. There was an L-shaped lug wrench sticking vertically from his stomach, fragments of bone, and chunks of red-stained brain matter clinging to the hexagonal socket end. Suspended three-quarters of the way up the shaft, a note dangled from its diameter, a neatly formed hole in the paper keeping it from sliding down onto the blood-soaked body. Surprisingly, there wasn't a lot of blood on the paper. The size of the hole suggests the note was on the weapon before the killer plunged it into the victim. I'm guessing the killer was holding the shaft below the note, taking most of the blood spatter on his hands instead. Real nice.

"It's too early to determine the cause of death with any certainty right now," Shane continued. "Based on the damage inflicted on the victim's face and head, the crushed skull, along with the remnants left on the lug wrench, I'd say he was bludgeoned to death. I think the impalement was just for show to get our attention."

"What the fuck is wrong with this 'Letter Man'?" Lowe blurted.

"What *isn't* wrong with him," I answered.

"There's some bruising on the victim's lower arm, as well," Shane stated, ignoring our comments, "and his wrist has been shattered."

He stopped for a moment, peered back quizzically, then mumbled, "I wonder if..,"

He shifted his eyes beyond us into the garage.

"Hey, Newman," he called to one of his crew members, "get me the GSR kit, would ya?"

"You thinking he was our gunman?" Hayes asked.

"Gun, bullet hole, broken wrist," Shane replied. "It makes sense."

"Well, who the hell is he?" Detective Murcur questioned.

Shane turned to look at the name patch on the shirt, but I already knew.

"It's Salvatore DeMarkis," I stated with confidence.

"The name says 'Sal' on his shirt," Shane confirmed.

"I don't know if this was intentional or coincidental," I spoke up, feeling I had a good grasp of what happened. "Ronan was the killer's target."

I heard Ben's voice in my head.

"The others were just collateral damage."

Then the killer's words flashed before me.

"Don't get in my way."

I felt the need to share. "Sal just got in his way."

I stepped away from the others, walking back toward the crushed victim, ready to earn my detective's pay by re-enacting the crime.

"The killer comes in and finds Ronan under the vehicle," I begin. "He thinks they're alone. Ronan doesn't immediately react to the killer's presence because he thinks it's his brother, who was probably in the office at that time." I pointed to the beige steel door located along the side wall, the words "no admittance" stenciled in black letters upon it. "The killer grabs a sledgehammer and whacks Ronan's leg. Unable to do anything from his position, Ronan screams out, but it's too late. The killer then knocks the jack stand out from under the car, crushing Ronan, and preventing him from screaming more. The sadistic fucker then begins to take the sledgehammer to Ronan's leg. Meanwhile, in the other part of the building, Salvatore hears the initial scream and comes running, but by the time he gets through the door, his brother's leg is crushed, and he's already dead or dying. He sees the killer holding the sledgehammer and runs to the tool chest where he has a gun tucked away." I point to an upright tool chest near the office door with one of its drawers conspicuously open. "The killer drops the sledgehammer." I open my hand and thrust it backward, simulating the motion of releasing the heavy tool. I then begin to sprint forward. "The killer runs at Salvatore, picking up a lug wrench off the floor along the way, and just as Salvatore points to shoot, the killer smacks his wrist with it." I swing my arm across violently. "The gun goes off, hitting the car door, Salvatore's wrist gets shattered from the blow, causing him to drop the weapon, and the killer proceeds to bludgeon him to death."

"That all sounds feasible except for one thing," Shane pointed out. "There's no blood anywhere by the office door. And I doubt the killer took the time to clean up after himself. All the blood is localized over here by the car - the seats, the door, the garage floor beneath the door. He was killed in the car."

"Okay, so the killer knocked him out by the office, then dragged him over to the car, where he laid him in the backseat. He walked over to the other side, opened the door to expose the victim's head, then did..," I pointed to the backseat, "*that* to him."

Shane lifted one of Sal's legs and studied the back of his shoe.

"Now I think you're on to something, Detective," he said. "Scuff marks at the back of his heels indicate he'd been dragged. If this whole detective gig doesn't work out for you, there's always a possible future in forensics."

"No thanks," I quickly replied, almost unable to get the words out fast enough.

Lowe spoke up, "Whatever the fuck happened, we've got two dead bodies. The killer is stepping up his game."

"It's not a game to *him*," I jumped in.

"And he's going to learn that the hard way when we catch him," Lowe added. "Officer Spencer..," he continued, turning toward Shane.

"Oh, just 'Shane' is fine, sir," the forensic officer replied.

"I want that note." Lowe pointed into the backseat.

"Oh, right," Shane complied, leaning over the dead body. "I'm on it."

"I agree with Officer Dooley on one point," Hayes began. "Ronan was the killer's chosen victim. The R on the door confirms as much. I'm not convinced, however, that Salvatore was just some unlucky victim of circumstance. It's too coincidental. R for Ronan. S for Salvatore. If this second body *was* a premeditated kill - and the letters certainly suggest it could have been - then I think we should prepare for the worst. Our guy is increasing his kill rate."

Everything she said made sense. I think I liked being in denial better.

Just then, Shane emerged from the vehicle's back door with the lug wrench in one hand and the speared note in the other.

"I did what I could to keep as much blood off the note as possible," he said, extending his hand toward Agent Lowe.

Lowe reached forward, hesitated, then gently grabbed the paper and pulled it from Shane's red-stained glove. He studied the words for a moment, then began to read aloud.

PEOPLE TAKE AND TAKE WHAT ISN'T THEIRS TO TAKE, UNCARING OF WHO OR WHAT THEY TEAR APART, ALL FOR THEIR OWN GAIN. THEY HAVE LITTLE REMORSE FOR WHOM THEY'VE TAKEN FROM. THEY CARE NOTHING FOR THE LIVES THEY'VE DESTROYED. IT WAS TIME SOMEONE TOOK SOMETHING FROM THEM – TO TEACH THEM WHAT IT'S LIKE TO HAVE THEIR LIVES TORN APART. HOW FITTING THEIR END SHOULD COME BY THE HAND OF SOMEONE WHO FEELS EVEN LESS REMORSE THAN THEY DO.

OR RATHER, THAN THEY *DID*.

DON'T LOOK FOR FINGERS OR TOES OR EARS OR TEETH; YOU WON'T FIND ANY. IF YOU MUST KNOW THE COUNT, YOU NEEDN'T LOOK ANY FURTHER THAN THE TOOL USED TO CREATE SUCH DAMAGE. FIFTEEN TIMES, S FELT MY RAGE. EIGHT FOR THE SINS OF HIS BROTHER, SEVEN FOR HIS OWN. IMAGINE HOW I FELT, LETTING OUT ALL THAT ANGER WITH EACH DEVASTATING SWING. IT DIDN'T HAVE TO BE LIKE THAT. R WAS SUCH AN EASY, CLEAN KILL. S COULD HAVE BEEN NO LESS. BUT THEN THE MISCREANT HAD TO CHANGE THE RULES AND PULL A GUN ON ME. THAT WASN'T VERY NICE. SO I WASN'T VERY NICE. CAN YOU PICTURE IT? UP AND DOWN MY ARM WENT. UP AND DOWN, UP AND DOWN, UNTIL ALL THAT WAS LEFT WAS THE MASTERFUL WORK OF ART YOU SEE BEFORE YOU. ISN'T IT MAGNIFICENT? I'D SAY THE LOWLIFE LEARNED HIS LESSON. WOULDN'T YOU?

MY WORK IS NECESSARY, MY WRATH UNRESTRAINED.

SIT BACK AND WATCH THE CARNAGE UNFOLD... JUST AS I HAVE WATCHED YOU FUMBLE WITH THE WRECKAGE I HAVE WROUGHT. I THINK YOU'LL LIKE WHAT I HAVE IN STORE. THERE ARE STILL SO MANY LESSONS TO TEACH. THEY WILL ALL LEARN.

THE HARD WAY.

MY WAY.

A

"What the hell do we do with that?" questioned Detective Murcur.

"*You* don't do anything with it, Detective," Agent Hayes answered. "The FBI will analyze the message and see what we come up with."

"The fucker certainly is pleased with his work, isn't he?" I stated, shaking my head. "He's comparing the dead bodies to artwork now."

"Well, it's certainly going to take an artist to make this guy presentable for an open casket," Shane added. "Though I wouldn't suggest it."

"So, what now?" Murcur asked, submitting to the Feds' lead.

"Now, we get these bodies to the morgue, where an official autopsy can be performed," Lowe responded. "I want every inch of this garage swept over with a fine-toothed comb. As for that piece of shit in the back of the cruiser, I want him brought to the station and processed. He'd better be ready for questioning when we arrive."

"What if he requests a lawyer?" the arresting officer asked.

"His lawyer will just have to wait until we're through with him," Lowe replied, nodding to Agent Hayes.

"You'll be wasting your time," I said. "Shane is right; he's not the killer."

"You got a better idea, Detective?" Lowe questioned, slightly annoyed at my comment.

"I keep thinking of what the killer wrote – that line about watching us fumble. Do you think he means in the literal sense?"

"Are you suggesting the killer is watching us?" Lowe questioned. "That he may have been watching us at the crime scenes?"

"I'm not suggesting anything."

"It's not uncommon for criminals to revisit the scene," Hayes stated. "Many have some twisted fascination with witnessing the outcome of their crime as seen through the eyes of an ordinary citizen."

"Yes, we're all well aware of that, Special Agent Hayes," Lowe interjected. "But most of the killer's victims have been indoors, away from the prying eyes of the public."

"Most," I jumped in, " but not all."

"So, what are you saying?" Hayes asked.

My thoughts shifted back to the peculiar person at the cemetery, staring at us through binoculars. I wanted to believe there was something there, but it had been months since the last time I saw him.

"Well, Detective?" Lowe asked.

"I'm sorry; what?"

"Special Agent Hayes asked you a question."

"Oh, yeah," I stumbled, shaking the cobwebs from my brain. "I mean, it's probably nothing."

"So then, tell us," Hayes encouraged.

"At the cemetery," I began. "The day of Karen's funeral, and also when 'O'.., I mean, Oliver was found half-buried in the dirt - someone was watching us."

"What do you mean, *'someone was watching us'*?" Lowe questioned. "Who? And why are we just hearing about this now?"

"I don't know who it was?" I replied. "He was by the roadside and had binoculars. I couldn't even say for sure if he was watching us or if he was maybe just some random birdwatcher. I just thought it was strange. But when I saw him the second time, something hit me, and I wanted to go after him, you know? But my wife went into labor, and suddenly, I couldn't think of anything else. But that was it. And it's been months with no other sign of him."

"It could be nothing," Hayes said, "but still, it might be worth looking into. Do you remember anything else about the person?"

"His car," I replied. "He drove a lime-green Hyundai."

"License number?" Lowe asked.

I shook my head, disappointed in myself, even though there was nothing I could have done.

"Well, that's great," Detective Murcur spoke up. "A green Hyundai. Not a lot to go on. Let's see.., Larson has a population of sixty-two thousand; Southbridge has seventy-four thousand. Between both, there could be a hundred vehicles that fit that description. Maybe more."

"I didn't say I had a lot, Murcur."

"It's more than what we had a moment ago," Hayes stated, reassuring me that, perhaps, I wasn't an idiot for suspecting something odd about the mysterious figure. "We can contact the DMV and have them send us what they can about matching vehicles. In the meantime, let's get everything we can from this double homicide. There's going to be a lot to sift through. We'll still want to question Mr. Dertich out there. If he's not our guy, maybe he saw something when he first arrived on the scene. I also want to continue our search for the remaining two Matthew Lynch victims."

"This case keeps adding more shit to the pile," I stated. "Aren't we supposed to be getting closer to catching this asshole instead of falling deeper into a black hole?"

"We *are* getting closer," Hayes stated. "Sometimes, it's a marathon, not a sprint."

"Well, I don't know about the rest of you, but I'm ready for this race to be over. I'm tired of feeling out of breath, knowing the killer is somewhere up ahead, ready to cross the finish line, while I'm at the back of the crowd, staring at everyone's asses, catching all their flatulence."

One of the uniformed officers chuckled at my comment. It wasn't meant to be funny or obscene humor. That only confirmed this case was turning us all into twisted fucks like the sick bastard we were hunting.

Chapter 29

Strong Desire

I glanced at the clock, thinking I had another hour in me, but when I heard the clomping footsteps approaching from down the hall, I knew the hour was up before it began.

"Mick, what are you doing?" Gina asked in her quiet, tender voice - the one she used when she was confused but also genuinely concerned. "It's 2 am. Why are you up?"

"I couldn't sleep," I whispered back. "I didn't want to wake you."

She stood over my left shoulder, gently gliding her right hand back and forth across my upper back. I could feel her inquisitive stare peering down at the scattered paperwork I had in front of me.

"How long have you been out here?" she asked.

"I don't know; maybe an hour." That was a lie. It had been two, but there was no sense worrying her. And for my punishment, Frank's voice rang out in my guilt-ridden head.

Everybody lies.

"Please tell me you're not going to let work keep you up all night again."

"No, just a few more minutes," I assured her. "You go on back to bed. I'll be right behind you." Another lie.

"Is this about that young man you put in the hospital? You said Frank was handling things."

"He's not handling anything. He just thought it best if we kept it quiet for a while. But no, it's not about that. Thanks for thrusting it back into my brain, though. Now I'll be thinking about *that* all night."

"Sorry, hon." Her hand slid from my right shoulder to the side of my neck, where her fingers began to rub a little harder to massage the tension out.

I needed it.

I reached across with my left hand, placing it on hers as I closed my eyes and dipped my head to let her work her magic. It felt so good. I wondered if this was her way of convincing me to give up my late-night struggle and go back to bed with her. I should seriously consider it. I tilted my chin up over my left shoulder to give her an appreciative smile and to let her know I had only one more page to review. In that single moment, the blood rushed from my face as my worst fear suddenly gripped me. The hand on my neck squeezed ever tighter while I stared into a man's cold eyes, his face hidden in shadow. A glint of light caught my eye as it reflected off the edge of a large butcher knife held in the man's left hand. Before I could react, he shifted his weight over his right hand and pressed down on my right shoulder, holding me in my seat.

"M is for Mick," the man yelled as he jabbed his left hand forward, plunging the knife into the side of my neck.

"NO!" I screamed, throwing the blanket off me as I sat up in bed, feeling my heart jump out of my chest. Gina jumped up in response.

"What, Mick!" she yelled. "What is it?"

I didn't respond right away, my senses on full alert as I glanced around the room, looking for anything willing to reveal itself in the invading moonlight that crept in from between the separation in the curtains.

"Was it a bad dream?" she questioned, turning her bedside lamp on.

"Yeah," I replied, breathing heavily. "It must have been. I mean, it felt so real."

"It's okay, hon. Whatever it was, it's over."

She rubbed her hand across my back, a similar gesture to that in my dream. Understandably, I didn't take to it as much the second time.

"Will you be able to get back to sleep?"

"Yeah," I answered, swinging my legs off the side of the bed from under the covers. "I just need to splash my face. I'll be right back."

"You sure you're okay?" Gina asked as I slowly made my way to the door.

"I'm fine. Go back to sleep."

That was easier said than done. Just as I opened the door, Stella began to cry. The girl had quite the set of lungs on her, made worse by the fact her cries were in stereo, coming not only from the open door but through the baby monitor speaker on Gina's nightstand. Gina threw the blanket aside to get up, but I quickly stopped her, throwing my hand up.

"Don't get up; I've got her. It's my fault she's awake."

"Are you sure?"

"Of course," I nodded.

I didn't know if I should feel insulted by her comment or not. Stella was *my* daughter, too. Did Gina think I wasn't capable of comforting her back to sleep? I realized she thought I took my job too seriously – and I do – but I'm a father now, and that was something I took *more* seriously.

I fumbled my way down the hallway toward the nursery, peeking into the bathroom on my way by and thinking about how nice that splash of water would have felt on my face if I had been able to do it. Parenthood was a bitch sometimes.

I let out a barely audible sigh as I reached the nursery, though it occurred to me that I could have belted it out, and nobody would have heard me over Stella's screaming. As I stepped into the doorway, my legs almost collapsed under my weight, and I felt an immense pressure on my chest as my body stiffened. I wanted to scream, but my mouth wouldn't obey my command.

My eyes locked on a darkened figure standing beside Stella's crib. He was holding a knife and staring down at her. I saw his head turn toward me as he noticed me enter the room.

"HOW MANY TIMES HAVE I WARNED YOU? LET THIS BE YOUR LESSON. SALVATORE WASN'T WHO I WAS AFTER, SO HIS DEATH DOESN'T COUNT. NO, DETECTIVE. I'M AFRAID S IS FOR STELLA."

Before I could move a muscle, the threatening figure swung his arm down, stabbing the knife into my little girl.

"Stella!" I screamed, jumping up from the bed and almost falling on my face as my ankle got caught in the sheet, tripping me up. Gina jumped higher than I did – and faster to her feet. She sprinted out the bedroom door in seconds before crying out, "What's wrong with my baby?" Untangling my foot and recognizing where I was, I realized I must have had a nightmare and had now unwittingly dragged Gina into my screwed-up world. She wasn't going to be thrilled.

I slogged my way to Stella's doorway and hesitantly peeked in, afraid of what – or *who* – I'd encounter. Gina stood beside Stella's crib, peering down at our little girl. Even in the dark, I could almost make out the relieved look on her face.

I was thankful Stella hadn't awoken. Gina had been having it rough lately, worrying about returning to work. Her lack of sleep had quickly been catching up to mine. If my outburst had disturbed Stella, Gina would have been awake half the night trying to get her back to sleep. No matter how much I would have offered to handle things, she would have stubbornly done it herself anyway.

I approached her quietly, nestling my arm against hers to let her know I was there.

"Sorry," I whispered. "Nightmare."

She kept her eyes diverted, staring at Stella sleeping.

"Is this going to end?" she questioned. "Are we ever going to get past this?"

I turned slightly to look at her, conflicted.

"What do you mean?" I asked.

"You know what I mean," she replied, stepping back and walking toward the door without even a glance in my direction.

I did know, but I acted like I didn't, following her out of the nursery like a confused puppy. Once back in the seclusion of our bedroom, I felt utterly helpless as I watched her drop her chin to her chest while she brought her palm to her forehead in defeat.

"It was him again, wasn't it?" she questioned. "Of course, it was," she jabbed. "It's always him. He's controlling your life."

"That's not what's happening here," I jabbed back.

"Isn't it? He's on your mind more than your own family is. You think about him night and day."

"That's not fair," I raised my voice. "And it's not true. The case weighs on me – we both know that, but nothing is more important to me than the two of you. That's why it's on my mind. All I can think about is keeping the two of you safe. I won't be able to sleep comfortably until that maniac out there is either dead or behind bars. I'm doing everything I can to catch the son of a bitch. Why can't you see that?"

Her hand dropped heavily to her side as she walked over to sit on the edge of the bed. She stared blankly at the wall for a moment before shaking her head. I watched as her facial expression changed from frustration to remorse.

"I *can* see that," she said softly, turning her eyes to meet mine. "I know you're doing everything you can. I just wish things could go back to the way they were. Before all of this – before The Letter Man."

I walked over to her, remaining cautious not to upset her more than she already was, and sat beside her. I placed my hand on hers and stared forward at the same wall that had kept her attention.

"Things will go back," I assured her, nodding. "I promise. If anything, you and Stella have given me more reason to want to catch this guy. And I *will*. We've got a few promising leads to look into. I'm sure they're going to produce results. I can feel it. Don't give up on me."

"I won't give up on you," she responded.

Then she flashed me a playful grin.

"Not yet, anyway."

I smiled and bumped her with my shoulder. Her face became serious again, and I wondered if I had gone too far with the nudge.

"I love you, Mick."

I felt my tense shoulders drop in relief.

"I love you too, babe. And I'd understand if you wanted to take Stella somewhere else until this was over."

"I wouldn't do that," she said. "We're in this together. Now, can we go back to bed?" she asked softly.

I smiled and nodded.

I began to crawl across the blankets to my side of the bed when a second question came.

"And hold me like you used to?"

I pulled the already messy covers aside and slid my legs under.

"Absolutely." I tapped the bed beside me with my palm.

Gina slowly accepted my invitation, slipping her lower body under the sheet that I held in the air for her. She slid her hips closer to me, turned away, and pressed her butt into my crotch. I wrapped my arm around her and pulled her back against my chest, squeezing her tight. She wanted me to hold her – that was easy. I wasn't letting this woman go. Unfortunately, as I lay there, our bodies mingled together, I couldn't get my troubled thoughts to let go of *me*. I thought of Gina's words from earlier.

He's controlling your life.

God, how I didn't want that to be true. It couldn't be. I wouldn't let it. Like Gina, I also wanted things back to the way they were. Holding her now – like this – gave me a strong desire to make sure I held up my promise. I wouldn't let her down. I wouldn't let *me* down.

I stared at the wall, knowing sleep was a failed effort. Since I was cursed to stay awake, I did what I could to make myself feel better. I thought of what I'd do if I.., *when* I caught that sadistic fucker. A smile came to my lips.

You'd better be ready for what I have in store for you, Letter Man. I'm coming for you. Your time is up.

Chapter 30

T

The morning didn't bring ease to my mind. I think I slept for maybe an hour. Since I was up early, I decided to head to work to focus my thoughts. It was a strange concept, but it worked for me.

The DMV had sent what they had on green Hyundai owners; I figured I'd get started on those. Unfortunately, there was a miscommunication, and they sent only the Southbridge residents' vehicle information to us, sending the Larson information to the Larson PD. That made it easier for me. As it stood, I had seventy-three vehicle owners to sort through. It would probably take me two solid days to vet them for possible suspects and then another two weeks to meet with and question them. Let Murcur and the Larson PD handle their own.

I'd already been at it for a couple of hours when Special Agent Hayes stopped by my desk to check in on my progress.

"How's it going over here; any luck?"

"I'm going crosseyed," I replied. "How about on your end? Any luck tracking down the two kids?"

"That's what I stopped by for," she answered. "We found one of them. Special Agent Lowe and I are taking a ride now to question him."

"Sounds fun."

Her eyes shifted to the stack of printed sheets in front of me. I watched her left eyebrow raise as she looked back at me.

"Wish I could say the same for you."

"Yeah, thanks," I responded sarcastically. "Now get out of here; I've got important reading to do."

She smiled and walked away, joining Lowe as he exited the briefing room. As I watched them depart, the kid in me took over, and I tried to raise a single eyebrow as she had done. It was a skill that always eluded me. And still, I had no luck, feeling both brows raise in unison. I even went so far as to use my fingers to lift one, thinking I could get it to stay once I released it. I didn't realize Detective Frazier was watching me and pointing it out to the others until one of them burst out laughing.

"Your face feeling a little droopy, Dooley?" Frazier announced, chuckling. "Looks like you're trying to give yourself a facelift."

"Shut the hell up," I shouted to mask my embarrassment. "At least a facelift would help my looks. There's nothing medical science can do to improve *your* chopped hamburger face."

"He's got you there, Frazier," one of the others stated, backing me up while laughing.

"You guys are a fucking riot," Frazier said heatedly, unable to take the same heat as he dished out. "You can all go to Hell."

I looked at the other officers and shrugged my shoulders. It was all in good humor. We all understood that. Well, most of us, anyway.

I went back to examining the files on my desk, which included a Hyundai catalog I had picked up at a local dealership. Had I known the actual green color of the vehicle, it would have narrowed down my search options. Instead, I was digging through files covering every shade of green Hyundai offered. Or, at least, those owned by Southbridge residents. Rockwood Green, Mirage Green, Green Grass, Green Apple, and Elm Green – who knew there were so many choices? Whatever happened to just "Green"? More importantly, did any of it matter? Would I even find the killer in this stack of names? I was pretty confident our guy wasn't a Southbridge resident. But we all had to do our part, even if that meant wasting time searching through a useless pile of information because the DMV couldn't get their instructions straight.

Just then, my desk phone rang, thankfully interrupting my mundane task and negative attitude.

"This is Detective Dooley," I answered.

A muffled voice responded.

"217 Schaeffer. He'll be waiting."

Then, the caller hung up.

I don't know why, but my first response was to look around the room, thinking one of the other detectives was messing with me. It seemed like something they would do, but they were all nose-deep in their own case files. I hung up the receiver and stared at the phone, wondering about the message. Was it even meant for me? Maybe it was the wrong number? Curious, I picked it up again and dialed *69 to call the number back. A second later, dual rings rang out – one coming from the receiver, one from

Frank's office. I stared forward through the open blinds in his window and watched him turn his head to his phone. A second ring in my ear chimed, followed by the same from his office doorway.

"What the fuck?" I whispered to myself.

I watched Frank pick up the phone. A second later, another ring sounded in my ear. In a heartbeat, I felt myself relax as I let out a silent sigh. A fourth ring came, followed by a fifth, before a message kicked on.

"You've reached the voicemail of Trevor Hicks. Leave a message; maybe I'll even get back to you."

I hung up, choosing not to leave a message. I immediately thought of the caller's words, "217 Schaeffer. He'll be waiting." Assuming that was an address, Schaeffer Rd was only four blocks from the station. Feeling something twist in the pit of my stomach, I got up and marched toward Frank's office. I leaned into his doorway just as he was ending his call.

"Yeah, understood," he grumbled.

Then, in true Frank fashion, he hung up without saying goodbye. He quickly turned his annoyed stare to me.

"What do you want, Dooley?"

"I just received a strange phone call telling me to go to 217 Schaeffer Rd. I don't have a good feeling about it."

Why? Who was it?" he asked.

"I don't know," I replied. "I called the number back, and it dumped me into the voicemail of a Trevor Hicks."

"What are you thinking?"

"Right now, only bad things. Trevor. T. I think you know where I'm going with this. It wouldn't hurt to check it out."

Frank shook his head as if wrestling with the decision.

"All right, you go ahead," he responded. "Bring Officer Marcus with you as backup."

"What about you?" I questioned.

"I can't," he answered. "That was Chief Copelli on the phone. He wants me in his office in a half hour."

"Uh oh. Something serious?"

He dropped his eyes to his desk. I watched his shoulders slump as he exhaled through his nose. He then looked back at me, his stare not as cold as usual.

"Just get going and check that address out, will you?"

I nodded, "Sure thing, Lieu."

I walked away, thinking something was up. It was a strange interaction. Frank wasn't acting like his usual self. It didn't matter; it wasn't my business. I had my own shit going on.

I grabbed Officer Marcus on my way out, explaining the situation. I didn't tell him what I was thinking, but I could tell from his expression he already knew. He wasn't looking forward to the trip.

We arrived at the address, a small ranch house, and parked out front. Small strips of wooded areas on either side of the house kept it somewhat secluded from the nearest neighbors. That wasn't promising. There was a pickup truck parked in the gravel driveway, its side panels covered in mud spray from the tires. Perhaps the vehicle was an indication someone was home.

"Let's get this over with," I said to Marcus as I opened my door. He followed my lead.

As we approached the front door, Marcus' training kicked in, and he stepped ahead of me, placing his hand on his sidearm. He knocked on the door while listening for movement. After receiving no response, he knocked a second time while announcing our presence.

"Trevor Hicks, this is the police. Please answer the door."

No sound, no movement. Maybe no cause for alarm. I wasn't buying it.

"I'll wait here," I said. "You go check the side door."

Marcus did as I asked, disappearing around the corner. A few seconds later, he reappeared, a nervous, almost frightened expression on his face.

"Detective, I think you need to see this."

That was one way to pique my curiosity. I followed Officer Marcus to the side door, where the reason behind his worried look was suddenly clear.

"Call for backup," I ordered, my eyes fixed on the door.

Smeared across the door's white paint, the words "Welcome officers" written in what appeared to be blood. Marcus got on his radio while I pulled my gun from my hip holster. When he was through, I nodded to him. He pulled his firearm and nodded back. I slowly reached for the knob while Marcus stood with his shoulder against the doorframe. The knob turned freely in my hand. He looked into my eyes, silently telling me he was ready, a line of sweat forming just below his hairline. I took a deep breath, my gun poised at my chest, and gave the door a quick shove, taking care not to disturb the bloody message. Officer Marcus charged in, his arms extended, ready to fire if the situation called for it.

"This is the police," he yelled. "Come out and show us your hands."

He cautiously walked forward, allowing me to enter behind him. We had come through the kitchen door but had a clear view into the living room. There was nobody in either room.

"Trevor Hicks," I called out. No response.

No surprise.

We made our way into the next room, scanning for signs of movement. To our right was a small half-bath, its door slightly ajar. In front of us, a narrow hallway led to a bedroom at the end, its door wide open. Halfway down the hall, along the right wall, another door - that one closed.

I signaled toward the bathroom, aiming to clear it before moving on. Marcus nodded, standing in the opening of the hallway in case of any activity from that direction. I slowly pressed the bathroom door open with my fingertips to get a clear look inside, my gun at the ready.

Nobody.

I glanced back at Marcus; he nodded sideways into the hallway. I joined alongside him. We took two steps forward when Marcus suddenly stopped and turned his head sideways as if listening for something.

"Do you hear that?" he questioned.

"Hear what," I asked.

"Listen."

I put my head down, concentrating on the sound of silence until that silence was interrupted by muffled groaning.

"It sounds like it's coming from behind that door," I whispered, pointing at the closed door ahead of us.

As we stepped closer, the moaning became louder. There was no longer any doubt. Someone was inside. Marcus took the lead.

"Trevor Hicks," he announced, "this is the police. We're coming in."

The sound of a man's grumblings became louder. Officer Marcus turned the knob and opened the door about two inches to catch a cautious glimpse. It was enough to notice a man lying face up on a bed, stripped down to only his boxer shorts. He was gagged with a leather strap, and his arms and legs splayed out, tied to each of the four bedposts like he was DaVinci's Vitruvian Man. Three or four belts connected together, drawn over his forehead, and wrapped under the bed frame, held his head pressed firmly against the mattress. It looked like an old movie scene - a patient in a psych ward, prepped for electroshock treatment.

The man's eyes shifted to us peering in at him, and he began to struggle violently, trying to make words where only incoherent mumbling sounded out. I noticed his eyebrows rapidly raising and lowering while his eyes nervously shifted to his right. Marcus became frantic.

"Holy shit!" he yelled excitedly as he went to push the door open.

"No, wait!" I yelled.

But it was too late.

The door flew open, and a thunderous bang exploded beyond the door. My instant reaction was to grab Marcus and throw him to the floor, thinking the killer had shot at us. When I saw Officer Marcus was unharmed and no more shots had been fired, I peeked around the doorframe into the room. That was when I saw the blood spattered across the far wall. The man on the bed, presumably Trevor Hicks, was no longer struggling, the side of his head blown out from a shotgun blast.

It was an elaborate setup – a shotgun clamped to the back of a wooden chair beside the bed, the barrel pointing at the victim's head, some fishing wire looped around the trigger, then fed through a hook in the ceiling like a pulley, with the other end tied around the doorknob. The poor son of a bitch tried to warn us.

We killed him.

I sat with my back against the open door, unable to move, feeling Officer Marcus' shoulder rub against mine as his chest heaved up and down.

"You okay, Marcus?" I asked.

"Yeah," he responded. "Are you hit?"

He still had no idea what had happened. I didn't know how to tell him that his opening the door just blew a man's head off. He didn't need to hear that. That type of psychological scar never really heals. He'd learn what happened soon enough without me saying a thing.

"No, I'm good," I answered, reaching up and grabbing the doorknob to pull myself to my feet. I quickly closed the door before Marcus could get to his and look in.

"Looks like backup is here," I said, pointing into the living room where flashing red and blue lights were strobing across the walls. "Go grab one of the senior officers, would you?"

He pointed to the closed door. "But what about..,"

"Just go," I barked.

He first shot me a confused look. Then his face changed when the realization hit. He knew. Still, knowing it in your head and hearing it aloud were two different things. Seeing it was off the table. I wish I had that luxury.

The Bomb Squad was called in to clear the room in case of any other hazardous devices. It then took another thirty-five minutes for Barry to get here and call it before Vera and her lab tech could begin their work. She wasn't happy about waiting, but there was nothing Barry could do; he was in the middle of an autopsy when he received the call. I'm surprised he arrived as quickly as he had. Special Agents Hayes and Lowe took even longer. They were in the middle of questioning the Matthew Lynch victim when they heard. It was better that they stayed and finished what they'd started to rule him out as a possible suspect. Officer Marcus stayed outside with a few of the other officers. I suspect he was regretfully second-guessing his actions over the last hour. I'm sure it would weigh on him for a while.

"What a fucking mess," Lowe blurted while rubbing his forehead.

"Sure is," Barry responded. "I'll be pulling pellets out of this guy for days – what's left of him, anyway."

"How could this happen?" Lowe asked, directing his question at me.

"We heard the man in distress," I answered. "How the hell could we have known about this goddamn contraption?"

"Shit!" Lowe stated.

Looking at the damage inflicted upon the victim, Hayes asked in a calm voice, "Is there any way of knowing if this is Trevor?"

"You'll have to get his prints and hope he's in the system," Barry replied. "I can't put his face back together, and there's not much dental work left."

"I've got a wallet," Vera belted out, looking into the top drawer of his nightstand.

She pulled it out and flipped it open.

"No license, but he's got an ID card. Trevor Hicks, 217 Schaefer Rd. Thirty-seven years old. Ugly as shit. A little uglier now."

"Jesus, Vera!" I yelled.

"Sorry; sometimes that shit just slips out. You know I can't control myself."

"Anything else in there, Ms. Snell?" Hayes asked. "And please try to contain yourself."

"Just a key," Vera replied, placing the wallet back in the drawer,

"Not exactly a plethora of information," Hayes responded. "How long will it take you to go through the room?"

Vera glanced around the room, but her lab tech, Danny, quickly spoke up ahead of her.

"About an hour. Give or take."

It was odd; in the ten months I'd known him, I think that was the most I'd heard him say.

"Well then," Hayes said, "we'll let you get started. Let's hope the killer left us more than just a mess."

We started to make our way out of the room to let Vera and Danny do their thing when another officer entered excitedly.

"Hold on, guys. We just found this in the other bedroom closet?"

He was holding a metal lock box in front of his chest. It wasn't the box he was drawing our attention to, but rather what was written on it. Scratched into the metal's surface were the words, "Open me," with a capital letter "T" beside it.

"Real subtle hint," I said.

"Open it," Lowe ordered.

The officer walked forward and placed the box on the chair where the shotgun was.

He rubbed his gloved hand along the front of the box. "It's locked."

"I bet I know what that key was for," Vera stated, grabbing the wallet again.

She pulled it out of its little pocket, dropped the wallet onto the nightstand, and excitedly marched to the locked box.

"It feels like Christmas," she announced. "I wonder what Santa brought me?"

Instinctively, I shouted a warning, "The Bomb Squad hasn't cleared that," but Vera was so anxious that she unlocked it and opened the lid before I even got the complete sentence out. Thankfully, there were no surprises.

All I could do was shake my head. She wasn't going to change; why fight it anymore?

"Well, hello," she said, peering into the box.

"What is it?" Hayes asked, beating me and Lowe to the question.

"We've got one, two, three.., six sobriety chips. Anyone care to guess why the man has no license?"

"The mud on the truck outside looked pretty fresh," I said.

"He's probably been driving illegally," Vera responded.

"Six chips," Hayes jumped in. "Six victims to go?" she questioned.

"Sadistic fuck," I let out.

"Oh, and look what we have here," Vera said, swiping aside the chips to access a folded piece of paper. She unfolded it and began to read.

A LIFE FOR A LIFE. IT SEEMED ONLY FITTING. ONLY, THIS MAN TOOK TWO. HIS ALCOHOL ADDICTION COST MORE THAN ANYONE SHOULD HAVE TO PAY. THE LIVES HE TOOK WHILE IN A DRUNKEN STUPOR BEHIND THE WHEEL WERE TOO HIGH A PRICE. WHY WAS HE ALLOWED BACK ON THE STREET? WHY WAS HE ALLOWED TO WALK FREE SO SOON AFTER THE ACCIDENT THAT KILLED HIS WIFE AND UNBORN CHILD? THE SYSTEM IS BROKEN. HE DIDN'T DESERVE LENIENCY. HE DESERVED TO GET WHAT HE'D GIVEN. DEATH. I AM THE BRINGER OF SUCH FATE. AND NOW, SO IS ONE OF YOUR OFFICERS. PLEASE THANK THEM FOR THEIR EFFORT. I COULDN'T HAVE DONE IT WITHOUT THEM.

THE SYSTEM MAY HAVE FAILED ITS PEOPLE, BUT I WILL FIND A WAY TO MAKE THE SYSTEM WORK FOR ME. ONE WAY OR ANOTHER, TRUE JUSTICE WILL BE SERVED.

I HOPE YOU'RE STILL HAVING FUN.

I ASSURE YOU, I AM.

A

"That goddamn piece of shit," I shouted.

"Calm down, Detective," Hayes stated.

"Fuck that," I snapped back. "You expect me to be calm after this shit? It's one thing to be a demented fucker, going around killing people because of some personal vendetta, but to ruin someone else's life by coming up with some twisted way to have them do it for you is too much. That rookie out there – Officer Marcus - will never be the same again, thanks to that asshole. We can't keep playing his game. We need to nail that mother fucker to the wall."

"We're all doing what we can," Hayes said unconvincingly.

"Well, it sure as hell isn't enough."

"Detective Dooley," Agent Lowe jumped in, "I think we've heard enough. Outside. Now!"

He pointed his finger out the bedroom door. I gave him a nasty glare, then turned it toward Hayes, thinking she'd have my back. Instead, she turned her head away. I should have known; even after all of her talk, in the end, she was just another Fed, sticking up for her partner. I shook my head in disgust and walked out. I hadn't realized Agent Lowe was following hot on my heels until I reached the front door. I stepped out into the front yard and whipped around to face him.

"What's your problem?" I yelled, ready for a fight.

He looked at me and calmly responded, "I did have a problem. That's why I had to get away when I did. I think I've gotten better."

"That's debatable," I responded snidely.

He took it well, responding with only a slight sneer. "Listen, Dooley," he continued. "I, more than anyone, know what it's like to let a case get under my skin. It'll consume you if you let it. You've seen it happen. I'm not proud of the way I acted. You've got to get your shit together before it takes you down. You're a good detective, but sometimes you need to reel it back some. You can't let the killer blur your vision, or you'll be blind when you need it most."

He stopped preaching long enough to look back at the open door of the house before looking back at me.

"You go back to the station and write up your report. Then get back to doing what you were doing to find this fucker. Special Agent Hayes and I have got things covered here. We've got the best Chief Medical Examiner, Mr. Hinkman, on the scene, and the best damn Forensic Officer, Ms. Snell, at our disposal. Southbridge is well-represented. If there's anything here that get's us closer to finding the son of a bitch, you'll be the first to hear."

I had to hand it to him; that wasn't half bad. I thought we'd be throwing punches, but he found a way to talk me down instead. I wanted to hate him, but he wasn't wrong. Early on in the case, I thought the guy was a ticking time bomb, spiraling more out of control with each new victim. He was now seeing the same from me. And he wasn't an asshole about it.

I nodded. "You're right. I need to take a step back to focus on the entire picture. I need to get my head on straight. We're going to get him."

"We will," he replied. "We've all just gotta stay clear-headed. Which is why you're getting out of here."

"Right," I responded.

I wanted to say more, but I wasn't sure I could; I didn't want him getting the wrong idea. It wasn't like this changed anything between us. We weren't friends. We just had a common goal. Still, as he turned to head back inside..,

"Special Agent Lowe," I called out to get his attention.

He looked over his shoulder.

"Thanks."

"No problem, Officer. Don't forget to take the rookie back with you."

Then he disappeared inside.

I'll do what he said; I'll go back and write up my report. Maybe getting it down on paper would calm my nerves. Then, I could get back to sorting through the DMV records. We had to catch a break sometime. Who knows, maybe I'd get lucky enough to track down the guy in the green Hyundai and find he was the killer all along.

Could I ever be that lucky?

Chapter 31

Down and Out

I could tell on the ride back to the station that things weighed heavily on Officer Marcus. He'd have to live with the decision of opening that bedroom door for years to come, questioning his actions and wondering if another officer would have handled it differently. But it *wasn't* another officer; it was *him*. Time would tell if he could learn to get past it. I could only tell him he wasn't alone and that he did what any responding officer would have done. Did it help? Of course not, but it was all I had.

We arrived back and parted ways at the entrance. I wasn't one to give advice, so I kept my thoughts to myself. Nothing I said would make it better. Nothing I said would relieve the overwhelming torment he placed upon himself. We all had our demons; that was now his.

I headed upstairs to the Detective Bureau, ready to relive everything on paper that that kid was reliving in his head. When I got to the top of the stairs, I immediately noticed Chief Copelli standing in Frank's office, along with a woman dressed in black pants and a matching suit

295

jacket. She was carrying a brown leather portfolio bag at her side. I didn't think anything of it until Frank spied me walking toward my desk and pointed at me. I instinctively threw up my hands, questioning what he needed. Chief Copelli promptly answered my unspoken question by leaning out the doorway.

"Detective Dooley, would you please join us?"

"Yes, sir," I stated, though I doubted he heard me since he was back in conversation with the nicely dressed woman.

I proceeded to Frank's office and stood in the open doorway, not wanting to interrupt the Chief's discussion with his guest. When things fell silent, Frank's voice rang out.

"Come in, Detective, and shut the door."

He said, "*Detective,*" not "*Mick*" or "*Dooley.*" That was when I knew it was a big deal. I did as he asked, still curious about what this was all about. Chief Copelli began, making it clear.

"Detective Dooley, this is Ms. Angela Keane from Internal Affairs."

"Internal Affairs?" I let out, feeling my stomach flop.

"She has some questions she'd like to ask you," the Chief said.

"Ask *me*?" I questioned, looking at the woman. "What about?"

"This isn't anything formal, Detective," Ms. Keane replied. "Not at this time."

"Okay then; shoot." That probably wasn't the best choice of words when dealing with IA.

"There was a young gentleman admitted to the hospital a few days ago; he'd been beaten pretty bad. He claims it was a police officer who did that to him. One of the paramedics said you were the officer on the scene. Is that true?"

"I mean, I showed up at the scene," I answered with a straight face. "I happened to be driving by. The kid was already unconscious by the time I pulled up."

"In fact," Ms. Keane continued, "you were the one who called an ambulance. Is that correct?"

"I did, yes."

"Did you.., happen to see anyone else around?"

"No. The street was pretty empty."

"And all of this is in your report, I'm sure."

"I.., haven't gotten around to filing a report yet."

"Oh?"

"In case you hadn't realized," I informed her, "there's a serial killer on the loose that's been a bit more pressing."

She shot me a snide smirk.

"Thank you, Detective," she said. "That'll be all."

"Sure," I replied, reaching for the door.

"Actually, Detective," she stopped me, "just one more question."

"O...kaaay," I said, releasing the knob.

She flashed me a deceptive smile. "The paramedic at the scene recalled your knuckles being scraped up and bruised. Would you mind telling us what that was about?"

I quickly glanced in Frank's direction while Chief Copelli and Ms. Keane remained focused on me. He subtly shook his head. I guess that meant I was going with the story I'd rehearsed.

"Oh, well, I had just left my sister-in-law's house. My wife and I had gone over for dinner. At some point, we had gotten into a little argument – I don't even remember what about, and my wife asked me to leave. At the time, I was furious, so when I walked out of the house, I punched this 4x4 post at the top of my sister-in-law's porch railing. Stupid, I know."

"A 4x4 post?" she questioned skeptically.

"Yup."

"I see. And the soft drink?"

"The what..?" I questioned.

"Oh, another officer we questioned stated your windshield had a soft drink cup on it – like, maybe somebody threw it at your vehicle."

"I don't understand," I responded. "I thought this was informal questioning. Should I have my union rep here with me or something?"

She gave me a fake grin. "I apologize, Detective Dooley. Sometimes, I get a little anxious about these things. I'm sure you can understand, being in your position. But you should know," she reached into her portfolio and pulled out some papers, "we'll be opening a full investigation regarding the case." She handed me the documents. "I hope, for your sake, you had nothing to do with it. Just the same, I would consider contacting your union representative if I were you. Oh, and one other thing - while we're looking into the matter, I've recommended to Chief Copelli that you be placed on administrative leave, effective immediately."

"What?" I shouted. "You can't be serious? There's a homicidal maniac out there."

Chief Copelli spoke up. "Detective Frazier will be fully briefed and brought up to speed on the case."

"I don't believe this," I said heatedly.

"These are strong allegations, son," the Chief said, a sour look on his face. "The department doesn't take this kind of behavior lightly. I have no doubt this will all get cleared up, but for now, I'll need you to turn in your badge and firearm, Detective."

"And," Ms. Keane added, "if what you said is true, this should go nice and smooth. You could be back on the job in just a few weeks."

"Unbelievable," I said, shaking my head. "We've got the worst killer this city has ever seen walking the streets, and you want to take me off the case because some punk asshole kid got beat up and blamed a cop?"

"'Punk asshole kid?'" the IA woman questioned. "It's odd that you would say that about someone's character. Especially since, according to you, you arrived *after* he was already unconscious."

"It's not difficult to determine what people in that neighborhood are like," I responded.

"I bet," she said, delivering an unbelieving stare.

I looked at Frank, hoping he'd jump in, but there was nothing he could do.

"Hand over your badge and gun, Detective," Frank ordered, tapping his index finger on the desk.

I knew I was only getting what I deserved, but it didn't stop me from hating it. I dipped my chin to my chest and shook my head in disappointment. It was my own fault. I had nobody else to blame. I unclipped my badge from my belt and tossed it onto Frank's desk. My gun was next. I pulled it from its holster and held it in my hand, looking at it like I was losing a part of myself. Wasn't I? This job was me, and I was this job. I now understood what Jimmy meant when he told me his suspension was the worst thing he'd experienced. Of course, that was before he learned his son was The Alphabet Killer.

I slowly placed my gun on the desk beside my badge, strangely thinking how glad I was Stella Mae was still an infant. I didn't have to worry about that kind of surprise.

"So that's it, then?" I questioned. "I have to grab my stuff and go?"

"I'm afraid so," Chief Copelli replied glumly.

Ms. Keane spoke up as I turned to exit. "Expect to hear from me in a few days to schedule a formal inquiry, Detective Dooley."

"Yeah, whatever," I responded.

I grabbed the door and yanked it open. As I stepped out to collect my things, I felt all the other detectives' eyes upon me as if they'd all known what was coming. I knew it was all in my head, but I couldn't shake it. I was too embarrassed to look anyone in the face. All I could do was trust in what Frank told me before. He said he'd make sure nothing happened.

He said he'd make this go away.

Chapter 32

Discovery

As miserable as being away from the job was, maybe this leave was a blessing in disguise. It had only been three days, but things were feeling good. I was making up for the paternity leave I *didn't* take when Stella was first born. My thoughts were still on the case - that wouldn't go away - but I was able to shove it back to the less frequented corner of my brain where it saw less daylight. Nighttime was a different story, though. Some habits were hard to break – especially subconscious ones.

My union rep had gotten in contact with me. Ms. Keane had scheduled a formal inquiry for the coming Tuesday. I wasn't worried about it anymore. Gina and I discussed it; I was going to come clean. Whatever happens, happens. We'd get through it together. I think we both just wanted it to be over.

Rosa stopped by this morning to pick up Gina and Stella to go shopping for some baby clothes. It gave me another opportunity to apologize to her for my unwarranted behavior the last time I saw her. It was a step in the right direction. Things were good.

I was going to take advantage of my alone time. I decided it was time to tackle the leaky sink in the bathroom. Gina had been after me for months to fix it. I thought it would be a nice surprise if I could get it done before she returned. I was about to settle into an uncomfortable crouched position beneath the sink when I heard a horn honk out front. At first, I thought it was only someone driving by, but then a second honk sounded. I couldn't ignore it. Whoever it was, they knew someone was home; both cars were in the driveway. I took that as a sign. It was obvious to me the sink was destined to leak forever.

I hadn't made it to the front door before another honk blasted. Someone was impatient. I opened the door to find Sanchez parked out front, his passenger side wheels at the edge of my lawn.

"What are you doing here, Rubio?" I yelled out as I made my way down the lawn. "They give you Larson boys days off?"

He hunched his head down to speak to me through the passenger-side window.

"You gotta come with me," he said excitedly. "Get in."

"I was just about to take apart the bathroom sink."

"Dude, the sink can wait. You're going to want to see this," he expressed. "It's about the case."

"Haven't you heard, Rubio, I'm on administrative leave. I can't be involved in anything police related."

"Don't worry; you won't be. Nobody knows about this. Now tell Gina you'll be back in a little bit and hop in."

"Gina's out with her sister."

"Even better," Sanchez said. "You don't have any more excuses."

"I don't know," I said, rubbing the back of my neck.

"Do you want to stop this guy or not?" Sanchez asked.

"Of course I do," I answered with conviction.

"Then get in the car, and let's go," he ordered, patting the passenger seat with his palm. "We don't have much time."

I had to admit, I was intrigued to find out what Sanchez was so excited about. Curiosity got the best of me. I relented. I got in the car just as Sanchez pulled out, barely giving me a chance to shut the door.

"Jesus, Sanchez," I barked, reaching for the seat belt. "Warn me next time."

"Sorry, man. Like I said, we don't have much time."

"Time for what?" I questioned. "What's this about?"

"Uh uh. No dice. You've got to see this for yourself."

"See what? Why are you being so secretive?"

"I'm not being secretive. It's just.., trust me, okay. You're going to thank me when we get there."

I shook my head in frustration. It was clear he wasn't going to fill me in on it.

"Well, where are we going at least?" I asked.

"Back to Larson. Where it all began."

I felt my heart thump. *Where it all began* was Karen's house. What the fuck was up? What did we miss? I suddenly found myself without words. Not that they would have done any good with my tight-lipped friend. All I could do was sit back and see where this took us.

We drove for a while in silence before Sanchez opened up.

"I'm telling you, buddy, you're not gonna believe this."

"It'd be easier if you'd clue me in on what this was all about," I responded.

"Nice try," he replied with a smirk. "Don't worry, we're almost there."

He turned onto Ledgehill, the dirt road leading to the old mine - the same road where Matthew Lynch's abandoned car was discovered, and eventually his body. I immediately straightened up and sat at attention.

"What the hell is this?" I questioned. "This isn't going to Karen's house."

"What? Who said we were going to Karen's house?"

"You said we were going back to where it all began."

"I didn't mean where The Letter Man killed his first victim. I meant where The Letter Man himself began. Didn't you tell me you believed Matthew Lynch was the one who set the killer on his path?"

"Well, yeah, but..,"

Suddenly, my voice stopped working as we approached our destination. My breathing became shallow. I could feel the blood fleeing from my face as I stared out the windshield. Just ahead of us, where Matthew Lynch's vacated car was previously found, a familiar green Hyundai was parked in the middle of the dirt road.

"What the fuck?" I gasped as Sanchez pulled up behind the vehicle.

Sanchez turned to me with a smile on his face. "Didn't I tell you?" he said, opening his door. "I said you had to see this for yourself."

"But how?" I questioned, stepping from the car and noticing the bumper sticker slapped across the back of the trunk that read, *"The dead walk among us."* That was what Charlene told us the killer spoke after stabbing her boyfriend Peter in the apartment hallway.

"This is the guy, right?" Sanchez asked, pointing to the sticker as he approached the vehicle. "The one who was watching us?"

"I...I don't know. I guess." I stumbled with my words, still in shock at what was happening. "I mean, it could be. Maybe. But where is the driver?"

"Ah, now that's why we needed to get here so quickly," Sanchez answered, opening the driver's side rear door to expose a man lying in the backseat, his arms and legs bound in rope. "We wouldn't want him waking up before we got back."

"What the fuck is this?" I questioned.

"I followed the fucker here," Sanchez replied. "The twisted fuck led me back to where Matthew Lynch's car was found. He didn't even notice me pulling up behind him until he stepped out of the car. He was acting all funny. You know, suspicious. I wasn't taking any chances. I pulled my gun on him and told him to get against his car. I just wanted to question him – to see if he was our guy. When I got closer to him, the son of a bitch went for my gun. That's when I knew it was him, for sure. I got lucky; I managed to knock the fucker out before he could get a hold of my weapon."

"Why didn't you call it in?" I shouted. "Jesus Christ, Rubio. If this is The Letter Man..,"

"It *is* him," Sanchez jumped in. "I know it."

"If it is him," I continued, "then we gotta bring him in. We can't take the chance of him walking on some technicality."

"Bring him in?" Sanchez shouted. "You've got to be kidding me. You've seen what this guy has done - all the people he's killed. Matthew Lynch. Karen. Fuck man. You, of all people, should know if we bring him in - he's not gonna get the justice he deserves. But we have a chance to end it now, once and for all. This fucker needs to pay for what he's done."

Sanchez reached into the backseat and pulled the unconscious man by the waist of his pants, sliding him out of the door and onto the ground. He sat him upright against the rear tire. That was when I got a better look at who it was.

I felt my eyes widen as the words stuttered out. "I.., I know him," I said.

"What? You know this piece of shit?"

"I mean, not well," I answered. "His name is Mort.., I mean, Lenny. Leonard Shurek. He used to be Southbridge's Chief Medical Examiner until a few years back when he was caught doing some questionable things."

"Like killing people?" Sanchez questioned snarkily.

"No, nothing like that," I replied. "Tampering with evidence – collecting personal things from the victims of The Alphabet Killer."

"That sounds like some serial killer shit to me."

"I can't believe it," I said, still in shock. "I never pictured Lenny as someone who could do the things The Letter Man has been doing."

"Well, believe it, buddy."

"There's gotta be an explanation for it."

"Really?" Sanchez questioned. "Are you really that naïve to think this guy can't be our killer? You caught him watching us. Not once, but twice. He led me right to where Matthew's car was parked, for Christ's sake. Hell, he's got a bumper sticker stating the same thing the killer said. Fuck, man, if this isn't our guy, I don't know who is."

I shook my head, wondering if it could be true. I'd heard Mort had moved out of Southbridge after he had lost his job. He felt humiliated and couldn't stand how everyone looked at him after what he'd done. Did it mess him up that bad? Was he taking his anger and frustration out on innocent.., well, *hardly*-innocent people? I needed to know for sure.

"We've gotta wake him up," I said. "I need to hear it from him."

"You still have doubts, huh? All right. Let's hear what the little fucker has to say."

Sanchez leaned over Lenny and began tapping his cheek.

"Wakey, wakey, mother fucker," he said.

After a few seconds, when Lenny didn't wake right away, the taps turned into slaps.

"I said wake the fuck up, scumbag." Sanchez pulled Lenny's head forward away from the car, then shoved it back, slamming it against the rear panel above the tire. The jarring motion was hard enough to cause Lenny's glasses to slip down to the tip of his nose.

Lenny let out a moan, letting us know he was conscious.

"Was that necessary?" I asked.

"It did the trick, didn't it?" Sanchez backed away, waving his hand forward. "He's all yours."

I stepped in front of Mort so he could see who he was dealing with.

"Mort." Just after it left my lips, I cringed. Sometimes it just slipped out. "*Lenny.* Do you remember me?"

"Mick?" he mumbled, squinting and squirming, trying to move his tied arms from behind his back. "What's this about? Why am I tied up and on the ground?"

"You first," I said. "Do you mind telling me what the fuck is going on here?"

His eyes shifted over my shoulder.

"He hit me!" He nodded his head toward Sanchez.

"Damn straight I did," Sanchez barked, stepping forward.

I put my hand up over my shoulder to wave Sanchez off.

"I mean, why are you out here? Why here?"

"I know how it must look. It's not what you think."

"Bullshit!" Sanchez snapped from behind me.

"Rubio!" I shouted, looking over my shoulder. "Take it back a notch."

I saw him roll his eyes and shake his head at me. I couldn't expect less.

I turned back to Mort, "Explain it to me."

"I wanted to check out the scene. I needed to see where the Lynch boy was killed."

"Why?" I questioned loudly.

"I don't know," he replied, shrugging his shoulders. "I just did. What if something was missed, you know?"

"Jesus Christ, Mick," Sanchez yelled. "Will you listen to this guy? He's a piece of work."

"It's the truth!" Mort cried. "You gotta believe me. I needed to see it for myself."

"Here's the thing.., I don't have to believe anything you say, Lenny. For all I know, you could be The Letter Man returning to the crime scene."

"Why would I do that?" he questioned.

"I don't know, *Mort*," Sanchez said mockingly, calling him Mort purposely to get a rise out of him. "Why would you be watching us that day at the cemetery?"

"Don't call me Mort," Lenny said through clenched teeth. "I wanted to see what was going on with the case. You don't know what it's like being away from the dead. They were all I had. That was my life. I miss it."

He was spouting some messed up shit. If he was trying to convince me he *wasn't* the killer, he was doing a lousy job of it.

"What about at Karen's funeral?" I asked.

"Yeah, *Mort*," Sanchez chided. "What about that?"

"I told you not to call me Mort."

"I'll call you whatever the fuck I want, you psycho."

"Will you knock it off, Sanchez," I yelled. "So how about it, Lenny? Karen's funeral?"

"She was *my* friend too, you know," Lenny shouted. "I wanted to pay my respects, but I couldn't show my face around you guys - not after..,"

He silenced himself, looking down at his lap.

"You're not buying this jackhole's story, are you?" Sanchez questioned.

"I don't know," I replied.

"I'm not lying to you, Mick," Lenny said softly, keeping his eyes down.

"Then what about the bumper sticker?" I asked.

"What?"

"The bumper sticker," I repeated. "'The dead walk among us.' Catchy phrase."

"They *do* walk among us," he said. "Even after you die, there's still a story to tell. There's *always* a story. Even now, right here, Matthew Lynch has a story to tell. Can't you feel it?"

"Matthew Lynch was a child molester," Sanchez cut in. "*That's* his story. Then you killed him."

"I didn't," Lenny responded, looking up to see Sanchez's disgusted scowl.

"Lenny, the killer was heard saying the exact words that are on that bumper sticker."

"What?" he questioned. "I...I don't know what that was about, Mick. Honest."

"Even if I believed you, Lenny," I began, "we can't let you go. We still have to bring you in for questioning. This behavior.., whatever this shit is – it's not normal."

"I say we put the sadistic freak out of his misery," Sanchez added.

"If I was the *other* me," I said, "I would probably be right there with you. But I'm not going back to that. Untie him. Let's bring him in."

"You're not serious?" Sanchez questioned.

"I am," I replied. "Let's do this the right way."

"The bastard's killed ten people."

"We don't know that. But we will. Untie him."

"Unbelievable," Sanchez griped, stepping forward to comply. "I'm telling you right now, I don't trust this guy."

He bent over Lenny's legs and began to work the knot free.

"Grab my cuffs, will you?" he said, pointing to his car. "They're in the center console."

I nodded and turned for the car. Sanchez belted out one last comment as I walked away.

"For the record, I think you're making a mistake."

"Not the first," I mumbled. "Won't be the last."

I ducked into the passenger side of Sanchez's car and opened the center console. There was a pack of gum, two pennies, and a used napkin, but no cuffs. I slid my hand between the console and the seat to see if they had fallen into the tight space. Nothing. I looked at the passenger floor, and still nothing. I opened the glove compartment next, thinking if they weren't there, I was making Sanchez find them himself. I shuffled aside some papers until something caught my attention. It wasn't so much the pair of blue latex gloves that forced my doubletake, but rather what was buried under them. I reached in, pulled out a Polaroid, and stared at the picture, my jaw clenching. It was a picture of Miguel Sanchez, Rubio's son, undressed and in a provocative pose like the other boys from the photos found on Matthew Lynch's dash. It was at that moment I felt the barrel of the gun pressed against the back of my head.

"I wish you hadn't found that."

Chapter 33

Twist of the Knife

"I wish you hadn't found that."

Sanchez's voice stabbed into my back harder than the gun pressed against my head. My brain caught fire, and I found myself questioning everything I thought I knew.

"What the hell is this, Sanchez?" I questioned, dropping the polaroid of his son to the seat. "What are you doing?"

"You've really put me in a spot here, Mick," Sanchez said. "This could have gone so much easier if you'd have just listened to me."

"Fuck you, Sanchez; this isn't funny. Put the gun away."

"You think I'm trying to be funny?" he responded. "You've seen the picture. Did that look funny to you? Now get out of the car."

"Okay, okay," I said, raising my hands and slowly backing out of the open door.

"That's it, nice and slow."

I stood up and glanced to my right to notice the rope had been removed from Lenny's ankles, but his arms were still bound behind his back.

"Why are you doing this, Rubio?" I asked, with my back still to him.

"Why? Why don't you ask my son? Oh, that's right, you can't because he's dead - because pieces of trash like that no good son of a bitch Matthew Lynch think they can do whatever the hell they want and get away with it. People like Matthew Lynch think it's okay to destroy lives – like the way he destroyed *my* life."

"The picture," I said, thinking about what I'd seen. "Miguel was one of the boys that..,"

"Shut up!" Sanchez yelled. "Get over there with your little friend, Mort."

He grabbed my upper arm and yanked me sideways toward the Hyundai.

"I'm going!" I snapped back.

He pushed me forward until I was beside Lenny.

"Sit down," Sanchez ordered. "Fuck. It wasn't supposed to be like this."

"What was it supposed to be like, Rubio?" I asked, sliding my back down the car's rear door to take a seat beside Lenny.

"I didn't want to do this," Sanchez answered. "I wanted this to stop. You were supposed to help me end this."

"I can help you now," I said, trying to reason with him. "Just put the gun away and let's talk this over. Nobody else needs to get hurt."

"You make it sound so simple."

"It *is* simple," I responded. "Let us go, and I'll make sure everything ends okay."

"I bet you would," he said, curling his upper lip. He shook his head. "Goddammit, Mick! You stubborn asshole. Why wouldn't you listen to me? I didn't want to keep doing what I was doing. I tried to stop. But you couldn't let it go. It ate you up inside that you didn't get your man, and you couldn't accept that it was over. I watched you turn dark, man. You were hurting Gina."

"No thanks to *you*," I interjected.

"Do you think I don't know that? Christ, Mick, it hurt me to watch you sinking like that. But then *this* guy comes along," he motioned toward Lenny, "acting all strange and shit. I mean, come on; spying on us with binoculars? Who *does* that? He even had *you* believing he was the killer."

"And the whole 'The dead walk among us' comment at Peter's apartment?" I questioned. "That was all just to play me, wasn't it?"

"Yeah, I thought that was a nice touch," he replied. "Didn't you? The blue medical gloves, the bumper sticker - fuck, man. After that day at the cemetery when I saw you run off after that peeping Tom a second time – yeah, that's right, I saw the car that day too – I knew what I had to do. I found the little inquisitive fucker driving around one day and followed him so I'd know where to find him when I needed him. When you called me that day and told me to keep an eye out for a green Hyundai, it all came together. The little creepy twerp was the perfect suspect, and he was the perfect out for both of us. It would have been so easy. We kill this mother fucker," he waved the gun at Lenny, "no more Mort, no more Letter Man. We could all move on with our lives."

"Don't call me Mort," Lenny jumped in.

"I told you to shut up!" Sanchez shouted, pointing the gun at Lenny.

Lenny recoiled, turning his head and closing his eyes, waiting for the gun to go off.

I threw my hands up. "Whoa! Relax! Just calm down, huh? You don't have to do this, Rubio. Lenny didn't do anything. I know that now, so there's no reason for him to be here. Let him go."

"I can't do that, Mick. You know that. He knows too much."

"Lenny's not going to say anything." I glanced in his direction. "Are you, Lenny?"

Lenny shook his head vigorously.

"See? Besides, who would believe anything this messed up, evidence-stealing liar had to say? Everybody knows what he did. He can't be trusted."

I hated saying those things, but I had to convince Sanchez that Lenny wasn't the threat he thought he was.

"No, no, no," Sanchez responded, pacing back and forth. "I *have* to kill him."

"That's bullshit, and you know it," I said, trying to de-escalate the situation. "You're The Letter Man; you're all about seeking justice. You don't kill innocent people. Lenny already paid his dues. He doesn't belong here. If anything, it's me you want. *I'm* the criminal here."

"What the fuck are you talking about?" Sanchez questioned.

"Don't you know why I'm on administrative leave?"

"Of course; it's about that kid who was beaten. Just another punk who wants to sully the badge and kick dirt in the face of the hard-working cops of the city, lying about police brutality and shit. They'll figure out you had nothing to do with it."

I looked into his eyes, showing him the truth in my stare. "But I did," I admitted. "It *was* me. I put that kid in the hospital. I wish I could say I didn't mean it, but that would be the *real* lie. When I had him on the ground, and I was hitting him over and over - deep down inside, a part of me liked it. A part of me wanted to keep lashing out at him. If I hadn't stopped when I did, I might have killed him. So, you see, if anyone deserves punishment, it's me. What do you say, Rubio? Do the right thing. Let Lenny go. He's got nothing to do with this."

Sanchez stood in front of us with a blank stare, motionless as if he were trying to process everything I'd just told him.

"Rubio!" I announced to get his attention. "Did you hear me?"

Life came back to his eyes.

"You think I'm a bad guy, don't you?" he asked.

"I never said that."

"You didn't have to; I can see it in your eyes. I'll show you I'm not as bad as you think I am." He pointed at Lenny. "*You*, stand up."

"What are you going to do to me?" Lenny shuttered, maintaining his seated position.

"You should be more concerned about what I'm going to do to you if you don't listen. Now get up."

Lenny looked at me as if seeking my guidance. I gave him a nod, hoping it wasn't a mistake. He bent his legs to make it easier to push himself up, but with his arms still bound behind his back, he struggled. I grabbed under his right elbow to offer support and helped him to his feet. Once standing, Sanchez immediately walked up to him and stood face to face, glaring at him threateningly.

"Today's your lucky day.., *Leonard*. Turn around."

Lenny did as Sanchez directed, turning to face the car as he kept his eyes downward on me, the look of fear gripping his face.

"Don't do anything stupid, Mick," Sanchez said, waving the gun back and forth as if I'd forgotten he'd had it. "We wouldn't want anything to happen to your little friend here."

I watched as Sanchez began to untie Lenny's wrists. I wasn't planning on attempting anything. It was too dangerous, especially with Sanchez appearing as unstable as he was. He finished loosening the rope enough for it to fall to the ground. Lenny brought his hands in front of his chest and began rubbing his wrists. I could see where the rope had dug into his skin.

"All right," Sanchez said. "Turn back."

Lenny nervously turned to face Sanchez. I imagined the thoughts running through his head. He must have been thinking this was it; this was the end. If he was going to be killed, it would ironically be when he was finally free of his bonds. Instead, something else happened.

"Now get out of here," Sanchez ordered.

I was shocked by what I heard.

Lenny didn't move, unsure of what to do. He looked at me and then back to our captor.

"You must be hard of hearing," Sanchez snipped. "I said, get the fuck out of here."

"Wh...what about Mick?" Lenny asked, pushing his horn-rimmed glasses higher on his nose.

"Mick and I have some unfinished business."

Lenny turned to me with concern in his eyes. "Mick?"

"It's all right, Lenny," I assured him. "Go. I'll be fine."

He turned back to Sanchez.

"Last chance, douchebag," Sanchez stated. "Take it, or leave it."

With that last offer (or perhaps threat), Lenny put his head down and walked around my legs toward the driver's side door. I heard him mumble, "Sorry, Mick," as he opened the door. He hadn't a chance to get a single foot in before Sanchez screamed, "Leave the car," catching us both off guard.

"What?" Lenny questioned.

"You're leaving on foot," Sanchez replied, pointing the gun up the road from where we had come. "Now go on; get."

Lenny hesitantly shut the door and started walking away. I dropped my head in relief, letting out a heavy sigh. Lenny was going to make it. Or, at least, that's what I thought. He made it as far as the trunk of Sanchez's car before I heard the gunshot. I looked up and saw Lenny on the ground, screaming and grabbing the back of his leg.

"You shot him, you son of a bitch!" I screamed.

"It was only in the leg," he snapped back, smiling from ear to ear. "I told you I wasn't all that bad. He'll live. For now."

"What the fuck, Sanchez? What happened to you?"

"What happened to me? You want to know what happened to me? I came home one day to find my son dead, hanging from the ceiling. That's what happened to me. All those years after his mother died, I thought her death was the cause of his depression. Turned out he couldn't live with the shame of what that fucking pedophile Matthew Lynch did to him. Ten years old, Mick. My boy was only ten when that piece of shit did those awful things to him. I told you he left me a note, but I wasn't exactly honest about what it said. He wrote it all out for me, every disgusting detail; that's what was in the note. He lived with the guilt and the shame for six years until he couldn't do it anymore. As if that wasn't bad enough, he left me a picture too - the one you found. What do you think that shit does to a father?

"Prison would have been too good for that mother fucker Lynch," Sanchez continued while Lenny's screams of pain echoed against the trees. "I wanted to kill him for what he had done. I was ready to. And then that day came when I heard the news. The Alphabet Killer had been caught. And just like that, an idea had hatched. Why should I ruin my life over that piece of shit child molester when a copycat serial killer could take care of my problem for me? It was *then* that The Letter Man was born. But I knew I couldn't go off half-cocked. I needed a plan.

"Almost two years I waited to exact my revenge. Can you imagine what that's like? That shit festers in your head, man. It does stuff to you. It changes you. And not for the better. I mean, it really fucks you up. But if I was going to do it right, it had to be big.

"I wish Karen didn't have to be the first, but I needed that connection with The Alphabet Killer. And with what I was about to start, I needed you all to understand how serious I was."

"So you killed an innocent woman?" I seethed, my teeth clenched.

"Innocent? Please. She didn't even want to see her own son. How disgusting is that? I'd give anything to see *my* son again. She had every opportunity but refused. That's not innocent. That's not a mother."

"You twisted son of a bitch!"

"Twisted?" Sanchez questioned. "You think *I'm* the twisted one? Those criminals out there, man," he pointed the gun down the road again, "those are the ones you should be worried about. I'm trying to rid the city of that garbage. *You* know what it's like, Mick. Wearing the uniform, we can only do so much. And too often, our efforts are wasted. The filthy dirtbags end up back on the street. But not in The Letter Man's world. Uh uh; they don't come back."

"Is there a point to all this, Sanchez? We need to get an ambulance out here."

"What, for *him*?" Sanchez questioned, turning and pointing the gun toward Lenny. "Fuck him. I should put another bullet in him to shut him up."

I felt my muscles tense up at that remark. He was further gone than I thought. I was losing him. There was no telling how this was going to end. If I didn't do something soon, Lenny and I would both be dead.

"You know what?" Sanchez continued, wiggling the gun in his hand. "I think I *will* do that, after all."

He turned and took a few steps toward the writhing ex-medical examiner. My heart jumped into my throat. He was going to kill Lenny. I couldn't sit by and watch it happen. I needed to act. As I pushed myself to my feet and charged at Sanchez, a flood of thoughts overwhelmed me. I knew this was the end; this was *my* end. But Lenny could still live. I'm sorry, Gina. I'm sorry, Stella Mae. I love you both so much.

Sanchez heard me coming and swung around to face me, but it was too late. I slammed into him like a linebacker, surprising him and knocking him off his feet. He hit the ground hard, knocking the gun from his hand, but not before it fired into Lenny's back window. Suddenly, I found myself in the same dark place I was that night on Hooker Highway. Sanchez was pinned beneath me, and I couldn't hold back my rage. With hardened fists, I began to beat him. Over and over again, blow after blow, visions of that kid flashed into my head, and I kept swinging. As I told Sanchez, someplace deep inside, I liked it. The sight of Lenny on the ground reeling in pain and the sound of his ear-piercing shrills stabbed into my brain, and I kept swinging. I saw Karen's blood-covered body, her severed fingers and toes on display like grotesque ornaments, and I kept swinging. I saw Lydon and Nancy, Oliver and Peter, Quinn, Ronan, Salvatore, and Travis, all of them dead at the hands of this psychopath, and my fists kept pounding away. I saw Gina and Stella Mae, and I...,

I..,

I let out a gasp and slumped to the ground, my hands bloody and stinging from the punishment they endured - from the punishment *Sanchez* endured. His face was battered and swollen, covered in red, and barely recognizable. He got what he deserved. He would have gotten more if not for..,

Thank you, Gina and Stella, for stopping me.

Sanchez would still get more, but it wouldn't be from me. Let Justice take its course.

I glanced over at Lenny, his wails still reverberating in my ears. I slowly crawled over to him, my body too exhausted to do much else.

"It's going to be all right, Lenny. You're going to be all right. It's over. It's all over. Let's get you some help."

Epilogue 1

Six Months Later

Everything was getting back to normal. I could sleep at night. Comfortably. For the first time in a long time. Rubio Sanchez, The Letter Man, and sad to say, a man I once called my friend, was convicted on ten counts of first-degree murder and one count each for aggravated assault, attempted murder, and conspiracy to commit murder. He was sentenced to serve ten life sentences without the opportunity for parole. It was a fitting end for someone as sadistic and manipulative as he was. He had us all fooled, how he'd pretend to be sickened by the different crime scenes - the very scenes *he* created. He was warped and twisted. And it was finally over.

As for *my* troubles, they unexpectedly disappeared. I escaped punishment in the beating case. My inquiry with Internal Affairs never took place. The kid, Roderick, spoke up again about the incident from that night, changing his story, claiming he'd been beaten by two members of a local street gang, though he refused to give their names for fear of retribution. It was a believable story, especially when that same gang began taking credit for it to bolster their reputation and send a message to rival gangs. It's like the cycle never ends.

I confronted Roderick about it one day. I wanted to apologize for what I'd done and to find out why he'd changed his story. He told me he'd learned I was the detective responsible for taking down The Letter Man, so he was cool with letting things go. It was his way of saying thanks for keeping his mom and little sister safe. I still felt guilty about the whole thing and wanted to come clean, but he told me not to. He said this city needed good cops like me on the street. I didn't know what to say; I got a little choked up, and my eyes shed a tear or two.

I've since taken him on a few ride-alongs. That was my way of saying thanks to him, as well. It turns out he's not a bad kid. He just needed clear direction and some positive guidance. He even expressed interest in joining the police academy. I hope he does. As he said, this city could use some good cops on the street.

I also had a long talk with Frank about our arrangement. I told him that as much as I appreciated his willingness to turn a blind eye to his officers' indiscretions - as he did with Jimmy and me - it would only lead him down a dark path if he continued. That's when he filled me in on a little tidbit. He told me he never did anything like that for Jimmy. He made the whole thing up. *Everybody lies*. He knew I was having a hard time with my situation and didn't want me distracted from The Letter Man case. He needed me firing on all cylinders. He told me if it wasn't for The Letter Man murders, he would have personally turned me in immediately after I originally came forward.

Mort.., I mean.., Lenny Shurek survived his non-life-threatening gunshot wound. I couldn't believe it - for all his screaming and writhing in excruciating pain, you would have thought he was going to bleed out right there on the road. Instead, it turned out the bullet only grazed him in the back of the leg, leaving him with barely a scratch. He walked out of the hospital that same day with only a gauze patch and an Ace bandage. And those were for his wrists. I almost felt like killing him myself after the way he'd been hamming it up.

As for Gina and I, things couldn't be better. When she learned of my ordeal on Ledgehill Road and how I could have been killed, the job became more real to her. She saw things differently after that. On my end, once The Letter Man case wrapped up, all the stress I'd been holding onto melted away. We both learned what was truly important in our lives - each other and our little girl.

Speaking of our little girl - Stella Mae has three teeth already, and she barely cried through any of it. That's my girl. She's a real trooper.

As I said, everything was getting back to normal. Things were feeling right. But, if everything was going so right for a change, why was I sitting on the couch, stewing about opening a letter I'd received from BrentRidge Penitentiary? The mailman hand-delivered it today, along with an apology. It was from Ben and had been postmarked six-and-a-half months earlier. The Post Office had somehow "misplaced" it. That was the professional way of saying, "We lost it for a long time."

I stared at the sealed envelope on the coffee table and nervously rubbed my knees with my palms. I'd seen enough letters from serial killers to last a lifetime. Did I *really* want to see one more?

I did.

I drew in a breath and let it out - then reached for the envelope. As I tore into the top flap, Gina marched into the living room, Stella in one arm, her other hand holding her phone pressed to her ear.

"Babe, turn on the TV," she announced excitedly. "It's all over the news."

"What is?" I asked, grabbing the remote and turning on the television.

"...refused to comment. We've since gotten word the State Police have managed to get the situation at the prison under control, though not without incident. The riots, which first erupted two days ago, have seen three guards killed and several others badly injured. In addition, this station has just received leaked footage from two days ago, shortly after the riots began. The disturbing footage you are about to see was taken from a State Police helicopter circling the scene overhead. This aerial footage captures three prisoners, seen here, running outside the prison grounds toward the wooded tree line with officers in pursuit, where seconds later, they disappear into the surrounding forest. We are being told that two of the escaped prisoners have since been apprehended - the third is still on the loose. State and local law enforcement are scouring the city for his whereabouts. Information is still trickling in, but citizens are being cautioned not to approach any suspicious person or pick up any hitchhikers in or around the greater Hobskinot County.

"Wait, ladies and gentlemen - we've just received word that the prisoner still at large is Benjamin Had-

dick, the notorious Alphabet Killer of Southbridge, who you may recall was responsible for the deaths of nine people during his killing spree from three years ago. The State Police and the FBI are asking for the public's help in locating the escaped convict. If anyone has any information on the whereabouts of the prisoner, they are encouraged to contact their state or local law enforcement as soon as possible. In just a few moments, we'll have the number to reach displayed on your screens. Again, citizens should not approach the prisoner as he is considered dangerous.

"Keep it here as we bring you live continuing coverage of the events as they unfold. We take you now to news correspondent Macey Constelou, reporting from outside BrentRidge Penitentiary. Macey?"

"Thank you, Paul. I'm standing outside..,"

I hit the mute button and stared at the torn envelope in my hand.

"Mick, that's crazy, isn't it?" Gina commented.

She didn't know how crazy it was, as I hadn't told her about the letter I received. My face must've given me away.

"Babe, are you all right?" she asked. "What is it?"

I held up the envelope.

"It's from Ben," I said.

"What? You have to tell someone."

"It's from six months ago. While The Letter Man stuff was still going down."

"Oh. Well, what's it say?" she questioned.

I pulled the folded paper from the envelope, opened it up, and read it out loud.

"I'm sorry I upset you, Mick. I hope you'll reconsider visiting with me again. I don't have anyone left in my life. I can't lose you too. I don't know what I'd do if I didn't have someone who knew me - the old me - before my world became dark and distorted.

"If you'll let me, I can earn your trust again. To show you how serious I am, let me help you out. Your killer was after Matthew Lynch; it's the only thing that makes sense. Not only was this the scene where the killer first dubbed himself The Letter Man, but Matthew's death took place outside, in the open, where his naked body could be stumbled upon by anyone. The killer wasn't only after revenge - he wanted Matthew to be humiliated and his name to be slung through the mud. This was personal. I suspect the killer knew one of Matthew's victims - maybe a close friend or family member. Hell, maybe even the killer's own son. Given the nature of the kills and how angry The Letter Man is, I'd wager the latter.

"Don't fall for the killer's comment about the dead walking among us. He wanted to be seen and heard for only one reason - to get you off his trail. I wouldn't be surprised if he's trying to frame someone else. Of course, this is just a theory.

"Speaking of theories - you're not going to like this one. I think the person you're looking for might be a cop. He knows quite a bit about the criminals he's been killing. That's convenient. How else would he be able to find them unless he was privy to their activities? What do you think? Does any of this make sense? Do you know any cops who have a damaged son? Wow, a 'damaged son.' Doesn't that sound a little too familiar? Maybe all cops' kids are damaged in some way. Don't let that hap-

pen to you, Mick. Keep your kid protected. Be a good dad. You were always a good uncle.

"I hope you get your man, and I hope to see you again soon.

"Ben."

I couldn't help but grin. The son of a bitch knew it all along. I should have been upset, but I wasn't. Ben tried to help. How could he have known his letter would get lost in the mail?

"Oh my God!" Gina expressed. "It's almost like he knew. The little fucker!"

I swung around to face her.

"Gina! The baby."

"Oh, shi..," she quickly covered her mouth, both out of shock for letting something slip and to prevent anything further from leaving her lips.

"It's okay, babe," I said. "Her dad's a cop. I'm sure that won't be the worst thing she hears."

As I said, everything was getting back to normal.

A week later, "normal" took a turn for the worse, when a second letter from Ben arrived. This time, it was post-dated only two days earlier. Gina was at the store when I grabbed it from the mailbox, so she never learned of it. And she wouldn't. *Everybody lies.* I sat down on the couch and read it.

"I thought you were different, Mick, but you're like all the rest. I practically handed you The Letter Man, but you still never came back to visit. I waited for you, think-

ing you'd do the right thing. I wasn't expecting a thanks. I just wanted a friend. I now know where I stand in your eyes. You'll always see me as a killer. If that's all I am to you - if that's all I am to everyone - then I'll give you all what you want. It's time I let the real me out. There's a lot of work to be done and a lot of streets to be cleaned of the filth occupying it. But I had it all wrong the first time around. Choosing my victims using the alphabet was a mistake. Letters are finite. But numbers.., numbers go on forever.

"Goodbye, Mick. Don't come looking for me; you won't find me. But if you try, it will upset me. And that would be very bad. Trust me.

"Ben."

I shook my head and placed the letter on the coffee table. I thought Ben was smart, but now I had to question it. He sent me a letter, telling me not to look for him. What was he thinking? I'm a cop. If you threaten the citizens of my city, do you think you can keep me from coming after you? Not a chance. Let the chase begin.

Just then, the doorbell rang, snapping me back to reality. I did my best to leave the negative thoughts behind as I made my way to the door. I opened it to find Special Agent Hayes standing on my doorstep with a taller gentleman standing behind her, facing away toward the street.

"Detective Dooley," she began, "we need to talk."

Then, the man standing behind her turned around.

"How's it going, kid? Long time no see. We need your help to take down my boy."

"Jimmy? What the fu..,"

Epilogue 2

Three Years Earlier

"I'm not sure we'll be able to continue our fun after this case."

"Shut up, Jim."

I did what I set out to do and to hell with the consequences. It's what I always did; it was my job. I was a cop. I could finally close the case. I had said I would catch the killer if it was the last thing I did. And with that thought, I felt my eyes close.

* * *

"Clear!"

It's strange, but I think I actually heard those words before the current shot through me, restarting my heart. I knew it wasn't possible and probably just a call-back to the many times I'd witnessed the same occurrence on other individuals who had succumbed to their injuries, only to be brought back moments later from the land of the dead. I could now be considered among their roster as my eyes fluttered open to see Marion sitting by my side in the cramped metal enclosure, her face distraught while tears ran down her cheeks. The EMT was leaning over me with paddles in hand, probably as surprised as I was by my sudden awakening.

"He's back with us," he said.

I felt Marion's hand on my forearm just as a relieved gasp fell from her lips. The gurney beneath me shimmied from side to side as the ambulance raced down the street en route to the hospital. If the paddles hadn't woken me, surely the jostling would have done the trick.

I reached for the oxygen mask covering my nose and mouth, the bothersome device making my cheek itch.

"Try not to move, sir," the EMT stated, wriggling the mask back into position after I'd knocked it ajar.

I slapped his hand away. Nobody tells me what I should or shouldn't do. I pushed the mask sideways enough to free my lips from capture.

"Why do you have to be so stubborn?" Marion asked.

"It's my undeniable charm," I answered through labored breathing.

"Try and relax," she continued. "We're getting you to the hospital."

"I think I'm a lost cause," I said.

"Shut up. They're going to fix you, good as new."

"I'm glad you're finally showing your positive side. Listen.., if I do make it..,"

"*When* you make it," she adamantly interjected.

"*If* I make it," I continued, realizing the severity of my injuries, "I don't want to go back."

"What are you talking about?" she asked.

"I don't want this life anymore. It's all shit."

The ambulance hit a pothole, and a pain shot through my stomach, causing me to tighten up and press my hand to my gut while I winced.

"Try to be still, sir," The EMT reiterated. "You've been shot."

"No shit, I've been shot," I howled back. "Tell your driver that, would ya? His driving is causing me more pain than the bullet."

"Jim, try to relax," Marion said.

"I'll relax when I'm dea..," I caught myself before I finished. Probably not the best choice of words at the moment. "Listen, Marion," I continued, reaching for her hand, "there's nothing left for me. I have nothing. My kid's a serial killer; he'll never see the light of day again. My ex-wife can't stand me. My boss can't stomach me. I can't do it anymore. I just want to be happy for a change. Don't I deserve that? Can't I be happy? Can't *we* be happy? Together?"

"What are you saying, Jim?"

"I'm saying I want to disappear. Isn't there something you can do to make the old me disappear? Give me a new identity or some shit?"

"I can't do that," she responded. "It doesn't work that way."

I felt myself getting weaker. "Why not?" I questioned. "The Feds give criminals new identities all the time. Are you telling me you can't do it for a cop? Besides, technically, I already died. What if.., what if I just stayed that way?"

"You could quit."

"I can't just quit. Not with what happened. As long as I'm alive, the job will find a way to feed off whatever's left of me until I'm a rotting carcass. People will always throw the case back in my face, reminding me who my kid was. Do you think I want that? I need to be gone. Forgotten."

"Do you even know what you're asking?"

"I'm asking for your help. Can't you contact your bosses in Washington and make this happen?"

"You're being ridiculous," Hayes replied. "It's not that simple."

"Isn't it?" I questioned. "If you can't help me, I'll find a way to do it myse..."

Things suddenly went black. I heard Marion cry out.

"Jim? Wake up, Jim. Stay with me."

Then, the paramedic chimed in.

"Ma'am, I'm going to need you to sit back. He's slipping away. I need to start chest compressions."

"Oh my God," Marion's voice slowly faded. "Don't do this to me, Jim. I'll do it; just come back to me."

Quieter and quieter her voice became until..,

Nothingness.

* * *

My eyes sprung open. I was looking up at ceiling tiles full of tiny holes. My mouth felt drier than a desert. I tried to lick my lips, but my tongue stuck to my lower lip like a fly on fly paper. I cleared my throat and called out in a raspy, barely audible voice.

"Hello?"

"I'm right here, Jim," the lovely sound of her voice responded. "Try to relax."

I was alive!

"Where am I?" I asked, looking up at Marion standing over me.

"You're at a medical facility in Pierre," she replied.

"Isn't that where your field office is?" I questioned. "What am I doing here? Wasn't Cooley General closer?"

"You were at Cooley General," she said. "After the surgery, as soon as you were stable enough to be transported, I had you transferred here."

"Why? What's going on?"

"We've still got a lot to do if we're going to pull this off."

"Pull what off?"

"I'm giving you what you wanted," she replied. "You're getting a new life. As far as people in Southbridge are concerned, Jim Haddick died in surgery."

I tossed her a smirk. "It was my comment in the ambulance about me dying that convinced you, wasn't it?"

"No, it was you *dying* that convinced me," she responded. "*Twice.*"

"What was that?"

"You died twice," she answered. "I thought I'd lost you that second time, you son of a bitch. That was when I knew.., I didn't want to lose you again. You promised me a good time after The Alphabet Killer case. I'm holding you to it."

"Are you playing with me right now?" I asked in all seriousness. "I don't think I'm in any condition for surprises."

"You don't want to know the kind of strings I had to pull to get you this far. And it's not over yet."

"Your bosses came through for you, huh?"

"My bosses don't know. And if they find out, I'll be in a world of shit. You'd better be worth the trouble."

"Probably not," I joked. "But it sounds like it's too late to turn back now."

"After what I've been through, if you even think about changing your mind, your death won't be faked. I'll kill you myself."

"Well then, I guess we'll just have to take it day by day and see what happens."

"Sounds good to me," she replied, smiling and holding my hand. "I can do that."

She rubbed her free hand across my forehead and brushed my hair aside.

"I should probably warn you, though," she continued. "I snore."

"Wait, what?"

A LETTER FROM THE AUTHOR

Dear readers,

I hope you loved *The Letter Man*, and if you did, I'd be very grateful if you'd consider writing a review. I love to hear what readers think, which helps me grow as an author, and it makes such a difference in helping new readers discover my books for the first time.

Check out my website at:

javo-publication.square.site

Where copies of all of my books (including signed copies) can be purchased. You can also find them on Amazon.

Thank you so much!

Jeff

Acknowledgments

I'll try to keep this short. I'd like to start by thanking the two people who have helped me the most during the process of writing this book.

My editor, Elizabeth Kelly, who still stands by me through all the mistakes I send her way, loves to use her red pen to cross off entire paragraphs and annotate her thoughts in the margins of the pages before sending them back to me. This time around, she crossed off entire pages and commented that an entire chapter had to be thrown out and rewritten. I think she ran out of red ink. I'm thankful she hasn't thrown me away. She claims she still enjoys my stories, but I think she's probably just a good liar.

Police Chief, John Cartledge, has had to endure my constant texts, asking him questions about police policies and procedures. I'm sure there were things he would rather have been doing than answering my 6:00 am and 9:00 pm texts about the stresses of the job and questioning suspects. He responded like a champ each time, always ending his replies with "Anytime, Jeff." I'm thankful to have such a friend in law enforcement.

Lastly, I'd like to thank my wife, Elena, who agreed to let me take my tablet along on vacation with us so that I could continue getting some writing in during our downtime (I was so close to the end). The best part is, you're reading the finished product of that decision now. I finished the book four days in.

YOU'RE NEXT ON HIS LIST

THE
ALPHABET
KILLER
A NOVEL
Jeff VanOudenhove

SECRETS NEVER STAY HIDDEN

Just
Listen
No secret stays safe forever
Jeff VanOudenhove
Author of The Alphabet Killer

SCREAMS IN THE DARK
AND OTHER
TWISTED TALES
JEFF VANOUDENHOVE
AUTHOR OF THE DARK SERIES

THE DARK SERIES

Jeff VanOudenhove has written several novels in the genre of dark fiction, including the **Dark Series** and the psychological suspense thrillers, **The Alphabet Killer** and **Just Listen**. His talent for storytelling combines unforgettable characters and dire situations, mixed with astonishing plot twists. **The Letter Man** is Jeff's ninth book. He lives in Western Massachusetts with his wife, Elena.